FACIAL JUSTICE

Leslie Poles Hartley was born near Peterborough on December 30th 1895 and educated at Harrow and Balliol College, Oxford, where he made some distinguished literary friends. In 1924 he published his earliest volume of short stories (*Night Fears*, 1924); and thenceforward he devoted his life to literature. From that time, his private existence, wrote a obituarist, 'so far as the public knows', was completely absorbed by his imaginative career. Twenty years after he began work, he concluded his famous *Eustace and Hilda* trilogy (*The Shrimp and the Anemone*, 1944; *The Sixth Heaven*, 1946; and *Eustace and Hilda*, 1947), an acute analysis of a complex personal relationship, which firmly established him as a novelist of considerable psychological insight and understanding. His later books, especially *The Go-Between* (1953), and *The Hireling* (1957), consolidated this reputation. He died in December 1972. A notably quiet and reticent character, he had, nevertheless, a wide circle of admiring intimates, which included almost every member of Virginia Woolf's Bloomsbury group.

Peter Quennell was born in 1905, the son of an architect and an artist, who between them wrote and illustrated a succession of highly esteemed popular social histories. Like Leslie Hartley he was educated at Balliol, among his Oxford friends being Evelyn Waugh, Graham Greene, Anthony Powell, and Harold Acton. Since then, his own productions have included biographical studies of Byron, Ruskin, Hogarth, Alexander Pope, and three autobiographical essays, *The Marble Foot, The Wanton Chase* and *Customs and Characters*. He lives and works today in Chelsea.

ALSO AVAILABLE IN

TWENTIETH-CENTURY CLASSICS

Nigel Balchin THE SMALL BACK ROOM

H. E. Bates MY UNCLE SILAS

John Bayley IN ANOTHER COUNTRY

Adrian Bell CORDUROY

Adrian Bell SILVER LEY

Adrian Bell THE CHERRY TREE

Arnold Bennett RICEYMAN STEPS

Hermann Broch THE DEATH OF VIRGIL

Joanna Cannan HIGH TABLE

THE ESSENTIAL G. K. CHESTERTON

Ivy Compton-Burnett A FATHER AND HIS FATE

Ivy Compton-Burnett MANSERVANT AND MAIDSERVANT

Walter de la Mare MEMOIRS OF A MIDGET

D. J. Enright ACADEMIC YEAR

Ford Madox Ford THE FIFTH QUEEN

Robert Graves SEVEN DAYS IN NEW CRETE

Patrick Hamilton THE SLAVES OF SOLITUDE

Pamela Hansford Johnson AN ERROR OF JUDGEMENT

Patrick Leigh Fermor THE VIOLINS OF SAINT-JACQUES

Sinclair Lewis ELMER GANTRY

Rose Macaulay THEY WERE DEFEATED

Vladimir Nabokov THE DEFENCE

Seán O'Faoláin BIRD ALONE

William Plomer TURBOTT WOLFE

Rainer Maria Rilke

THE NOTEBOOK OF MALTE LAURIDS BRIGGE

Saki THE UNBEARABLE BASSINGTON

Osbert Sitwell BEFORE THE BOMBARDMENT

Lytton Strachey ELIZABETH AND ESSEX

Rex Warner THE AERODROME

Denton Welch IN YOUTH IS PLEASURE

H. G. Wells KIPPS

H. G. Wells LOVE AND MR LEWISHAM

Edith Wharton ETHAN FROME *and* SUMMER

Leonard Woolf THE VILLAGE IN THE JUNGLE

L. P. HARTLEY

Facial Justice

———◆———

INTRODUCED BY
PETER QUENNELL

The spirit that dwelleth in us lusteth to envy.
ST. JAMES

OXFORD UNIVERSITY PRESS
1987

Oxford University Press, Walton Street, Oxford OX2 6DP

Oxford New York Toronto
Delhi Bombay Calcutta Madras Karachi
Petaling Jaya Singapore Hong Kong Tokyo
Nairobi Dar es Salaam Cape Town
Melbourne Auckland

and associated companies in
Beirut Berlin Ibadan Nicosia

Oxford is a trade mark of Oxford University Press

First published 1960 by Hamish Hamilton
First issued, with Peter Quennell's Introduction, as an Oxford University Press paperback 1987

British Library Cataloguing in Publication Data
Hartley, L. P.
Facial justice.—(Twentieth–century
classics)
I. Title II. Series
823'.912[F] PR6015.A6723
ISBN 0–19–282057–5

Printed in Great Britain by
The Guernsey Press Co. Ltd.
Guernsey, Channel Islands

DEDICATED
with homage, acknowledgments and
apologies to the memory of
Nathaniel Hawthorne

INTRODUCTION

BY PETER QUENNELL

ONE'S own face, whether one likes or dislikes it, is an essential part of one's existence. Behind the image we observe in the looking-glass, sometimes with mild affection, sometimes with active distaste, now and then with real repulsion, lurks the secret of the Ego. There we find a record, written up in an indelible script, year after year, of almost everything the self has thought and done.

Would one change one's face if one could? Leslie Hartley's novel, first published twenty-six years ago, depicts a social system where that choice is no longer left to the individual; for individualism is a trait that the current rulers detest and despise, and believe should be vigorously subdued. Mankind has been divided into categories that range from Alpha to Gamma; and 'Alpha is anti-social' the heroine humbly agrees, explaining why she has found it safest to submit to the draconic forms of 'Facial Justice' and adopt a fresh mask, based on a certain 'stock model'. Jael's previous looks were considered capable of arousing social Envy; and 'Equality and Envy . . . were in the moral sphere the positive and negative poles' around which the New State regularly revolved. Other women, she tells her plain friend Judith, had begun to criticize the enviable effect she made: 'it was my eyelashes they mostly picked on, for being too long and curly. My fault, of course; I should have cut them'. But, alas, she had occasionally forgotten. 'One woman complained that she has lost several nights' sleep just thinking about my eye-lashes. She felt they were digging into her, she said.'

I

In other respects, too, life in this grim new world is severely regimented; all its inhabitants are obliged to wear sackcloth suits, 'differently cut and trimmed, but unmistakably sackcloth.' Nor is a woman encouraged to wash her hair: 'Some foreign substance had lodged in it; something grey and gritty. Could it be ashes?'

Such are the gloomy conditions the novelist describes in his imagined England of 'the not very distant future, after the Third World War', a cataclysm that has devastated the whole country and, for a while, driven humanity underground, whence a few citizens, officially labelled 'delinquents', have at last emerged to help build a new society on earth, and assent to the implacable rule of a mysterious, invisible Dictator, whose radio-transmitted voice follows them during every action they perform and, at 'the Equalisations (Faces) centre' and similar centres of authority, keeps them constantly aware of the faults they must avoid and the rules they must obey. Hartley spares us nothing; each horrid detail of this nightmare world is expertly driven home. As his earlier books show—not only his collection of ghost-stories, *The Travelling Grave*, but his fascinating domestic saga, the excellent *Eustace and Hilda* stories—he was acutely sensitive to the terrible and the horrible in life, a characteristic I should scarcely have suspected from our brief, but enjoyable friendship. Smoking a cigarette at one of Lady Ottoline Morrell's garden-parties, he bore some resemblance to Lewis Carroll's Dormouse, perfectly wide-awake, it is true, but always comfortable-looking, calm and sedate among far noisier companions like Lytton Strachey, Duncan Grant, and Clive Bell.

He was evidently a determined individualist; and *Facial Justice* I regard as both a dramatic fantasy and a brave defence of the Ego against the many attacks with which a 'collective' society threatens it. In the past, he has had

2

many precursors and certain distinguished opponents. The self was hateful—'*le moi est haissable*—Pascal had coldly announced; whereas his great adversary Montaigne, in whom Pascal saw the odious type of Natural Man, held exactly the opposite opinion, and declared in his *Essays* that he had spent most of his life composing a gigantic self-portrait. His eyes, he informed his readers, were 'incessantly turned upon myself'; and he had conceived 'the ferocious and extravagant design' of producing a 'living likeness' of his own character, since he, after all, was the one human being he could claim he really knew well. On the rafters of his study he had also had painted various salutary maxims, including the classic phrase '*Know theyself*', which the ancient builders of Delphi had placed above the main door of Apollo's famous shrine.

We must be true to ourselves, he insisted again and again, and thus achieve the inner quietude and sense of order, that alone can bring us peace and happiness. How the stern directors of Hartley's imaginery future state would have abominated Montaigne's influence! Nor, considering eighteenth-century literature, would they have had a good word to say for that deleterious sage Jean-Jacques Rousseau, a peculiarly self-centred prophet, whose *Confessions* are a long painstaking essay in impassioned self-scrutiny.

Although he was much preoccupied with the betterment of society and the re-education of his fellow men, Rousseau's chief interest, particularly as he grew older, was the personal pursuit of happiness, which once or twice he had nearly achieved, first at Annecy during the course of his earliest love-affair; many years later beside the romantic Lac de Bienne, the sound of whose wavelets rippling against the shore has somehow chased away his sorrows. Above all else, he decided, a man must learn to be himself—'*il faut être soi*—and derive the blessings of

3

self-sufficiency from the simple consciousness of living.

This privilege Hartley's main personage, the once-attractive, long-lashed Jael, has been brutally denied; and she is intensely conscious of the deprivation:

Tears started to her eyes and trickled down her rain-proof cheeks. She wept for her lost self, the self she knew, for she associated it with her old-time face; she wept for her present self, the self she did not know, for her new self was faceless; she did not know, and did not permit herself to know, what she looked like. She had denied herself that assurance of identity; sometimes she mentally groped for her own image, as someone might who has long been blind.

Meanwhile, in other members of the New Society, subversive impulses are now stirring. Disasters break out; shouts are even heard of 'Bet on yourself' and 'Down with the Dictator.' 'Can't you hear the noise?' citizens ask one another, when the cries grow more and more audible, and 'a sound louder than the sighing of the March wind' drifts towards them through the windows.

Not that all amusements are forbidden them; and from time to time a coach-tour is arranged to visit and examine some relic of the 'Bad Old Days', as they are taught to call the pre-war past. Such an historic monument are the ruins of Ely Cathedral. The East-Anglian landscape, once so pleasing and verdant, has tragically changed, however, and so has the noble building it surrounds. The fields, centuries ago reclaimed from fenland, have gone back to a featureless, ill-smelling marsh, with 'no trees, no vegetation, nothing to attract the eye.' Although, before Jael and her fellow tourists set out they had been dosed with 'Joyful Journey' tablets, she experiences a deep depression. But then an entirely new feeling arises: it is a feeling of strange expectancy—she knows that she awaits something.

4

Of the Cathedral itself, only a single broken tower remains; but her expectancy is soon realized; the tower's splendid grace and height 'fills her mind with awe and terror'. On the rest of the bewildered gathering it has the same revolutionary effect; they begin to sing and dance, the women like maenads, the men revealing an athletic joyfulness, of which their normal bearing gave no hint, until they collapse on the earth, as if 'the Angel of Death was passing over them'; but above their heads still 'soared the tower, expressionless and unconcerned, unchanged . . .'

While I was re-reading *Facial Justice*, a companion, much younger than myself, asked me if I assumed that the book had any 'message' for the last half of the twentieth century; and I replied that, although I was not at all convinced that delivering a message, or teaching a social lesson, was the proper business of a literary work of art, I felt that it represented a profoundly sympathetic point of view. The self is by no means hateful, whatever Pascal may have told us. Indeed, a regard for the Ego, and a judicious appreciation of its merits and demerits, have long been the basis of European culture.

We must know ourselves, as the priests of Apollo declared, should we hope to understand the world; and we cannot afford to ignore the questions put by the image in the looking-glass. Montaigne was certainly right; Pascal, that stern ascetic, on this occasion altogether wrong. Compulsory self-abjection, whether it is enforced by a political dogma or a religious creed, stultifies and cripples the aspiring human spirit, and ultimately has disastrous results.

In Hartley's tale—or, perhaps we should say, his fable—these results are given a dramatic form. Smouldering discontent explodes into senseless violence; and, among scenes of growing chaos, the Dictator's insidious voice—the tyrant's true identity is exposed in the final chapter—is heard on the radio for the last time. Thus the New Society gradually dissolves, and the individual is again free. But here, as has happened during many real revolutions, the sudden recapture of freedom proves to bring some serious dangers:

The recognition, by each member of the community, of a self-hood that must suffer, and suffer alone, involved a refusal of all their mental processes that acted on them like madness . . . Relying on the stimulus of what others thought and felt, they had no idea how to meet a situation which was to affect each one of them alone . . . the thought was so frightful that many went mad as soon as it had penetrated into their consciousness, while others died from shock.

Leslie Hartley does not describe what was the fate of more resolute survivors, what, for example, would be the future life of his gallant young protagonist Jael; but he allows us gleams of hope. The self is a burden as well as a blessing; yet, once boldly confronted and appraised, in the looking-glass, it may at length turn out to be a steady friend.

PART I

Ev - 'ry val - ley   ev - 'ry val - ley   shall be ex - alt - ed,

CHAPTER ONE

In the not very distant future, after the Third World War, Justice had made great strides. Legal Justice, Economic Justice, Social Justice, and many other forms of justice, of which we do not even know the names, had been attained; but there still remained spheres of human relationship and activity in which Justice did not reign.

Two girls were walking up the shallow curving steps of the Equalisation (Faces) Centre. Each was absorbed in her own thoughts; and one, to judge from an occasional twitching of the shoulders, was crying. They did not look at each other, rather, they looked away; but as they reached the top and began to converge upon the tall glass swing doors, the one who was crying fell back to let the other go in front of her. They turned and their eyes met.

'Jael!' cried the one whose voice was better under control.

'Judith!'

They drew apart and stared at each other with looks of horror and dismay. Each felt that she was seeing her old friend for the first, and also—it simultaneously occurred to them both—for the last time.

Judith saw a pretty, fair-haired girl slightly above middle height, whose mouth trembled and whose eyes were reddened by weeping. She had a faint scar on one cheek, but it did not spoil, it gave point to her prettiness. Jael saw a dark, plain, thick-set young woman whose features were only redeemed from positive ugliness by a pleasant expression and a look of intelligence. Now, her face corrugated by bewilderment and concern for her friend, she looked a fright. Both were in their early twenties.

A stranger to their world would have been struck, as they

9

were, by the contrast in their looks, but he would have been still more surprised by something which they appeared to take for granted: the clothes that they were wearing. In each case it was a suit of sackcloth, differently cut and trimmed, but unmistakably sackcloth; and he would have noticed, with a repulsion which they did not feel, that their hair—for they wore no hats—looked dirty. Some foreign substance had lodged in it, something grey and gritty: could it be ashes?

Having looked their fill the two girls dropped their eyes, as though the spectacle was too painful to look at.

Judith was the first to speak.

'I didn't expect to see you here, Jael,' she said in a low voice.

'Nor I you, Judith.'

For a moment this seemed all that they could say, then Judith stole another glance at her friend's swollen and tear-stained prettiness, and murmured:

'I might have guessed.'

'But you, Judith——' began Jael, and stopped.

Well as she knew Judith she could not put her thoughts into words that would not sound insulting. But Judith spoke for her.

'You see, he wanted it.'

'Who?'

'Well, Cain.'

'Oh, *no*.'

Much less upset than her friend, Judith answered steadily, and almost defensively:

'Well, he's a man, after all.'

'So he may be, but——' She could not face the 'but', but Judith could.

'You mean I'm not so ugly? I was Gamma minus, you know, at my last Board.'

'I can't believe it,' Jael said, not looking at Judith.

'So I've qualified for a rise. Any Gamma is, of course, below Gamma plus.'

'They must be blind,' cried Jael, indignantly. 'I . . . I love your face, and so should he. You don't want to change it, do you?'

'No, I'm used to it, you see. I'd rather have been born Beta, of course. But if he wants it——! Getting the permits was the worst part. I minded that.'

'You never came to me.'

'I went to strangers, mostly. You know, the professionals. You have to pay, of course, but you get secrecy.'

'Does that matter?' Jael asked. 'Everyone's got to know in the end . . . What . . . what model did you choose? Number 5?'

'Oh, don't you know? There's no personal choosing now —that's been cut out, it was found to be too expensive. They choose one of three stock models. I wanted Oval, but Cain——' Judith stopped, feeling she had talked too much about herself, 'likes heart-shaped best. What . . . What . . .' Judith hesitated; in her turn she was unable to put the question. She saw her friend's tears falling afresh; she knew the cause; there was really nothing to say.

'I was going to choose 5,' said Jael listlessly. 'But now you tell me it's been cancelled.'

'Yes, this afternoon. It was given out at three o'clock. Where were you?'

'At the Litany. I always go there for my half-day. Where were you?'

'I was at the Casino,' Judith said. 'I hadn't been for quite a long time. Actually I prefer the Litany, but it doesn't do to show a marked Personal Preference.'

Jael was hardly following. 'I suppose not,' she said.

'No.' Judith was firm. 'It leads to inflammation of the ego. But I'm so sorry for you, Jael. Number 5 would have suited you so well. Tell me . . . Tell me how it happened.

Of course, I'm not surprised. Everyone knew you were an Alpha—and Alpha is anti-social,' she added reluctantly.

'Alpha is anti-social,' repeated Jael with bowed head. After a moment she went on: 'I only just failed the Misses.'

'I know,' said Judith.

'That was three years ago. I've been in danger ever since. I thought that when I cut my cheek with the razor——'

'Then it wasn't an accident!' exclaimed Judith.

'No. I thought it would make me B——' She shrugged her shoulders. 'Oh well, put me into a lower category. But I hadn't the courage to do it properly, and my next Board passed me Alpha, but Failed Alpha.'

'What bad luck! Oh, I mustn't say that—luck is a leveller.'

'Luck is a leveller,' repeated Jael. 'And then the complaints began coming in again. The Ministry warned me yesterday that I'd had my twenty-fifth.'

'Were they all genuine?'

'So the Ministry said. They vet them pretty carefully, you know. I'd have had thirty, but five were disallowed as frivolous.'

'I wonder who——' Judith began.

'Oh, they don't tell you. I can guess a few, of course. Electra 90 was one, I'm sure. Maybrick 903—she's always had a down on me. And there are several more whom I suspect. That makes it so unpleasant. It might have been anybody, Judith, it might have been you.'

'It wasn't,' Judith said.

'I shouldn't really blame you if you had. They nearly all complained of E—Bad E,' she added hastily. Equality and Envy—the two E's—were in the moral sphere the positive and negative poles on which the New State rotated. The one attracted, the other repelled. Either word, once uttered, involved the speaker in a ritual dance—a few jerky, gymnastic capers for Envy, a long, intricate, ecstatic exercise for Equality. Some were excused both on medical grounds but

12

the rest did their utmost to avoid these verbal pitfalls. The abbreviations Good E and Bad E were exempt from ritual consequences, as were their facetious counterparts, Good Egg and Bad Egg. A curtsey for Equality and a token spit for Envy were concessions to time-saving that came later.

'It was my eyelashes they mostly picked on, for being too long and curly. My fault, of course, I should have cut them, but sometimes I forgot. One woman complained she had lost several nights' sleep just thinking about my eyelashes. She felt they were digging into her, she said.'

'How do you know it was a woman?' Judith asked. 'It might have been a man—it might very well have been a man.'

'The complaints all came from women, I was told. Most men don't really mind you being pretty.'

'On principle they ought to,' Judith said.

'Yes, I suppose so.' Jael was resigned. 'We ought all to be e——' 'Equal' she was going to say, but she bit the word off, to avoid exposing herself to the most dreaded of the booby-traps that the Dictator had introduced into conversation. To get through the ensuing ritual with credit one needed the grace of a ballet-dancer; indeed, the proper performance of it was taught at all dancing classes. Done well, it was a beautiful and touching *pas de deux*, but the movements had to be so precise and identical that very few could do it justice. An Inspector had the right to ask any passer-by to perform it for him—or her, for there were women Inspectors too, Misses as they were called. But the right was seldom exercised, except by the more officious Inspectors. The mere fact that one person could acquit himself better than another fostered the very element of competition that the ritual was designed to discourage.

'Of course, we must all be level,' said Judith confidently, for the word 'level' had no ritual consequences. 'All the same

I have always thought——' she lowered her voice—'that we ought to be levelled up, not down.'

Jael said nothing.

'You are quite pretty enough to be one of the Misses,' Judith went on indignantly. 'I can't imagine why they failed you.'

'On my nose,' said Jael. 'It's too . . .'

'Too retroussé?'

'Yes. When I was hoping to be elected I tried all sorts of things to . . . to lengthen it. But it was no good. Then I cut myself to be Beta——'

'Beta is best,' said Judith perfunctorily.

'Yes, Beta is best. It's so lonely being a Failed Alpha.'

'Alpha is anti-social,' put in Judith, but without much conviction.

'Yes. Failed Alphas suspect each other. We're betwixt and between—not one thing or another. And to cause Bad E is the worst thing you can do. I shall be much happier B——' She nipped the word off, and looked through the glass doors into the circular hall in which nurses wearing white aprons over their sackcloth were passing to and fro. 'I could be one of them,' she said. 'There are no openings for us, as you know. We can only get temporary jobs, subbing for other people. It's so restless and unsatisfactory. And yet somehow I can't reconcile my-self——'

'Why should you?' asked Judith, suddenly. 'Why should you, Jael? It isn't compulsory.'

'No, but it may become so, if enough people don't volunteer . . . Perhaps we'd better go in now, Judith. I'm only keeping you.'

Irresolutely she moved her hand towards the door. But Judith restrained her.

'I don't see why you should,' she exclaimed. 'It's not your fault that you're an—oh, blast the word! I believe someone's pushing you into it.' She looked at Jael keenly. 'There! I knew I was right.'

'It's Joab,' Jael murmured. 'Don't tell anyone.'

'What, Joab 98? Your brother? But what's it got to do with him? Besides he's a Failed Alpha, too.'

'Yes, but only for brains, and it doesn't matter for men, that's what's so unfair. He's got a good job as a statistician, and he's terrifically keen on the régime, it's his religion. Being his secretary, I see a lot of him, and he's always nagging me, just as Cain, I suppose, nagged you.'

'I like that!' exploded Judith. 'Your own brother! But all the same——' she resumed her normal voice—'if I were you I wouldn't. There are masses of other Failed Alphas about, and I don't believe that anybody envies them. It's different for me—no one will mind if they never see my face again, and I shan't either. I shall be just another Beta.'

'Beta is——'

'Oh, cut it out. I shan't have to bother how I dress. Hats stock-size, stock-shape, stock-colour. All the shops have Bargains for Betas. You've no idea what I used to go through, trying to make the best of myself, while anyone could see I was a low Gamma. People who valued their aesthetic sense wouldn't be seen with me. Oh yes, the second letter of the alphabet is best. It won't change my nature; one's personality isn't in one's face, as some of the malcontents try to make out. I shall be the same underneath.'

'Shall you destroy your Gamma photographs?' asked Jael.

'One is supposed to, of course. I expect I shall be glad to. It's an offence to keep them after you've been altered. I've only had one photograph taken since I was old enough to know what I really looked like and that was for my registration card. I shall have to get a new one for that, I suppose.'

'Will you?' said Jael. 'Won't any second letter do as well? I mean, they all look alike. You can buy the photograph of a stock-face off the peg.'

'It's like finger-prints, you know,' said Judith. 'Experts can tell the difference—and, and . . . people who know you well. And there's one's figure,' she added, with a self-deprecatory giggle. 'That doesn't alter.'

'I know,' said Jael, who was busy with her own thoughts. 'But Maybrick 903 always has to tell me who she is now that she's got her stock-face.'

'She never had much individuality even when she was an anti-social,' said Judith, who was better than Jael at by-passing troublesome words. 'It's my belief that she had herself lowered out of vanity—people didn't mind her type of good looks all that much. Now it's different with you, Jael. If you get yourself lowered, something will be lost.'

'Do you think so?' asked Jael, doubtfully.

'I'm sure of it. And Joab's a pig to want you to.'

'Well, you see, he remembers the war, and he says that any sacrifice——'

'We all agree to that, and we know that Excellence belongs to the Elect——'

'Excellence belongs to the Elect,' repeated Jael, humbly. 'We mustn't try to rise above each other.'

'But you're not trying. You were born good-looking. It was natural——'

'Nature is nasty,' Jael said.

'Nature is nasty,' repeated Judith. 'But even the Dictator——'

'Darling Dictator,' put in Jael quickly.

'Darling Dictator, then. Even he has said that one must not be in too much of a hurry to condemn the natural. The natural, he said, is only to be condemned when it transgresses the rule of E—and you know which E I mean.'

Confusion between the good and bad E's was so frequent that some of the more devout and law-abiding members of the New State found it safer to abstain from abstract discussion.

'But in my case,' Jael said sadly, 'nature has transgressed. That's just it.'

'But not too badly,' Judith tried to reassure her. 'You remember Article 31 of the Constitution—attributes of E. Even E—Good E—has blurred edges—we are advised not to inquire too closely where the blur ends. Well, Jael, you are the blurred edge. And in Chapter 19 of the Revised Pandects it says: "Life is to be lived fully within the limits of the Law. A river must not be content with its bed: it must explore its banks." '

'What a memory you have,' said Jael, admiringly. 'I'd forgotten that one.'

'But it's most important. And somewhere else he says: "Ours is not a negative philosophy; and it is not for the delinquent to have a more delicate conscience than the Dictator." '

'When did he say that?' asked Jael, obviously unconvinced. 'He changes his views so often.'

'Not long ago. And he only changes them in matters of detail—respected be his name.'

'Respected be his name,' echoed Jael, reverently.

A nearby clock struck six.

'Great Dictator! It's time for me to go in,' said Judith briskly. She turned first rather red, then rather pale. 'My appointment for a rise is at six o'clock.'

'Mine, too,' said Jael, beginning to tremble.

'But you're not going to keep it,' said Judith. 'You're not going to keep it, Jael, do you hear? I . . . I forbid you to!'

Jael's tears were beginning to flow afresh and she looked the picture of irresolution and despair.

'But I'd get it all over!' she wailed. 'All . . . all . . . the

17

mental pain of making up my mind! You've no idea what I went through! I haven't slept for nights! It was like . . . like deciding to die! And I *shall* die, in a way—you won't see me again! Not the me that I am now. I know the me doesn't matter——'

'The me doesn't matter,' repeated Judith, in an unwilling voice.

'But somehow I can't bear to lose it!'

'That's what I said!' cried Judith. 'You mustn't lose it! You're not to lose it! You're going beyond your orders!' Pointing to her shrinking friend she raised her voice and said: 'You are transgressing Chapter 19, sub-section 3, of the Revised Pandects.'

Jael was obviously impressed by this but she became still more agitated.

'But what shall I do? How shall I face Joab? And I can't, I can't make up my mind again! Oh, how I wish I had been born Beta! And I wish I hadn't run into you here, Judith! I shouldn't have, if we hadn't both kept the dear Dictator's command to be a quarter of an hour early for every appointment! And he only gave it out last week! Oh, how miserable I am, how miserable I am!'

Wringing her hands she swayed to and fro. Judith looked at her friend in concern and pity, then took a quick decision.

'Go back now,' she said, 'and I'll explain to your Bureau that you aren't well enough to be put down. Then you can think it over quietly. I'll come in tomorrow and you'll have a good laugh when you see me Beta. The operation's hardly more than having a tooth crowned. Goodbye, Jael 97. Kind thoughts of the Dictator.'

18

THE glass door swung ponderously to and fro sending out gusts of warm, conditioned air, and Jael was alone. Still crying and hardly knowing what she did, she began to descend the steps. The sharp breath of the spring twilight revived her—the rounded, pinkish buildings smiled at her. The peacefulness of what she saw stole into her, calming her agitation. Her mind was still topsy-turvy—she felt herself already Beta, but knew that she was still Alpha—but the confusion of the two realities did not hurt her as it had. Timidly, experimentally, she raised her finger to her face and touched the little scar. Her skin, her own dear skin, not that nasty, cracked-up substitute, 'Win-Skin', that the Betas wore, with its ready-made, water-proof, weather-proof make-up. 'Be Beta and you won't have to beautify!' ran the slogan on the hoardings. But she enjoyed making-up; she expressed herself that way; tiny variations of colour to suit different occasions, different moods. To have to look always aggressively healthy, as the Betas did ('Betas are buxom'), even when you were feeling very much the reverse! To faint without changing colour—to die, even, what a horrible thought!

She wandered on, whither her footsteps led her, along the uneven roads, along the weedy pavements, and at every step she began to feel lighter, as though she had avoided some tremendous danger. At the back of her mind a sense of guilt persisted but was held in check by the spontaneous joy that surged up in her body. How precious it was to be still herself! And not hidden away behind a win-skin, easy to put on, all but impossible to take off! Cases had been known where the mask had to be taken off because the flesh suppurated beneath it. People had got terrible skin diseases and one or two had died. As a rule, however, the transformation was perfectly successful, and nearly all the converts, as they were called, rejoiced in their Beta-hood. Security made the Betas smug. They were disapproving to the Failed Alphas and condescending to the Gammas. In fact they had the makings of a caste apart. But there was a flaw in the solidarity of the Betas, a line of demarcation, for the born Betas looked down on the converts, and called them skin-flints, safety-skins, skin-tights, skin-deeps and other opprobrious names.

All three grades had catch-phrases of their own which they used among themselves to distinguish them from the others. Jael had learnt some of them in preparation for her Beta-hood. 'It was all beautiful and beta,' for instance, as a term of praise. Gammas would say: 'How gloriously gamma!' The Failed Alphas were more chary of using their language. Overheard by lower grades, such expressions as 'How absolutely alpha' sometimes produced raised eyebrows and shrugged shoulders. The Failed Alphas were not exactly Ishmaels, but they existed on sufferance, and they knew it.

Pondering these things, trying to readjust herself to her old ambiguous status, which in her mind she had relinquished, Jael wandered on. Here was a knot of people gathered at the kerb, Betas most of them with just a sprinkling of Gammas. (Anyone, even a child, could classify a newcomer at sight.) Jael was naturally sociable; she wanted to join the throng, but hesitated because a Failed Alpha sometimes got a frosty reception. However, curiosity overcame her.

They were planting a tree! They were actually planting a tree! This explained the excitement. Two workmen, wearing the unadorned sackcloth of their labouring hours, were holding it tenderly, this strange brown spidery creature of roots, trunk, twigs and branches; while two more were digging the grave which was inexplicably to give it life. What was it? Where had it come from? Only the Dictator and his Executive, that anonymous band of the Elect, could say. The event must have been advertised on the wireless, but when? It suited the Dictator's puckish humour to spring these surprises; all the same, Jael felt the twinge of guilt that every citizen felt when they had failed to inform themselves of the latest proclamation. Perhaps while she was talking to Judith . . . Now the crucial moment had come; the act of faith was being performed; the tree was being lowered into the ground. The onlookers craned their necks and those behind, including Jael, shifted their positions to get a better view. The faces of the workmen holding the tree became transfigured; the mystical ecstasy that animated them began to spread to the crowd. A deep hush fell and Jael could hear the soft sound of falling earth as it was shovelled back on to the roots of the tree. Long sighing breaths escaped from the spectators. There followed much patting of earth and then—was such a sacrilege really justifiable?—the workmen, still with their intent, closed faces, trampled the place down with their heavy boots. Next, one of them detached himself and fetched a watering-can, and with incredible nonchalance directed a shower of water on the base of the tree. The last drops fell; all four men drew away; a shiver of relaxation went through the crowd. Many of them turned and exchanged with their near neighbours smiles of an almost imbecile happiness and delight. Jael, too, essayed a timid smile, but it seemed to her that the responses she received lacked warmth. Lights were coming out along the streets. For the first time she felt the chill of the March twilight creeping through her sackcloth. To the mixed feelings of the past hours—the alternating resignation, apprehension, elation, guilt—was added a new one: loneliness. She looked about for a class-companion in

21

whom she could confide as easily as the Betas confided in theirs—no introduction needed, just a basic similarity of feature. But there was none.

Sadly, with bent head, she turned away; and as she did so there loomed up before her, coming she knew not whence, for he had certainly not been there a moment ago, the figure of an Inspector. His high shining boots, his white breeches, his golden helmet with its nodding plume, and above all the three B's embroidered on the breast of his white tunic, made him look god-like. He stood looking down at her. In silence Jael salaamed three times and waited for him to speak.

'Alpha is——?'

'Anti-social,' replied Jael promptly, surprised and relieved at being asked such an easy question.

'You're wrong,' said the Inspector. 'Think again.'

Jael stared up at him in dismay. But she took courage from the thought that he must be a kind man: the Inspectors were not obliged to give one a second chance.

'Anarchic?' she ventured.

The Inspector's smile broadened.

'No good. Try again.'

Familiar as she was with them, every disparaging epithet beginning with A fled from Jael's mind. But the Inspector's smile had deepened, and she brought out, almost pertly:

'Awful?'

The Inspector shook his head and the plume dipped and flourished, making a half-circle above his handsome face.

'Antiquated,' he said. 'Five shillings, please.'

Jael fumbled in her handbag and brought out her roll of shillings. Coloured purple, the token money was held together like the bus-tickets of an earlier day. They were not transferable and each was stamped with her identity number.

'Why, you haven't used up any!' exclaimed the Inspector, admiringly.

Sadly, Jael counted out five tickets, and tore them off.

'I don't get much opportunity to,' she said.

'What, a pretty girl like you!'

'Inspectors shouldn't talk to delinquents,' said Jael primly, but without much conviction.

'No, it's you who mustn't talk to us,' replied the Inspector in a lordly manner. 'Name, please.'

'Jael 97.'

'Address?'

'Tophet 518.'

'Now I know,' said the Inspector, with satisfaction. 'Now I know,' he added in a conversational tone; 'I was a Tophet man myself before I was elected. Nice place. Good wireless reception. No excuse for this sort of thing.' He shook his head reprovingly, making the plume dance.

'I was out,' said Jael. Gracious as the Inspector was, she could not feel at her ease talking to him.

'But what about the loud-speakers?'

'There didn't happen to be one where I was,' said Jael feebly. She felt wretched. Among the many emotions of the evening exhilaration had been one, but it had worn off, leaving her empty and despondent: and she felt she could hardly bear this extra stroke of bad luck. But the law must be obeyed. She handed her fine to the Inspector.

But to her astonishment he waved it away.

'Alpha is——?'

Making a prodigious effort Jael remembered.

'Antiquated.'

'Yes, but you're not,' said the Inspector, 'and don't forget it. Sweet thoughts of the Dictator.' He saluted and strode off into the twilight, and the gleam from his uniform left a glow in Jael's heart long after he was gone.

23

CHAPTER THREE

THE Dictator had ruled for fifteen years and was not unpopular.

The Third World War had all but eliminated the human race, and when the end came the twenty million survivors were living underground in the caverns they had excavated before and during the catastrophe. Nobody really believed that it was over, for there had been many false alarms. Deceived by these, reckless and enterprising persons had gone up to explore and not come back. The Governments of each cavern then proclaimed that anyone making investigations on his own would be punished with death; the guards at the cavern entrances were doubled and redoubled. Any attempt to reconnoitre the upper element, it was given out, must have official sanction. (Telephonic communication existed between the various national caves and in some cases, though not in many, they were connected by corridors, heavily guarded. These corridors were hardly ever used and it cost a lot to keep them in repair, but such cave-countries as possessed them were intensely proud of them.)

Perhaps the guards at the entrances were corruptible; at any rate dauntless individuals did manage to slip out and a few of them got back, bearing news which, unobtrusively and judiciously circulated, eventually induced the Governments to send out exploration parties. They were in no hurry to do this because not only had a great many formalities to be gone through, innumerable forms filled up, and special and very expensive ray-proof suits manufactured (the original explorers had gone in their ordinary clothes), but far the greatest proportion of the various surviving people had no wish at all to regain the upper air, or go aloft, as it was called. They were conditioned to the ways of life below, and many had gone through such experiences on the earth's crust that the mere thought of them brought on a nervous seizure. These dissidents brought pressure to bear on their Governments to leave the upper air alone; their own air was plenty good enough, they said; it was sucked down from above and filtered and the temperature and the seasons never varied. Every day was exactly like the last, and this was what they liked. Indeed, the smallest variation in their routine, such as the substitution of a blue food tablet for a pink one (all food was taken in tabloid form) had a disastrous effect on their nervous systems. 'Daylight is dangerous,' was one of the passwords of the cave-dwellers; people wandering too near the mouths of their caves had been known to faint at the sight of a reflected sunbeam. Screens were put up to keep out the daylight, and all the cave-dwellers lived by artificial light, except the guards, who were furnished with strong spectacles.

When it became known, as it did almost simultaneously in all the underground countries, that the surface of the earth was now fit for human habitation, their Governments were faced by a problem more serious than any that had occurred during all the years of their subterranean existence. In each case mass-observers reported that the people were divided roughly into two halves—those who wanted to go up and those who preferred to remain below. The second group was largely composed of the younger members of the community, who had been nourished on tales of the horrors of the Third World War and had been conditioned to a life of absolute routine. Their whole beings, like their gastric juices, worked by the clock; any interference with their time-table had the effect of a grain of grit on a motor engine; they jammed and seized and let out horrid screams.

25

The Governments, not unnaturally, took the side of the stay-at-homes; the younger generation was in all essentials their creation, their hold on it was complete, and their power depended on identifying themselves with its interests. Emigration from the caves was forbidden by law under penalty of death.

It need hardly be said that by this time scientists had devised ways of making people physically and mentally uncomfortable of which we, in these unenlightened days, know nothing. These inventions were rigorously applied and for a time there was no more talk, at least no more open talk, of going aloft. But in spite of everything the longing for it, in many breasts, was not appeased, and in each country arose a leader round whom resistance gathered. These followed each other in quick succession to the grave but others took their places, and do what the authorities would they could not stop a constant leakage through the cave-mouths and other bolt-holes which sleepless ingenuity either made or discovered.

Yet such was the force of organisation that in many countries the revolts were stamped out altogether. But in a handful it lingered on and I needn't say that one of these was the English community, some two million souls living somewhere beneath East Anglia.

The leader who ultimately succeeded in getting the Israelites out of Egypt adopted a new policy and one which baffled the Government. He did not appear; he was a Voice. And such a strange voice, very clear, but over long words it stumbled, though generally it managed to get them out somehow. The listeners-in (and everyone was a listener-in: the radio and television had largely usurped the place of conversation, and talking, though still taught, was an accomplishment many people dropped when they left school) were puzzled and so was the Government. A price, of course, was laid on the Voice's head, and the capture and immediate liquidation of its owner hourly expected; but hours turned into days and days into weeks and still it went on, preaching the doctrine of the Upper Air, in spite of all attempts to jam it. Needless to say, in caverns so extensive there were many corridors and passages that had escaped the vigilance of the Government Survey; patrols were constantly sent out to explore them, but always without success, until one day, in the middle of the day (though the term had not much meaning, for the divis ons of time were purely arbitrary and had no bearing on the position of the sun), the culprit was discovered. He was standing in the Government Square, the place where proclamations were made, in full view, with his microphone, which looked so like a toy that everyone believed it was a mouth-organ until he began to talk through it. Then the loud-speakers on all sides blared forth, completely drowning the sound of the speaker's own voice. It was the moment when people were eating their eleven o'clock pastilles, which were coloured violet and had an E engraved in them; the Square was crowded, but everyone, including the police, was so astonished that for several minutes no one lifted a finger to stop the flood of treason pouring out. Just as the speaker had reached the words 'An ampler aether, a diviner air' a posse of policemen dashed forward and arrested him. He was a child of five years old.

The laugh was against the Government. Even below ground laughter went on, though it was strongly discouraged by authority. People were allowed five minutes a day in which to laugh and get it over, like the interval for coughing which, in earlier days, was sometimes conceded to bronchial subjects at a concert. To encourage them in this, the radio told stories intended to raise a laugh, but these were not, judged by a past standard, really funny. They were either purely nonsensical—attempts to detach the microbe of humour from its context in daily life, jokes in tabloid form, like food—or they were scientific howlers, such as saying the earth is flat, though in fact they were much more recondite than this, since the audience possessed a good deal of scientific knowledge, indeed it was almost the only knowledge they did possess. Fortunately for the Government, the infant traitor was apprehended only two minutes before the interval for compulsory indulgence in mirth was due; so the Government had some pretext for pretending that the guffaws which greeted the arrest were really a response to the official witticisms which almost immediately began to pour out. However, the thousands who were present at the scene knew better, and, since humour dies hard, during the remainder of the day and for several days to come the police had to report outbreaks of hysterical and pointless giggling, which only ceased after the strongest measures had been taken.

As for the child, he was another problem. The first idea was that he should be publicly beheaded, on the very spot where he had been caught red-handed—in fact the day and hour of the execution were fixed. But the mass-observers reported that there was a strong feeling against such a measure, not only among the articulate members of the population, but also among those who could only speak by signs. The Government, therefore, who paid some attention to whatever public opinion there was, proclaimed that by an act of extreme clemency the sentence would be commuted to one of imprisonment for life. Meanwhile, the child would be subjected to a searching interrogation.

It was soon apparent that the child was not politically minded. He could not answer the simplest questions about the Constitution and in other ways was backward for his age. The Investigation Department decided, very reluctantly, that he must be someone else's mouthpiece. But whose? Every known form of truth-finding was applied (and by that time many more were known than we know

28

now), from old-fashioned devices like making the child stand in the corner, or sending him supperless to bed, to ingenious tortures and truth-evacuating drugs. But to no purpose. All the child would say was: 'The pretty gentleman, he told me.'

Living so long below ground, and on exiguous though sustaining fare, had not improved the looks of the population; they were as a whole thin and scrawny, with bellies permanently distended by wind. But among them were quite a number to whom the epithet 'pretty gentleman' could be applied; and these very naturally shook in their shoes. (Indeed, it has been said by social historians that the prejudice against good looks which is to some extent the subject of my story dated from that day.) The suspects were rounded up and questioned; but the job was not as simple as that; many of them, seized by sudden modesty, maintained they were not pretty at all and would hate to be called so. 'Prove it,' they said, and, of course, it was very difficult to prove; they produced witnesses, aestheticians, art-critics, and others, to swear they had no claims to good looks and were, in fact, particularly ugly men. They also took pains to look their worst for the interrogation, refraining from shaving, and even from washing. The Government, who liked to grace their proceedings with a show of legality, were nonplussed, and after a mass-execution of pretty gentlemen had been threatened, the whole inquiry was discreetly dropped.

This was not the signal act of clemency that it was made out to be, for it had occurred to the Investigators that the child, having been brought up almost exclusively by women, was scarcely in a position to know any gentlemen, pretty or otherwise. He was not what was known contemptuously as an 'F.C.' or Family Child. Families were still permitted but they were very much frowned on, and the majority of children were brought up in crêches of a

29

hundred, fifty of either sex, and cared for (if that be the word) by women chosen by lot for the purpose. Until the age of seven their entourage was exclusively feminine. The little traitor's provenance was soon discovered: he belonged to kiddykot 81. The Government then began to set about the ten nurses or kiddy-kuddlers, as they were somewhat euphemistically called, but they displayed unexpected firmness. With the political sense that women sometimes have, they divined that the Government was embarrassed, if not actually on the run; one and all they declared that Kiddy (m) 19167 (for each child was allotted a number instead of a name) had never been out of their sight, and could never have been in contact with any pretty gentleman (a contact, indeed, they would have taken special pains to guard him from). To a woman they were loyal to the regime, they said; but if they had to put up with any more of this sort of thing they would strike. Striking was, of course, forbidden, but the idea, if not the fact, of it still existed, and the Government were alarmed. No member of the community would or could do any job, except the job that he or she was trained for; and at the thought of 200,000 children behaving exactly as they liked, without surveillance, the imaginations of the legislators boggled . . .

So not for the first time women played a decisive part in constitutional history.

Then for a time things simmered down; but while the episode was still fresh in men's minds, the crisis boiled up again. Again the Voice was heard, high, piping, clear, not the same voice, it was generally agreed, but speaking the same message.

Thrown into a panic, the Government immediately took repressive measures. This time neither pretty gentlemen nor kiddy-kuddlers were spared; their ranks were decimated, the victims being chosen by lot. The reign of terror recalled the worst moments of the war. By no means all the deaths were caused by Government action; the two parties inflicted wholesale massacres on each other, and many men with no particular political convictions took advantage of the general disorder to go about wounding and murdering. Still the voice fluted on; its demand for fresh air and sunlight could be heard above the rattle of machine-guns and the volleys of firing squads. The Government retired to their most secret bomb-proof, gas-proof, ray-proof, germ-proof shelter, and there it was that they ordered the Slaughter of the Innocents which brought the dispensation to an end.

For hardly had the shots rung out and the toddlers toppled over than the second child appeared. No shouts of laughter greeted him, only aghast faces and a horrified, despairing silence. He said nothing, but beckoned and slowly walked away; and by ones and twos people began to follow him until it seemed the whole crowd was on the move. Nobody tried to stop them as they passed down the long corridors, and when they came to the mouth of the cave the guards stood up and saluted them. So they went out into the daylight, about a million in all, half the population of the English Underworld.

CHAPTER FOUR

ALTHOUGH it was summer by the calendar, many thousands perished of exposure as well as of starvation, for the effect of the bombing had been to alter England's climate (and possibly the climate of other countries, too) to that of a perpetual March. An east wind blew, and grey clouds, which the sun never quite got through, though its position was visible behind them, scudded across the sky. The divisions of day and night followed the old seasons, otherwise there was little to distinguish them, since the temperature did not vary and there was no vegetation to speak of to mark the time of year. But gradually the creative forces of life asserted themselves, houses were built, trade established itself, the rhythm of work and leisure became more even.

Among the casualties of the exodus was the child who led it, the mouthpiece of the Pretty Gentleman. While food and shelter were being improvised the weakest went—not to the wall, for there were no walls—but out of the struggle for survival. At any rate he disappeared. Some said he was still alive and a few claimed to have identified him. In the New State Truth held no privileged position (privilege of any sort was frowned upon); as sources of information, hearsay and legend were much preferred and carried far more weight. The fluting, piping voice that had rallied the freedom-lovers in the Underworld was silent, and a great, golden voice, a voice by far more sonorous and plausible than the dry voice of Truth, was heard instead. Heard everywhere, indoors and out; for no room, however private, no country spot, however remote, was sound-proof to it. It could not be switched off.

In the confusion that reigned for a short time the boy might easily have been absorbed into the children's quarter, for among the many institutions that the New State took on from the Old, was the segregation of children. At first the Dictator's golden voice proclaimed that children should be brought up by their parents: every child should be a Family Child. But this didn't work. For one thing the children were too delicate to be brought up by medically inexperienced persons. In the New State they were exposed to lingering influences of radioactivity that the Underworld had escaped—just as their parents were: the percentage of sterility was much higher above ground than below. The survival of the race was the Dictator's prime concern. So once more the children had to be segregated and were seldom seen about the streets; someone coming new to the place might have thought it was an exclusively adult community.

There was another argument for segregation. Most of the children were so inured to communal life and being in an age-group, that they did not take kindly to solitary confinement with their parents. Except through mass-suggestion, they could hardly think or act at all; personal approach, individual attention, left them resentful and bewildered; their parents seemed to them another species and a hostile one. So both sides gained, in peace of mind at any rate, by being kept apart.

The Dictator, however, declared he wanted to keep the idea of family life alive, and among the many ballets prescribed for patients and delinquents of all ages was the Family Dance. The grown-ups did it and the children did it; in each age-section the parents were chosen by lot, the others played the parts of children. Among the grown-ups it was a favourite ballet: love, care, tenderness, all the most ideal feelings of parenthood inspired it, and so responsive were the adult children that the performance often ended in

33

tears of ecstasy. Among the children it was a favourite, too, but given much more sparingly, for the child-parents treated their child-families with the utmost severity and harshness: smacks, blows, scuffles were the order of the dance; and though it, too, often ended in tears, they were tears of pain and rage.

If the Dictator's theory was that vicarious and counterfeit emotions were safer than real ones, then both ballets were successful, for the children's was always called off before they had time to hurt each other.

He called his subjects Patients and Delinquents (the shortened form was Ps and Ds) to remind them of their common fallen state, confirmed by three World Wars; and he sometimes promised that, when they deserved it, he would address them by a different style, and a more complimentary one. Meanwhile, further to remind them of their shortcomings, he obliged each one of them to take the name of a murderer or a murderess. The Department of Criminal Nomenclature had a good many on its books (Biblical murderers were most people's choice) but not enough to go round. To supplement the shortage each name was followed by a number, the first figure of which indicated the district that the person lived in: thus, Jael was Jael 97, and Judith, Judith 91.

If, the Dictator said, patients and delinquents learned what it felt like, even nominally and vicariously, to have committed a murder, they would be less likely to commit one.

The Inspectors, however, were exempt; no criminal association clung to them. They were named after the Seven Archangels. Officially they, too, had each a number, the Number of the Elect; but it was only known among themselves. None of the laity would have dared to ask; to the laity they were Michael, Raphael, and the rest.

It was a relaxed and invalidish civilisation. Everything

about it suggested weakness and convalescence. A sort of toadstool architecture was invented, in which circles and curves predominated; corners were allowed, though sparingly, but right angles were forbidden, and no house might be higher than two storeys. Traffic was horse-drawn and whips were taboo. Any form of hurry was discouraged. Churches, casinos and cinemas were erected in every township. The cinemas showed films of the horrors of war and attendance was compulsory twice a week, unless a doctor's certificate of exemption could be produced. In the churches the Litany was intoned all day long; the Dictator promised that when the population merited it, other forms of religious service would be allowed. Attendance at the Casino was not compulsory but one earned good marks by attending, though very little money changed hands, since everyone had the same income and money was only transferable in return for an official receipt. Of course, a great many black-market transactions took place; culprits were always being dropped on by the Inspectors, and fined or made to wear their sackcloth plain, or worse still, to wear it on the one day a week when sackcloth was excused. On those days the offenders usually preferred to stay indoors; for if they ventured into the street anyone could challenge them to perform a ritual dance, and the Inspectors, who formed at least a tenth of the population, saw to it that they did. The townships were so small that the Inspectors knew everyone by sight, and had lists of each delinquent's fines and legal disabilities. So non-compliance was always a risk, though many took it.

On the whole, the penalties were not very severe; they were equivalent to wearing an overcoat on a hot day or going without one on a cold day, at worst to wearing a hair shirt. There was a great deal of compulsion in the air, but it was chiefly intended to make recreation obligatory; people were not encouraged to work, though everyone

35

had to work a little and no one was prevented from working if he had a mind to.

How did the Dictator enforce his discipline? Partly through the radio, through which with startling suddenness he announced his decrees, and partly through the Inspectors. The Inspectors were a caste apart, and were chosen by examination either for beauty or brawn or brains. Some had all three qualifications and were known as Three Bs. These they wore as decorations and were entitled to three salaams or whatever mark of respect was the order of the day; the Dictator kept changing them, as he changed so many things. But among themselves the Inspectors were virtually equal. There were women Inspectors, too, but it was considered inexpedient for them to patrol the streets; they either married the male Inspectors and made homes for them (homes were gradually returning to favour) or they held administrative posts, behind doors and windows. In any case, they were not entitled to marks of public recognition. Some said the Dictator was a woman-hater; but others said you could not expect a man to kow-tow to a woman, still less a woman to another woman.

The third method by which the Dictator maintained discipline was also the most criticised. Every citizen, before clocking in for his or her daily employment, and there were special arrangements for the unemployed, had to drink a daily dose of bromide, the strength of which was carefully calculated to suit the patient's temperament (everyone, except the Inspectors, was regarded as a patient). Attempts to evade this were frequent and sometimes successful; but when detected they were severely punished, either by long spells of ritual exercises or by compulsory indulgence in some sport for which the culprit was known to have a distaste: two rounds of golf was one of the severest. Those whom bromide brought out in spots were permitted other sedatives; but you could safely say that nine-tenths of the population below the Alpha, the Inspector class, who were exempt, were kept permanently below par as far as impulses towards rebellion, or any form of throwing their weight about unduly, went. Slogans such as 'Betas like Bromide' were put about to gild the pill, and though many people grumbled few regarded it as a real hardship. Many positively enjoyed it and were, in fact, bromide-addicts; while others found that when they succeeded in evading it their nerves began to trouble them with symptoms of anxiety and guilt.

But perhaps the chief reason why the Dictator kept his hold was that many people still remembered the horrors of the Third World War and the lesser but still considerable horrors that preceded the exodus from the Underworld. It almost seemed as though this time humanity had learned a lesson from experience.

All the same, there were critics who complained that the régime was too namby-pamby; and one of these, shortly before my story begins, gave his complaint existentialist sanction by committing a murder—the first of the new dispensation. Everywhere the little townships were plunged into mourning; even the Inspectors were put into a form of sackcloth and for a week every cinema and television set showed nothing but close-ups of the body of the murdered man. It was realised that none of the existing penalties was adequate to meet the situation. *Ex postfacto* legislation was quickly passed and it was arranged that the murderer should be Returned Empty to the Underworld, which would know how to deal with him, in exchange for one of its own malcontents whose offence had been political deviation.

No one knew what 'Returned Empty' meant, but the most terrifying suggestions were put about, and the letters 'R.E.' (everyone in the New State was initials-minded) came to symbolise the worst thing that could happen, far worse than death, which being common to all, was looked on with less horror. Some denied that the sentence was ever executed; even among the male population the distinctions of individuality were rather faint, and a number might slip in unobserved with other numbers. But by the majority the incident was held to prove that the Dictator still had diplomatic relations with the Underworld.

He was in touch, too, it was thought, with the other States which had escaped from bondage when the English contingent did. For the movement had been simultaneous among the cavern-dwellers of all nations; their Governments had been powerless to prevent it; half the remaining population of the world was liberated.

In the absence of transport and communication these countries were only names to most sub-Alpha English people, but names they were, and most important names, for each had its own epithet attached to it. This epithet the population had to learn, and it might be changed at any time without other notice than the voice of the loud-speaker. It was invariably a complimentary epithet, for the Dictator had declared that the thought of another country must always be a pleasant thought. But the epithets themselves varied continually. Thus, Belgium might be beautiful one day, brave the next, bountiful the next, businesslike the next, and so on through all the alliterative adjectives that made Belgium sound beatific (the Dictator was addicted to alliteration), and Denmark might be delightful, delicious, distinguished, dutiful, or even duty-free. The population had to keep themselves informed of what was the current epithet; and anyone who, when challenged by an Inspector, could not give it, was liable to a fine. If in exasperation he or she said that Belgium was beastly or bloody, and Denmark dirty or detestable, the fine was trebled. France was friendly, Germany generous, Spain splendid, Italy inimitable, Uruguay unparalleled, but only from one day to another. Theoretically, international relations could not have been better, for the name of every foreign country evoked an earthly paradise; and theoretical they seemed destined to remain.

Many such verbal booby-traps had official sanction; it was said that they kept people mentally and harmlessly on the alert, and were valuable agents of civic instruction. But for the Underworld no epithet, complimentary or the reverse, was ever promulgated. It was itself, no adjective could add to or subtract from it: a symbol of absolute dread.

The Dictator's dealings with it, whatever they had been, led to a new departure, the results of which will be told in the next chapter.

CHAPTER FIVE

AFTER her volte-face, so to speak, at the Equalisation (Faces) Centre, Jael felt like someone who has broken off an engagement of marriage: at once guilty and relieved. Relief would have carried the day, for she was a girl of sanguine temperament, but for one thing: her brother, Joab. Joab 98, to give him his full title, was, like his sister, a Failed Alpha; but as he was a man this carried no social or moral stigma. Had his other intellectual attainments been as undeniable as his gift for statistics, he might have been a Full Alpha, an Inspector; but they were not. He took his position as a high-grade civil servant very seriously; his detractors (for he had them) said that the only time during the day when he was really happy was in the five minutes set apart for serious thought—the 'S.T.' as it was called, during which no one was allowed to laugh. It might occur at any time, according to the Dictator's whim, and every day produced a new crop of petty delinquents, who had to pay a forfeit: it had even interrupted the midnight call to duty, though it was then very difficult to enforce.

Joab was Jael's senior by four years: he had been eight, she four, at the time of the Exodus fifteen years ago. They were orphans and had been brought up in the same kiddikot in the Underworld, and were allowed the same privilege in the new—for the Dictator had taken over a great many of the old institutions—too many in the opinion of some, too few in the opinion of others. Zeal for the New Order was paramount in Joab; it was said that he was spiritually married to it, and would never seek another spouse; but he was fond of his sister in his way and had great influence with her. It was almost as much for her sake as for the State's

40

that he wanted her to standardise her appearance; he thought she would be happier if she did. Neither fish nor flesh, looked on askance by their fellows, few of the Failed Alphas were really happy and Jael was a conformist at heart, as Joab knew.

To make her position more tolerable he had given her a job as his secretary. To do this he had had to compromise with his conscience, for, in the allotting of jobs, Betas and even Gammas were given preference to Failed Alphas. But the régime was, let us face it, rather corrupt; civil servants had many privileges. Joab, though more strait-laced than most, was prepared to avail himself of them. Besides working in his office, Jael also kept house for him, so she saw a great deal of him.

Jael told him about the planting of the tree, and how exciting it had been; she was going back to look at it, she said, in the luncheon interval. 'Supposing all the flowers had been killed, too,' she added, 'as well as the trees! I wonder where they found it,' she went on. 'A flower is rare enough, but only think, a tree!'

'Flowers were better protected,' said her brother, 'because of their nearness to the ground. It was the things that stuck up that were destroyed. The proportion of flowers to trees is—I could give you the exact figures—but roughly three to one. We don't need either, of course. The plastic substitutes are better in every way.'

'But think of something *growing*!'

'You're just being romantic. Besides, remember what the flowers suffered!'

It had been discovered that flowers could feel as much as human beings, or more; the few that remained were taken immense care of and it was forbidden, under serious penalties, to pick them. Among the many sins and crimes that historians of the régime imputed to previous ages, cruelty to plants came high. 'Imagine living in a time,' said

41

Joab, 'when plants were so tormented! The most precious things we have, and yet they were treated far worse than human beings in concentration camps.

'They were picked, which was in itself an appalling shock to their nervous systems (imagine how you would feel, Jael, if someone tore you in half), and left to die slowly in water, a lingering death from drowning and starvation, and then, often before they were dead, they were thrown on a rubbish heap to perish of thirst. It's almost inconceivable, the barbarity of those days.'

Jael agreed, for it was no use arguing with Joab. To change the subject—for she often told him things about herself that she suspected he might not approve of, for fear of losing touch with him, a danger that constantly threatened their relationship—she went on to relate her encounter with the Inspector.

'You mean to say he really let you off the fine!' said Joab, frowning.

'Yes,' said Jael.

'I think it's a pity Inspectors can't be reported,' Joab broke out. Then checking himself: 'Well, perhaps not. The Dictator knows best. Darling Dictator.'

'Darling Dictator,' repeated Jael.

'Still, another time I think you should protest. And by the way, have you taken your bromide?'

Jael admitted that she hadn't, and hastily turning the cock of the urn, poured herself a stiff dose of the sticky stuff.

Sitting down in front of her typewriter, which in certain moods reminded her of Joab, she addressed herself to her correspondence. Gradually the familiar deadening of sensation stole through her, a gentle tide, calming her agitation, putting the things that worried her further off, blurring their outlines in a film of whitish mist, but bringing nothing that she wanted nearer, confusing positive and negative, desire and aversion, until she could think of things she liked

42

and disliked without feeling there was much difference between them.

'Are you sure you haven't taken too much?' asked Joab, eyeing the medicine glass. He spoke as if he was warning a confirmed toper against excess, but there was real concern in his voice and Jael was touched by it, though she suspected it was due to bureaucratic zeal that she should not exceed the prescribed dose.

'Well, I felt a bit nervy,' she said.

'Why?' he demanded.

Jael sighed. It was so difficult to explain anything to him. 'Oh, it's all to do with my face, I suppose,' she said.

'Your face?' said Joab, staring at it.

'Yes, wondering whether to have it betafied.'

'You haven't had it betafied!' Joab exclaimed.

'No, hadn't you noticed?'

'Not till this moment,' Joab said. 'I had taken it for granted that you would. Oh, Jael!' he added, in sorrow as well as in anger. 'What an example to set!'

'Don't you like my face as it is?' asked Jael wistfully.

'I quite like it as a face,' said Joab, as if that was very little to like it for. 'But as a potential breeding ground of Envy' (Joab went through the motions of spitting: he never used euphemisms or shirked the consequences of ritual words), 'I heartily dislike it. I heartily dislike it,' he repeated, 'and you know that, Jael. No wonder you feel nervy. By keeping your face you have transgressed the first law of our common life. What you take to be nerves is guilt. Don't you feel guilty?'

'Not altogether,' confessed Jael, still anxious to be to him a person in her own right, not a reach-me-down but made to her own measure. 'It's my own face after all. I suppose I have a right to it,' she said with some spirit.

'You have a right to nothing that is liable to cause Envy in the heart of a fellow-delinquent,' said Joab, pursing his

43

lips for the ritual spit, and using the word 'delinquent', which, as one of the official terms for an inhabitant of the Upper World was more commonly used than 'patient'. 'Our constitution and way of life are based on it.'

Jael looked at him, as kindly as she could.

Joab's looks were definitely Gamma, and though standardisation of looks among men had never been considered necessary, before Joab achieved his present eminence some ill-natured men friends had sent him more or less facetious petitions begging him to have his face altered as it offended their aesthetic sense. His marked indifference, indeed harshness, towards good-looking women may have dated from that time.

Jael felt she must defend herself.

'I know that Envy is the worst thing possible,' she said, moistening her lips for the gesture she knew that Joab would expect of her. 'But——' She stopped, for to make an adverse criticism of the régime or its dogmas was almost impossible to her. 'Don't you think,' she went on, 'that there is another side to it—in my case, I mean? Don't you think that when people see me looking pretty—if I do—it makes them feel more cheerful? There's no harm in feeling cheerful, is there?'

'None,' said Joab, grudgingly. 'For reasons I won't go into, your face might make certain men feel cheerful. But supposing they are married men—and most delinquents are married, as you know, the State rightly imposes fines on bachelors—I might have been forced into marrying myself if——'

'But you *are* married to yourself!' Jael exclaimed.

Joab looked at her repressively and went on: 'The cheerfulness you might inspire in married men can only cause Envy'—his face worked—'in their wives. And that we simply cannot allow. Cheerfulness as you call it—I should give it a different name—is all right in its place, but if it excites a single twinge of what you would term Bad E, then it must be stamped out. Better a population of long-faced delinquents'—he attempted a smile—'than of smirking floosies' (the word had a strange effect coming from his lips) 'out to break up homes.'

'I'm not out to break up homes,' said Jael. 'Anyhow, there aren't many homes to break up.'

'The home is still on trial,' said Joab. It was characteristic of him that he did not hesitate to impart information which was perfectly well known to his interlocutor. 'It may be discontinued at any moment. Homes are a hot-bed of—well, of everything we want to eradicate. You will say' (Joab often put a vulnerable argument into an opponent's mouth) 'that all delinquents' homes are uniform, and that uniformity is the outward expression of Equal——'

Their eyes met.

'The shortened form, I think,' said Joab quickly. He made a creditable bow and Jael dropped a curtsey.

'They are as uniform as human hands can make them,' he proceeded. 'But each has something particular to itself—perhaps an ornament, or the arrangement of the furniture—which makes it individual and therefore a standard of comparison. You will hear people say, in the words of the old song, "ours is a nice house, ours is," meaning that it is nicer than other people's. Of course, all houses are alike, and they are the property of the State; but the idea of possession still survives in them: I recognise it, like a bad smell.'

'But we have a home,' objected Jael, 'and I'm proud of it.'

'Proud of it?' echoed Joab. 'What do you mean?'

'It answers to something in me,' said Jael, 'something that I aspire to. I don't know how to put it.'

'By aspiration,' demanded Joab, 'do you mean a perpendicular or a horizontal movement of the mind?'

Jael saw the catch in this.

'Well, perhaps horizontal,' she ventured.

Joab sniffed.

'So long as it isn't upward,' he said. 'Remember we can all touch the ceiling.'

'We can all touch the ceiling,' Jael repeated.

'And betafy means beautify,' continued Joab.

'Betafy means beautify.'

'Well then, why didn't you keep your appointment at the Ministry of Facial Justice?'

Jael moved uneasily in her chair and involuntarily her fingers went to her face.

'I don't know . . . I don't know . . . somehow I would rather look myself.'

Joab shrugged his shoulders.

'Well, there's no accounting——' he began.

He checked himself and added, rather sternly: 'But, of course, there is no such thing as tastes. There is only taste.'

Then, seeing that Jael was on the point of tears, he got up and awkwardly kissed her.

Jael said, chokingly: 'They say that Betas don't feel kisses.'

'Why not?'

'Because their faces don't feel in the same way—they aren't sensitive.'

'Oh, that's all nonsense,' exclaimed Joab. 'Of course they feel them.'

'How do you know?'

The question slipped out before she was aware of it. But she needn't have been afraid that she had wounded him.

'How do I know?' he repeated. 'Because I've been told. How else can one know anything?'

Jael said nothing, and was turning back to her papers, when suddenly he asked:

'What are you going to do this afternoon?'

It was unlike him to take an interest in her movements.

'I thought of going for a drive,' she said, uneasily.

'Oh, Jael!'

Drives were motor-coach trips, and were notoriously intended for the weaker members of the community. Private motoring was not allowed: it was considered dangerous, decivilising, individualistic, and ideologically unsound. Nearly all machinery was in the hands of the Inspectors; they did not need motors, for they had their own ways of getting about.

But the Dictator, so he said, was indulgent and compassionate; he knew that the pre-war generation had set great store by motoring and he did not want to forbid, as they all knew, any form of innocent corporate recreation. Accordingly, for those who wanted them there were motor trips into the countryside; but they were not popular with the authorities, suggesting that the pre-war state of mind still persisted in some reactionary hearts. Intending trippers had not only to pay the fare but a small fine as well. In spite of this, the expeditions had been growing in popularity: queues lined up and the unlucky ones had to be turned away. Jael had never before thought of going on one of these expeditions; she knew that it would mean a bad mark with the authorities. But since her nervous crisis at the Ministry she had suddenly felt an overwhelming impulse to go.

She was trying to explain this to Joab, determined that he should know what her feelings were, when suddenly the red light came on and the familiar opening phrase of 'Every Valley' was played three times.

'A triple warning!' exclaimed Joab, putting on his most official manner. 'Please take it down, Jael.'

The pen was hardly in her hand when the Voice began.

'Patients and Delinquents,' it said, 'it has been brought to our notice' (for important announcements the Voice spoke in the first person plural) 'that more and more of you are

47

making use of the Motor Expeditions (Country) Service. This Service was inaugurated, as you will remember, simply as a concession to those members of our community who had been accustomed before the Third World War to travel in these dangerous, unsightly, and (when in private hands) flagrantly anti-social vehicles. But for the representations of our Psychiatric Service, who were of opinion that motor-minded delinquents would suffer severe mental disturbance if deprived of their favourite pastime, we should never have consented to the revival of this noxious and unpleasant form of locomotion. More than any other single cause (unless it be cruelty to flowers) it has been responsible for the hardening of the moral arteries (sclerosis moralis) which has been the curse of the twentieth century. Motorists (as they used to be called) were utterly irresponsible in their dealings with each other and with the pedestrian public; for their benefit homicide was legalised. The basic principles of Equality were flouted, while the opposing principle of Envy was disastrously encouraged.'

At this point there was a pause ... Jael, while automatically going through the prescribed motions, watched through the window the passers-by who had been caught in the street by the announcement, also performing their ritual exercises. After two or three minutes the Voice went on:

'It has been said that in the case of each possessor of a motor-car, the ego was monstrously distended; psychic Y-ray photographs have shown as much as a thousand per cent enlargement. And not only that, but each car was to its possessor a badge of social superiority to all his neighbours who could not afford an equivalent vehicle, or perhaps a vehicle at all; while to the owners of more costly machines, these same motorists exhibited a demeanour of grovelling servility. We will not distress your ears by using again the word we used just now. Suffice it to say that unless under the influence of alcohol (as they often were) these motorists' (the

Dictator's normally suave voice hissed the word) 'were totally without the sense of solidarity, of the absolute fusion of interests between man and man, without which our race cannot hope to survive.

'We do not mean to suggest that the Motor Expeditions (Country) Service would lead to a recurrence of the lust for private property; but we wish to reaffirm our conviction that this antiquated method of progression does preserve the smell, we might almost say the stink' (a derisive note crept into the Dictator's voice) 'of the bad old times.

'Patients and Delinquents!

'We shall not abolish the Motor Expeditions (Country) Service, for we are well aware that the New Dispensation is more readily absorbed by some than by others. But we intend to modify it. In every future excursion one of the six vehicles that compose the Service's fleet will meet with an accident. The drivers themselves will not know which vehicle has been selected for this purpose. There will be discomfort; there may be casualties; we hope there will be no fatalities, but this even we cannot tell.

'Patients and Delinquents! We are confident that none of you will wish to take this risk, but it is for you to decide.'

Jael and Joab stood up with expressionless faces, and then sat down again.

Joab said: 'Well, Jael, do you still want to go for a country jaunt?'

'I don't know,' said Jael. 'Perhaps not today.'

CHAPTER SIX

CAMBRIDGE—for so the settlement was named—was built on the supposed site of the famous University town, not a vestige of which remained. It was a place of about ten thousand inhabitants. Ten thousand was the upward limit allowed to any one town except London, and communication between towns was not encouraged. A few roads had been built but they were worse than third-class. 'The sense of distance must be restored,' the Dictator had said. The Inspectors, on the other hand, could get from one end of England to the other with miraculous speed. No one knew how they travelled: some said on flying saucers. The Dictator, of course, seemed to be omnipresent. His voice was heard not only in every town but in every room and there was no way of silencing it. Radio sets were so constructed that even when they were turned off his voice still came through.

One handicap that the Motor Expeditions (Country) Service had to face was the fact that, during the Third World War, nearly all the Ancient Monuments had been wiped out. As far as the works of man went, there was nothing to make an objective for an expedition. And to some extent this was also true of the works of God. The atomic weapons had not spared them either. Not only had they stripped the countryside of verdure, replacing green with a colour like mud, but colder, greyer and less luminous, they had also, in many places, levelled the hills and filled up the valleys—the prophecy enshrined in the Dictator's signature-tune had come literally as well as figuratively true.

With one exception, there was nothing for the gaping trippers to look at—no beauty spot, no view, no 'sight'

50

of any sort. The expeditions, however, took different routes, in so far as there remained different routes to take, and these were numbered, for the sake of convenience, A1, A2, A3, like the roads of the pre-war world. Most of the expeditions-addicts (as they were called) took whichever coach happened to be going, without inquiring its destination; and this was the accepted practice. Others, however, professed to find one route more satisfactory than another, and would fiercely champion the hillock visible from A1 against the pond that, five miles from the start, was visible from A2. These arguments sometimes grew quite heated, although, strictly speaking, they were out of order, since the whole idea of preference was taboo.

Those were on safer ground who admitted frankly that they favoured one route rather than another because they had a prejudice in favour of certain numbers and figures; A1 or A2 had an almost mystical attraction for them. For with public and official opinion the irrational had much more weight (and was treated with more respect) than the rational. An argument was a proof of being out of line with official theory; a prejudice had the authority or at any rate the excuse of the sub-conscious mind to back it, and was a matter for compassion and the psychiatrist.

The post-war landscape, then, was, all over the country, featureless and dull. But in the neighbourhood of Cambridge there was an exception to this. Owing to one of those freaks in the process of destruction, of which the Second World War had given many examples, the western tower of Ely Cathedral still survived. The rest of the church was flat, its ruins scarcely distinguishable in the mud that heaved around it, but the tower still stood, a gigantic and awe-inspiring landmark. Indeed its effect was so overwhelming that beholders had been known to faint at the sight of it, and even the least sensitive were moved with tumultuous feelings for which they couldn't account.

Those few who remembered the great building in its glory would sometimes try to describe it but they got no encouragement to do this, for nostalgia of any kind was looked on askance. Not that the Dictator frowned upon religion; he even encouraged it as a necessary outlet of the human spirit; but it had to be the contemporary religion of his own brand, and the Litany was the only form of it that he permitted to delinquents. The Litany in which everyone was equal, equal in sinnerdom. The tower of Ely Cathedral, piercing the heavens, spoke another language.

All the same, excursions to visit Ely were allowed, and although they were far the most popular they had to take their turn with the others, and like the others were known by a number, in this case A5.

Jael did not talk much about her project. Few people did, for it was as unwise to broadcast in advance a proposed peccadillo as it would have been to say you meant to ride your bicycle on the footpath (bicycles were allowed) or get drunk on Saturday night. (Drunkenness was treated very leniently by the regime.) But the Dictator's pronouncement led to a buzz of conversation about the expeditions as a whole, and it was generally agreed that by making them unsafe he had snuffed them out altogether. No one would go at the risk of life and limb. Would passengers who had already taken tickets get their money back? Or would they lose their ticket-money and their fine-money as well? Jael listened, and commonsense told her that her best plan would be to try to get her money back. But it would be a compli-cated and time-taking business and the official would be short with her, as he had been when he issued the ticket. He had made her feel that she was out of step, letting down the side. But that slight embarrassment would soon be over, it didn't really count. What did count was the simple fact that she wanted to go, and that mysteriously the threat of the accident only inflamed her desire. People might say what they liked; she would go!

The worst moment was when she had to break the news to her brother.

'I can't understand you,' he grumbled. 'Ever since you started this face-saving business you've been a different creature. By rights I should report you to the Ministry of Psychiatry.'

'But you wouldn't do that, would you?' asked Jael anxiously.

'Only because you are my sister and Relations Needn't Tell.'

'Relations Needn't Tell,' repeated Jael.

'But they can, of course, and I should be doing it for your sake, not mine.'

'Of course,' said Jael, automatically.

'Don't think I don't realise the difficulty of your position. As a Failed Alpha you represent the Voluntary Principle. The Voluntary Principle, as the Dictator has said, is like the appendix in the human body—it is of no use, but unless it gives serious trouble it had better be retained. If it gives serious trouble——'

'Yes?' said Jael.

'Well, there might be an order for the V.P. to be removed. By clinging to your face——'

'I don't exactly cling to it,' objected Jael.

'Well, by refusing to be betafied, you have shown that your Voluntary Principle is unhealthy, and if you now go on this expedition you will prove it is inflamed. Besides——'

'Besides what?' Jael asked.

'Besides there is the danger of an accident.'

Jael thought a moment and her eyes brightened.

'Oh no,' she said decidedly. 'Not to me. Nothing ever happens to me. Have you ever known anything happen to me, Joab? And if it did——'

'If it did?' repeated her brother.

'Well, it might be rather fun.'

Joab shook his head disgustedly.

'I don't know what's come over you, Jael,' he said. 'If worry had not been forbidden, except in certain well-defined cases, I should worry about you. I might ask for a permit to worry——'

'Oh, please don't do that!'

'I might, if I thought it would bring you to your senses. Jael, I sometimes suspect you of secret worrying.'

Jael changed colour.

'Of course I don't.'

'Worry is Waste of Time,' said Joab.

'Worry is Waste of Time,' repeated Jael. 'What makes you think I worry?'

'I can see it in your face. If you had been betafied——'

'Yes!'

'You wouldn't show it. Betas don't show their feelings.'

'I know. That's what I don't like.'

'But why? They can show feelings. The choice is almost endless. You can have any one of ninety-nine expressions.'

'I still prefer my own.'

'Jael, aren't you rather conceited? Let me read you some of them,' Joab went to a filing cabinet and opened a drawer. He took out a sheet of cardboard, rather like those which customs-house officers used to give travellers from abroad to remind them of what they had to declare.

'Amiable,' he began, 'affable, agreeable. What's wrong with any of those?'

'But I don't always feel amiable, or affable, or agreeable.'

'Perhaps not, but wouldn't you rather look as if you did? Well, here are some more—compounds of Beta. Beta-Beauty (that's a general favourite), Beta-Belle, Beta-Buxom, Beta-Birdie (perhaps that wouldn't suit you), Beta-Bright——'

Jael shuddered.

'I should hate to be always bright.'

'But other people would like you to be. Then there s Busy-Beta (a play on busy bee, of course), British-Beta—that's a good, hard-wearing expression, I believe.'

'I don't like any of them,' said Jael. 'Not for keeps, I mean.'

'Well, let's leave the Betas. "Pert, pensive, patient, provocative"——'

'Would you like me to look provocative?'

'Well, I'm told that women want to.'

'Yes, but not all the time.'

'Stern, serious, saucy, side-long,' Joab cocked his eye at her. 'How would "side-long" do?'

But Jael could bear it no longer. Her eyes smarting with tears she jumped up, and ran into the next room, which she occupied as Joab's secretary. Work in plenty lay upon her writing table but she stared at it with unseeing eyes.

Presently Joab followed her in, and sat down awkwardly on the other chair.

'I'm sorry, Jael,' he said. 'I never realised you were such an emotional type.' He glanced at her tear-stained face and red, swollen eyes. 'Betas can't cry, you know,' he went on kindly, 'at least they can, but it runs off, the surface is water-proofed. Wouldn't you like Beta better?'

Still sobbing, Jael shook her head.

Her brother rose. 'I'll leave you now,' he said. 'Take it easy this morning and in the afternoon go for a good walk.'

'But I'm going to Ely,' spluttered Jael.

Joab turned back.

'Oh no, you won't. You'll see, nobody will go. A few may turn up, but the buses won't start unless they have a proper load.'

Jael said nothing.

CHAPTER SEVEN

JAEL started early for the Square where the coaches were accustomed to assemble. As she went she kept asking herself why she was so restless and unhappy and there seemed to be only one answer. 'Because you're out of step! Ever since you refused to be Betafied you have been feeling the whole weight of the Community's disapproval. They may not look disapproving because disapproval isn't one of the recognised Shades of Expression; but underneath they are; if they could pull a face at you they would! And what have you got out of it? Only the doubtful blessing of your own face. You may be a Failed Alpha and prettier now than most people; but soon you will be old and plain, whereas Beta faces don't change, or only once, when they get their Older Women's Replacement! You'll never be happy until you can think and feel and look like other people. Remember what the slogan says: "You can't be happy off the Beta Track." '

And now she was off the Beta Track again. Perhaps she was the only member of the whole community who was going to Ely.

She looked around for confirmation of her fears. But they were not confirmed. Others were going the same way she was, some singly, some in groups of two or three; they had a furtive, excited air, and talked in snatches interspersed by peals of high-pitched laughter. The March-day climate, with its chilly wind and pallid sun that never quite came through, tended to keep pedestrians on the move; but these were walking fast, sometimes running to keep up with each other. Jael had her seat reserved, but she couldn't help hurrying, too.

Round the next bend the Square came into sight, square in name, but oval in shape, because of the Dictator's aversion to angles and straight lines. And it was full, or nearly full, of people. Jael could only see the tops of the six coaches, for the crowds that were surging round them. For a moment she thought that they all meant to board the coaches; she would never get in. A sharp stab of feeling, half disappointment, half relief, ran through her. Slowly she edged her way to where a placard, 'A5', reared itself on a pole beside a bus. Sure enough, people were trying to get in and the conductor was fending them off and shouting: 'Show your tickets!' Jael showed hers. 'Make way there, make way there!' shouted the conductor, and she managed to squeeze through the throng and climb into her place. Once there, she looked down on a tossing sea of faces, upturned towards the coach; and though the great majority were Betas, and therefore incapable of much facial expression, their eyes were eloquent, and what did she see in most of them? Envy, Bad E—envy of her good fortune. It took her a moment or two to recognise it, for hitherto it had only been a name and an idea to her; now that she saw it lift its ugly head she was as appalled as if she had raised the Devil.

In the half-hour before the coaches were due to start, and while they were filling up, the Square was filling, too, and the pandemonium increased. The crowd had come to see the coaches off, the conductor said: it was the news that one of them would have an accident that had drawn so many people. But the fascination of the risk had taken such a hold that many of the spectators wanted to go, too; it wasn't fair, they declared, that only ticket-holders should go: everyone should go in the name of Equality! When this word was heard some tried to perform the appropriate ritual dance; but there was no room for it, and lacking this outlet, tempers rose, fists were shaken, and eyes blazed through impassive faces. Some mounted the steps of the coaches and

57

clung there; some perched themselves on the bonnets, and when the moment came to start, the drivers dared not, for fear of mowing down the mob. It looked as though an impasse had been reached and the expeditions would have to be abandoned, when suddenly the first phrase of 'Every Valley' soared slowly into the air. It was repeated twice, and silence fell, then a voice thundered:

'Patients and Delinquents!

'What is the meaning of this disgraceful disturbance? Are you even crazier that we have always thought you? Disperse to your homes quietly and in shame, and attend the Litany which until further notice will be the only form of entertainment permitted to you. Tomorrow at noon we shall have more to say and it may be our sad task to read the list of casualties which the Voluntary Principle has claimed from among you.'

The Voice ceased, the men put on their hats, the women curtseyed. Its tension gone, the huge crowd sagged and flopped. People looked at their feet, at the horizon, any-where but at each other. The drivers of the coaches sounded their horns imperiously, at which the crowd fell back and made lanes for them to pass through. As they lumbered off a feeble cheer was raised, but Jael scarcely heard it, she was thinking of the Dictator's closing words.

'I don't mind if there are casualties,' she told herself, 'and I don't mind if I'm one!'

The coach groaned, plunged and shuddered over the pot-holes of the Ely road. On either side the land once reclaimed from the fen had gone back to marsh, featureless, malodorous and unhealthy, differing little in aspect from the higher land, except that this was wet and that was dry. No trees, no vegetation, nothing to attract the eye; she might as well have been blind, Jael thought, for any visual stimulus the landscape gave her. She could have described it without seeing it; it was just what people said it was; they were right who declared that a guide-book to England could be written on a single page. And yet there was something in being out among it all—something she wouldn't have got if she had stayed at home thinking about it—a kind of exhilaration. Where did it come from? Not from the movement of the coach which, when the novelty wore off, only brought discomfort, not from the conversation of her neighbours, not from the sour smell of the marsh, not from the taste of the Joyful Journey tablets with which she fortified herself, not from anything to which she could give a name. Yes, she could—it was expectancy, she was waiting for something.

Before all this, before she had decided to reject betafication, she never waited for anything—it was all laid on. Nothing tempted her spirit out of its retreat; her mood was one of passive and, it must be admitted, pleased acceptance. Everything was arranged for her; there were no surprises. She moved with the general movement, she was part of it, like a drop of water in a river. That general movement was going on round her now. If anything disturbed the unbroken contour of the landscape, a hillock or a hollow, it might be, or a patch of darker or lighter coloured earth—all eyes turned to it at once. Nobody had to say 'Look!' If an unusual sound made itself heard above the general uproar, everyone listened simultaneously. And if anybody laughed, everybody laughed, without asking what it was about. They were like a flock of birds, telepathic to each other's thoughts. Thoughts, but were they thoughts? Were they not rather manifestations of instinct, of a common consciousness, which reacted to stimuli in precisely the same way, and excluded thought? The Dictator wants to replace intelligence by instinct, someone had said. Perhaps he was right. With nothing outside one to invite comparison, indeed with the whole idea of comparison frowned upon and virtually forbidden, what was there left to think about? If personality expresses itself by acts of discrimination, and discrimination, besides being taboo, has no material to work on, what becomes of personality? It shrinks, it atrophies, it dies.

Oh this flatness, within and without! Yet once Jael would not have minded it, did not mind it; she had accepted it with everything else that made up the Horizontal View of Life, of which, at lectures and on the wireless, everyone heard so much. Of course, there were jokes about it, cartoons depicted patients and delinquents in all stages of non-erectness, at every slope and angle, bending, kneeling, going on all fours, stretched out, prone or prostrate; many of them were improper, for in matters of sex the Dictator was not puritanical, he thought that indecency was an aid to relaxation. But, for all that, the Horizontal View of Life, or On the Level as it was sometimes more familiarly called, was generally accepted.

Without knowing why, Jael looked up. Everyone was looking up. Straight ahead, through the window beside the driver, she saw something breaking the line of the horizon, something sticking up. It might have been a puff of smoke, but it was too solid for that and did not move. Somebody said, 'There it is!' in a tone of awe, and a silence fell.

The next moment the tower disappeared behind the driver's head, but it had left its presence in the coach, a most disturbing presence, like a thought that had found its way into one's mind and would not be expelled.

Soon the tower reappeared; sometimes it was on one side of the coach, sometimes on the other, sometimes straight ahead, but always it was growing larger, and as it grew so did the thought grow in Jael's mind.

When the tower was half-way up the window and perhaps only a mile or so away, for the stonework of its structure was becoming visible, somebody called out: 'Let's go back!' 'Yes, let's,' cried someone else, and Jael, from some inner compulsion, was going to say the same, when the thought seemed to swell in her and choke her utterance. 'No, no,' she heard herself saying, 'we must go on!' and when she had said this others took it up. 'We must go on!' The sense of public disagreement was almost new to Jael; in an assembly she expected to feel what everybody felt: now she wanted her will, her private, personal will to prevail; she felt the other wills arrayed against her, trying to thwart her will. 'Go on! Go on!' They went on; she had carried the day.

Now they had reached the foot of the hill on which the tower stood, this monstrous mound of earth which had somehow survived the bombs. Of the tower itself, only the lower part was visible, blocking the windows, shutting out the light. 'It will fall on us!' a man cried, but still the coach went on, painfully climbing upwards, until suddenly, when no one was expecting it to, it stopped.

'Ely Cathedral,' the conductor said.

But nobody got out; nobody moved; they seemed to be frozen in their places.

Then Jael felt a loosening of her limbs, as though an enchantment was letting go its hold, and she stumbled out and stood under the tower, and looked up.

The western transept had been broken away, only the tower remained, and its immense height filled her mind with awe and terror. She thought she might be going to faint but the feeling passed, and she took two or three uncertain steps towards the tower, raising her hands towards it as she did so.

By now others had joined her, and joined their terrors to hers, as the reality of height took possession of them, driving from their minds the two-dimensional world in which they had been brought up. Hysteria seized them, they dropped writhing to the bare earth, covering their faces with their hands. 'Stand up! Stand up!' cried Jael,

61

striding in and out between their heaving bodies like a fury. 'Stand up and look up!' Some scrambled to their feet and shading their eyes forced their gaze to travel slowly up the crumbling masonry which had so miraculously been spared. To them, as to Jael, their first realisation of the idea of height brought an overpowering sense of sin; they were doing the forbidden thing, and every faculty they had protested; but soon it established itself as something awe-inspiring and worshipful. Craning their necks towards the four round turrets of the summit, they felt they could never have enough of it. The beautiful Galilee chapel had gone; they had never seen it so they did not miss it; but a torn arch led into the tower, and through this Jael, the first to recover her volition, made her way. Here, in the confined space between the four walls, the effect of height was still more overwhelming; arcades of rounded arches, tier on tier, led—not to the roof, for the roof had long since crashed—but to a patch of sky at once darker and more luminous than the grey sky outside. At this they gazed, drawing deep breaths of longing, which, when their lungs were tired, expired in sighs.

Somehow or other Jael found herself outside, at first panting and exultant, then with a crazy desire to dance and sing. Soon she was doing both, though to no steps or tune she knew. Others came out and joined her in the impromptu ballet; they took hands and there were just enough of them to make a ring round the base of the tower. Encircling it they danced and danced, all singing what they had come to think of as 'the Height Song', picking up the words from each other by the power of instinctive transmission:

> Hail to height!
> Which gives to sight
> A new delight!
> Which gives to thought
> A treasure, brought
> By fear in flight.

What if it made no sense? It had a meaning for them. On and on they danced, the women with streaming hair like Maenads, the men with athletic gestures of which their normal, ordinary bearing gave no hint whatever, until the current passing through their linked hands seemed to sweep away the barriers of individuality and leave a single personality, as homogeneous and indivisible as a wedding ring. What bliss was theirs! And what vital energy and endurance their bliss gave them! They felt themselves tireless, sustained by an inexhaustible inflowing strength; and when at last they did tire, they tired at the same moment: the current was switched off and they lay with twitching limbs on the caked, dun-coloured earth as though the Angel of Death was passing over them. Above their prostrate bodies soared the tower, expressionless and unconcerned, unchanged to the eye but transfigured to the mind, like a vessel that was empty and now is full, like a god that has received a sacrifice.

CHAPTER EIGHT

JAEL was in too much pain to think, but between the bouts she dimly wondered whether the darkness meant she had been blinded. Or could it be the bodies pressing on her, crushing her face, where the pain was worst, and nearly stifling her? When she tried to move, the pains increased, when she lay still she was being suffocated——

'I'll get you out of this,' she heard a voice say.

But did it speak to her? And how could she be rescued? she asked herself, before she fainted. Then, later, was she stationary or was she moving? Was she on the earth or in the sky? Was she awake or dreaming? The pain seemed to have retreated to some distance from her; she knew it was there, she could almost touch it, a dull, red circle round her, but she could not feel it.

The voice said: 'We shan't be long now.'

Not long? Not long? She had forgotten about time; there was nothing, where she was, to count the minutes by. Could they last for ever!

He seemed to be bending over her, she did not merely feel him as a presence that his voice had conjured up, she could see him; it was as though the gleams and flashes that came from him, sometimes uniting into a general radiance, had given her back her sight. That nodding plume! Of course he wasn't really wearing armour: it was the gold and silver the Inspectors had about them, the badges of their rank, which caught the light and shone reflected in his eyes. All the light there was seemed to come from him.

'Why am I so comfortable?' she asked him stupidly.

'Because I've seen to that. Now don't be anxious; I've got you where I want you!'

64

'But where's that?'

'Don't ask. It's the way that we Inspectors travel. You oughtn't to be here, really.'

'Shall I have to pay a fine?'

'You're paying it now.'

Had he kissed her? She thought she felt the touch of his lips on hers, but she wasn't sure: what had happened and was happening and might happen all seemed to run together. Of course she had had an accident . . . But it was so strange to be alone with him. Joab excepted, she hadn't been alone with anybody much. Any kind of pairing off was discouraged: even married couples weren't supposed to segregate themselves, unless they had to.

'Do I look very awful?' she asked. 'I know my face is bleeding.'

'No, you look sweet.'

'Shall I have a frightful scar? I gave myself one once, you know, a little one, but I ought not to tell you that. Perhaps this is a punishment.'

'Well, you won't be a Failed Alpha now, if that's a consolation.'

Jael's heart turned over.

'What shall I be?'

'I don't know, but a lot lower in the beauty scale.'

It was like a sentence passed on her. For a moment Jael felt the pure sense of loss, unalloyed by any more bearable emotion, that only comes in dreams. She almost wished that the encircling ring of pain would close in on her and crush her. Miserably she murmured:

'But you won't like me, then.'

'I shall like you more than ever.'

'Why?' she asked, trying to overcome disbelief.

'Because you'll be more yourself,' he told her tenderly. 'I liked the little scar, why not the big one? I shall call you scar-face.'

She became aware of an exquisite sensation that surely must be motion, a gliding like the flight of a swallow.

Presently she asked: 'What has happened to the others?'

'The others?' he repeated. 'I don't know what has happened to the others. Someone will have been detailed to look after them, I expect.'

'Were many hurt?'

'Oh, quite a few.'

'Worse than . . . worse than me?'

'Much worse. Some of them are dead.'

'But how did you——?'

'Spot you, were you going to say? Well, I'd been keeping an eye on you.'

'But why?'

'Perhaps just to collect a fine. You slipped up once before, you may remember.'

Jael did remember. 'How kind of you,' she said.

'Oh, not at all. That's what we're for, among other things.'

'What other things?'

'That would be telling.'

'But shouldn't you be looking after someone else?'

'Yes, all the Jaels are my province.'

'I thought so,' Jael said. 'To you I'm only a human unit, am I? Do you really distinguish between us?'

'I'm not supposed to, but I can do what I like.'

'Do what you like?' said Jael aghast. It sounded blasphemous to her. 'But doesn't the Dictator——?'

'Darling Dictator.'

'Ah, even you say that. Darling Dictator,' repeated Jael devoutly. 'But doesn't he mind if you——'

'Use my discretion? No, that's what we're for.'

'I don't feel I ought to——'

'Monopolise me? That's for me to say. Now just relax.'

Luxuriously she stretched her limbs. How could the sky be like a bed? How could it yield to her and yet support her?

66

How could the act of living be so effortless? How above all could the pressure of time have been removed? She had the strangest feeling about Time; she seemed to be lost in it, almost without location; as if it was coming to meet her, instead of her going to meet it.

'When shall we be there?' she asked.

' "There"?'

'Well, we must be going somewhere.'

'Why?'

'But isn't one always?'

'Not necessarily,' he said. 'But we *are* going somewhere, as a matter of fact.'

'Is it a nice place?'

'If I can make it so.'

She detected the reservation in his voice.

'Am I going to be punished?'

'Not more than you deserve, I hope.'

'Hasn't the D.D. told you?'

'We only get general orders.'

Jael thought about this.

'Have you ever seen him?' she asked, boldly.

'Yes, once, when I was commissioned.'

'What is he like?'

'Quite ordinary-looking. But we only see him in a mirror, so we're not quite sure if it's him.'

'A sort of portrait?'

'Well, I suppose the reflection comes from somewhere.'

'Is he very angry with us for——'

'For looking upwards? Time will show.'

'But you are not?'

'Officially I am, of course. But, as I said, I make distinctions.'

He had twice told her this.

'When shall we be there?' she murmured.

'Oh, any time. Now if you like . . . or, or later.'

'Please let it be later.'

Were they going forward or back, soaring, hovering or sinking? Whatever the movement was it eased, as movement often does, the surface tension of her mind; and she wondered: Am I now where I wanted to be, when we were dancing round the tower, earthbound? Does it mean, because I no longer feel the aspiration I felt then, can't even conceive it, that it has been fulfilled in this element, wherever or whatever it is? But, except for the gleams and flashes, the darkness round her was absolute; none of her senses told her where she was. Nor did she want to know; for the first time in her life her physical whereabouts was a matter of indifference to her. Have I died? she thought. Yes, to myself I have, but my being is somehow linked to this other's. His arms are not about me; I can't define or delimit his nearness; I'm not even sure that he is touching me. All I have is his presence, but it's all I want to have.

Suddenly she knew the pain was drawing nearer; she could feel it as well as see it; her head began to throb; the dampness on her cheek was running into her mouth—she could taste blood; and she recalled with a stab of terror what this would mean to her as a woman—a scarred lopsided face which people would turn away from just as they had once turned towards it. At a lower level than her vanity her whole conception of herself was shaken; in company or alone she must revise her habitual estimate of herself, prepare, as an old woman does, for being disregarded, for not counting, for being devalued, not worth her face-value.

In an access of terror she cried: 'Can you see me?'

'Why, yes,' he said.

'I can't see you, not properly.'

'Some little trouble with the optic nerve.'

'Then am I blind?'

'Of course not.'

'But you can see me?'

'What else do you suppose I'm looking at?'

'I don't know. But do you like what you're looking at?' she almost shouted.

'Yes, or else I shouldn't.'

'Do you mean that?'

'Has all my behaviour,' he asked, 'been quite inexplicable to you? Do you suppose I winkled you out of that damned coach by chance? I told you I've had my eye on you, ever since——'

'Yes, but I'm not the same now,' Jael cried.

'How not the same?'

'I'm—I'm disfigured. I'm cut, horribly cut. I know I am.' Her voice sank; she could hardly bring herself to say the words: she was branding herself with her own shame, trying, by self-mortification, to forestall his criticism of her. 'My face——'

He laughed, and she was bitterly offended.

'Well, what about your face?' he said.

For a moment she was too deeply hurt to answer; then she said: 'How can you ask?'

'But it's *your* face I like!' he protested. 'After all, it's still your face—your dear face, if I may say so, and that's all I care about.'

At last she was convinced, but with the overwhelming happiness of that certitude the pain drew nearer and began to clutch at her. It reminded her of her body and her body reminded her of him—not simply as a presence, but as a man. Where was he? She stretched out her arms towards the void; they touched him and his arms encircled her. Their steady pressure added to the pain; made it excruciating but made it bliss. She closed her eyes against the darkness, feeling she could see better so, see in her own mind the picture that was denied her by the darkness.

'We're nearly there,' he said. She didn't know what he meant, but in this rapture of the night she swooned away.

CHAPTER NINE

THE screens had been taken away, and Jael was lying in a bed like all the other beds. The pattern of a hospital ward had not changed with the other changes; anyone from the not too distant past would have recognised it without having to rub his eyes. Indeed, the Dictator had said more than once that surviving humanity's living quarters should aspire to the condition of a hospital. 'You are all delinquents, and all delinquents are invalids,' he had said. Except in the case of some infectious diseases, private wards were not allowed. One of the advantages of the New Dispensation was that people were not ill so often as they used to be. The hardships of war and underground life had killed off many of the weaklings; such as survived were hardier than their forebears. But the chief reason why the hospitals were never crowded was the lack of accidents. Accidents there were, for accidents will happen; but the occasions for them had been greatly reduced. For instance, since nearly everyone lived on the ground floor nobody could fall downstairs: as the hymn, frequently sung and quoted, said:

> He that is down can fear no fall,
> He that is low, no pride.

Industrial accidents were few, partly because industries were few, and those there were involved the use of little machinery. The machines the Inspectors used—and some said they were mostly made of immaterial substances, by-products of thought—were constructed behind walls and gates with sentries mounting guard; the sight of them gave one goose-flesh; but curiosity had reached such a low ebb, thanks to the daily dose of sedatives, that hardly anyone wondered what went on inside them, or would have understood it if they had.

But the main reason why accidents were scarce was, of course, the scarcity of motor-cars. Some maintained that the Dictator lagged behind public opinion; others that he was always a move ahead of it. His mind was very devious. In some quarters it was even said that he invented the jokes against himself which went the rounds, and that he designed the cartoons, some of them quite savage, that appeared in the papers; but no one really knew. It was generally thought that he believed in a doctrine of safety-valves as a cure for unrest. He had his ear to the ground, he knew when discontent was brewing. The motor-coaches were a safety-valve, designed to allow the population to let off steam. But the pressure was still too high; the thirst for violence had not been slaked. Hence the accident; the accident had been a kind of purge.

Jael's first visitor was her brother. He said: 'Well, Jael, how are you?'

'I'm all right,' said Jael. 'My face feels a bit stiff, though.' She tried to smile.

'It's bound to be,' he said, 'it's bound to be.' He looked hard at her.

'Am I very changed?' she asked with an effort. 'You see, they don't give us looking-glasses here . . . not until later. You would have recognised me, wouldn't you?'

'I'm not sure I should have,' said Joab with devastating truthfulness. 'The nurse brought me in and when I saw your card and index number over the bed I recognised you at once. I don't look at people much.'

'I know, I know,' said Jael, and tears came into her eyes. 'But after all, I am your sister, and I thought——'

'You think too much about appearances,' said Joab, not unkindly. 'About your own appearance, I mean. You look nice, you really do.' At that she felt her face brightening.

Oh, how stiff it was. 'But it's what you feel that really matters.'

'How can I tell how I feel till I know how I look?' moaned Jael, and then seeing a shadow cross her brother's face she added: 'Yes, I feel all right. It hurts me to move, though.'

'You were very foolish,' broke out Joab, with the air of one who had wanted to say this for some time but had for reasons of delicacy refrained. 'You might have been killed, and then where should I have been?'

'You could easily have found another secretary,' said Jael.

'It isn't only that, and I'm surprised that you should say so—surprised and hurt. I'm as fond of you as one human unit can or ought to be of another. Believe me, I should miss you as well as your typing. You are necessary to me—more necessary than I am to you, I dare say. To lose you would quite upset the rhythm of my life. Can I say more than that?'

'No, indeed,' said Jael humbly, for it was perpetually being dinned into them that life consisted of a pattern and a rhythm which must not be disturbed. 'I should have . . . I should have broken the chain. I've always been a weak link, I suppose; but what else can a Failed Alpha be? It's different for men, men Failed Alphas don't have the disabilities that we have; they aren't discriminated against, or hardly at all. That's where the Dictator shows his sex solidarity.'

'You mustn't say that, even in fun. Darling Dictator.'

'Darling Dictator,' repeated Jael, half-heartedly.

'Female human units,' went on Joab,' 'are $77\frac{1}{2}\%$ more liable to personal vanity than we are.'

'I know men say that, but I don't believe it,' said Jael, rebelliously. 'Men may not be as vain as women are, but they're much more conceited.'

'Conceit is A.S., of course, but vanity is nine times more disruptive. Vanity is the incubator of Envy——'

The word slipped out. Joab turned away and performed a token spit in the direction of the beds. To comply with the regulations Jael also screwed her mouth up, but the effort hurt her, and the spit was hardly audible.

When they were face to face again, Joab said:

'Anyhow you are safe, and that's the great thing. My present secretary, though a good Beta girl, is not efficient and shows distressing signs of——'

'What?' asked Jael.

'Of . . . of developing feelings for me which are utterly irrelevant and redundant. It happens in about 51% of cases where a woman secretary is employed. Thank goodness you were never fond of me——'

'Well, not in that way,' Jael said.

Joab looked shocked.

'That is one reason why I shall be glad to have you back. If I have occasion to criticise your work you don't burst into tears.'

'When shall I be back?' Perversely, tears pricked Jael's eye-lids; perhaps it was suggestion.

'You were judged curable in thirty days. There are nine and a half days still to go. But, of course, there is also the question of punitive action——'

Jael's heart missed a beat. 'But what I did wasn't illegal,' she said with spirit. 'We were officially allowed to make the expedition.'

'I agree, it was a marginal action, not a true deviation, and as such would have been overlooked. But you were, I gather, also the ring-leader in an act that *was* illegal. Ring-leader in the literal sense. You incited some weaker units to form a ring about that totem-tower, that phallic emblem from the bad old days, and . . . and . . . look upwards. Twenty-three people had to be treated for stiff-neck afterwards: twenty-three. The Dictator was merciful. That was their only punishment. But you—you *seduced* them.'

'I didn't,' cried Jael indignantly. 'I——'

'You knew the rule "Look your own height—there is nothing higher." Why did you disobey?'

'Because I felt like it.'

Joab was horrified.

'But only Inspectors can do what they feel like. Except in the abstract, as a dimension, which scientists and others have to take into account—it sometimes comes into my own work, I regret to say—height must be regarded as inadmissible, if not non-existent.'

'What will they do to me?' asked Jael, trembling.

'No one knows yet. But the Dictator is merciful and I have put in a plea for you.'

'Thank you,' said Jael, humbly.

Joab, whose first experience this was of hospital-visiting, found his stock of conversation drying up. He fidgeted and began to look about him.

'That's rather a measly flower they've given you,' he said, bending over the blue cineraria on Jael's bedside table. 'It looks shop-soiled to me. They oughtn't to have fobbed you off with this.' He put on his spectacles and his glance travelled round the ward, noting the blue plastic cinerarias that adorned each bedside table. 'Look, they're as fresh as paint,' he said, 'and all of them the latest model, too, not a leaf nor a petal different, absolutely identical, all but this one, this seedy-looking thing. It isn't fair, whatever you may have done, Jael, that you should be florally underprivileged. The Dictator himself has said: "A flower must never be a stigma." I shall complain about it.'

He looked round for someone to complain to.

'Oh, don't do that,' cried Jael. 'It does quite well for me. I'm used to it now—I shouldn't want another.'

'You ought to want another,' Joab grumbled. 'They wouldn't let you keep this one if it was prettier than the others. I shall certainly speak about it.'

'Please don't,' cried Jael, getting more agitated and afraid that Joab would notice, though he didn't seem to. 'We're only allowed seven complaints a week each, and I've used mine up,' she lied. 'You'll get me into trouble if you say anything.'

'All right,' said Joab, unwillingly. 'But I don't like to see you victimised, it's against the regulations and you must be suffering tortures from Bad E.' He frowned portentously. 'Am I allowed to kiss you?'

'Ask the Sister,' Jael said.

The Sister happened to be passing by. She looked at Jael doubtfully.

'No, better not. At this stage, any undue excitement——'

'I shouldn't excite her,' Joab protested. 'I'm her brother.'

'A kiss inflames the ego,' said the Sister. 'We are trying to keep Jael's ego down, aren't we, Jael? Kisses are for later on.'

'Oh,' said Joab, 'of course, in that case!'

He retreated, trying not to show relief at being let off an endearment that did not suit his temperament. 'So long, my . . . my . . . my dear. Kind thoughts of the Dictator.'

'Kind thoughts of the Dictator,' Jael repeated.

Jael didn't know where the flower came from, but she had a shrewd suspicion, which sometimes swelled into certainty and sometimes dwindled to the feeblest hope. Coming round, it was the first thing she saw, but she didn't look at it specially; it was just another of the flowers that all the patients had. She didn't even ask its name. One day her neighbour in the next bed said to her: 'That flower of yours looks rather droopy, Jael. Why don't you give it some water?' and they both laughed at the idea of watering a plastic flower. But just for fun Jael did; and to her astonishment the flower revived. Its recovery aroused no comment, for it still looked sicklier than its fellows; but Jael had seen the reawakening life in it, and marvelled. How could it be

75

alive? And yet it must be—the only flower in all the ward that was. Surreptitiously she tended it; under cover of darkness she caressed its leaves, and felt something pass from it to her.

But how had she come by it? Who had given it to her? Only one person could have.

'But don't you *know* who sent it?' she would ask the Sister, in those early days.

'No, dear, we don't. A man brought it, an ordinary human unit, Gamma or Gamma plus at most, he was—if you look at men that way.'

'But who *told* him to bring it?'

'Sheaves of forms came with it, all signed and counter-signed. But not the original order; that's always given by word of mouth.'

If he had sent it surely he would come himself? The memory of her flight with him made all other experiences savourless; she lived for their next meeting. But was it real or had she dreamed it? She couldn't be sure; all she could be sure of was the bliss that overtook her whenever she looked at the flower. The flower was a proof that it hadn't been a dream.

'How did I get here?' she asked the Sister. 'Did I come with the others?'

'Well, not exactly. You came first, as a matter of fact.'

'You mean I had priority?'

'Well, only in time. Someone has to be first. There is no other priority.'

'Of course not,' Jael said. 'And yet——'

'You came a good half-hour before the others,' volunteered the Sister. 'You came before we heard about the accident.'

That must have been his doing . . . sooner or later he would come again.

Her next visitor was Judith.

CHAPTER TEN

MUCH more vividly than Joab had, Judith brought back the outside world. Jael enjoyed gossiping with her. Cain was their first subject—Cain who had egged on Judith to betafication. They had been married while Jael was in hospital: 'And, my dear, you can't think how he's changed for the beta! You hadn't heard that one? Well, it's fairly new. A bit obvious, perhaps, but then it's beta to be obvious.'

'It's beta to be obvious,' Jael repeated.

'Yes, and he's so improved you'd hardly know him from any other nice, good-natured man. He used to fly into rages and have fits of sulks. I had to be so careful with him, and humour him and try to placate him—and then he would apologise to me. Such scenes we had!—and all because I was a Gamma. He liked me but not my face. Now he likes both, and takes both for granted, and never gets into a rage. Why, sometimes I hardly know he's in the room—he might be anybody's husband, and what more can you say?'

'Isn't it a bit dull?' asked Jael.

'Gracious Dictator, no! Sometimes I wish he was, well . . . more ardent—as he used to be, oddly enough, in my Gamma days—but that was partly his nasty temper—you know the way men are, or if you don't, you will! I verily believe, when they make love, it's because of what they don't see in us, not what they do! They're taking it out on us for not being their ideal! I'll teach you to be a Gamma girl! But when you *are* their ideal——' Judith shrugged her shoulders—'then they don't bother any more.'

Did a sigh escape her? At any rate she changed the subject.

'Clytemnestra 98 is going to have a baby—isn't it wonderful? One takes it for granted that one's friends are sterile. Good old Clytie! Let's hope it won't be born dead, as they so often are, or turn out to be a monster! Are you sterile, Jael? I am, or was, when I was last examined. Of course, it doesn't really matter much. Cain doesn't mind. Men aren't put off, or women either, most of them! Think how they used to go in for contraceptives in the bad old days! It seems so funny now, when some people would give their eyes to have a child! I shouldn't want the bother of having one. State-born babies are best, don't you think? The State can regulate the supply to meet the demand. You don't want a baby, do you, Jael?'

'Do you know,' said Jael, who hadn't spoken for some time, 'I rather think I do.'

'Well, it's legal, of course, and some people actually think the better of you, but it's liable to raise the quotum of personality to danger-point. What is yours now? Have they told you?'

'17½%, I think.'

'That's all the self one is allowed?'

'Yes, but I don't think anyone takes the tests very seriously.'

'A child would be bound to lead to hypertrophy of the personality.'

'Why?' asked Jael. 'Surely a child would draw some of it off?'

'It might, but mothers and fathers can't help being self-important. They preen themselves on having done what most people can't do . . . Any family tends to be A.S., it's self-defensive. Even the D.D. has said so. Parents, yes, but not family life.'

'All the same,' said Jael, 'I think I'd like to risk it.'

'Is there . . . is there anyone?' asked Judith.

How should she answer that question? How did she answer it to herself?

'I . . . I don't quite know,' she answered, strictly truthful.

78

'That means there is.' Judith took a good look at her friend, opened her mouth to say something but thought better of it.

'You're looking well, you know,' was what she said.

'Oh, am I?' Jael's face brightened. 'I haven't seen myself. They don't let us have looking-glasses. Everybody here except me is Beta, and Betas don't need mirrors. I thought I should have a frightful scar, but I can't feel one.' Experimentally she ran her finger down her cheek.

'There isn't one,' said Judith. 'They've certainly made a good job of your face. These plastic surgeons . . .'

'You would have recognised me, wouldn't you?' asked Jael anxiously.

As Joab had, Judith hesitated a little before answering.

'Well, I was a bit bewildered at first, seeing such rows of women! But yes, of course, you'll always be the same old Jael.'

Jael turned her face restlessly on the pillow.

'Do you know, I'm a bit disappointed.'

'Disappointed?'

'Disappointed at not having a scar. I made myself one once, do you remember, a tiny one, but that seems to have gone, too.'

'Why on earth should you want a scar?'

'Oh, I don't know. Perhaps because it would make me feel more real—more myself, I mean.'

'But why do you want to feel more yourself? It's just what we're supposed not to feel. I don't feel half as much myself as I did when I was Gamma.'

'I know, but somehow I do want to. And, Judith——'

'Yes?'

'Come a bit nearer, I don't want the others to hear.'

Judith pulled her chair closer to Jael's bed.

Jael whispered: 'I shouldn't have been ashamed of it, the scar I mean. I think I got it in a good cause. I suppose it

79

would have spoilt my looks—I'd have been Gamma or even Gamma minus, and people would have avoided me on aesthetic grounds and perhaps informed against me, but when they saw me they couldn't help remembering——'

Jael's voice grew still lower.

'Yes?'

'Well, what I did at Ely. It was the proudest moment of my life and I don't the least regret it——'

'Jael!'

'It wasn't the happiest moment—that . . . that came afterwards, but I couldn't have had the one without the other.'

'I'm afraid I don't quite understand,' said Judith, coldly.

Jael heard the disapproval in her friend's voice, but she meant to have her say out.

'Sometime, perhaps, I'll tell you. But you see, I led them, I made them look up, I made them see and feel what was above them. They hadn't seen, nor had I, until that day. Height! Height!'

'Darling, you mustn't,' Judith pleaded. 'Please, please, don't say any more.'

'And then I went right up into it, I can't tell you how, but I did, and it was all I thought it would be, and much more. I can't tell you what it was like, because we haven't anything down here to measure it by or compare it with, not even words——'

'Hush! darling, hush!'

'No, because I must tell somebody, and who can I tell but you? Do you know, I can hardly bear the thought of getting well and creeping about, an insect with the other insects!'

'I suppose I'm an insect,' Judith said. 'And I'm quite content to be one. Ever since I was betafied——'

'Oh, darling,' cried Jael, suddenly all contrition. 'We've never talked about that, not properly, never since we parted at the door of the Ministry, and you went in and I stayed outside. You wanted me to, do you remember? You thought it would be better for me to go on being a Failed Alpha. And I'm so glad you did. But have you changed your mind?'

Judith looked at her friend hard and Jael tried to read her expression; but it was always difficult to tell with a Beta: their faces moved, of course, but only their eyes registered what they were thinking.

'Well, perhaps I have,' said Judith at last. 'At the time it seemed different for you: you would have been going down and I was going up. Not up in the sense you meant just now, that sounded to me as if you were running a temperature. "Height means fever," we were always told.'

'Height means fever,' repeated Jael automatically, and could have bitten her tongue with annoyance at the slip.

'Ah, you remember it. Well, since I was betafied I've felt a different creature. Being subnormal isn't as bad as being above normal, because it means that some people are sorry for you instead of env—well, you know. But most of them rather despise you and quite a number show it—in small ways, you know. Pushing in front of you, not answering when you speak, little slights and pin-pricks. I know it's against the rules for anyone to be rude to a Gamma but in practice they often are, you have to take a back seat, literally a back seat when it comes to the Collective Photograph. Was my face red? I could hardly hold my head up sometimes, and, of course, it got worse, as more and more women went in for betafication. We're so much in a majority now, we show the others up——'

'We are?' interrupted Jael. 'You mean, you are.'

Judith gave her a Beta's wooden look.

'I was speaking for all of us. It isn't that we look down on the Gammas—you shouldn't look down or up, you should only look ahead, your own height—we just feel, if a

Gamma comes along, that she's different. We don't despise them, but they embarrass us. We don't know what to say to them, any more than you know what to say to somebody who's ill—you have to choose your words, and put on a special voice——'

'I hope you don't feel like that with me,' said Jael.

'Of course not. You're an old friend, and besides . . . You're not ill any longer—you'll be discharged soon, won't you?'

'Tomorrow week. But I don't know what's going to happen to me. They don't tell you much here. I may be up for trial.'

'Oh, I should doubt it. Just a fine, perhaps, which you'll easily be able to pay, having been so long in hospital economising.'

'You think so?' Jael said. 'I don't altogether fancy coming out, a Failed Alpha and all that, and then the Ely affair on top of it. I'm not flattering myself, or trying to make myself out more important than I am; but the Dictator will have heard of what I did, for he hears of everything.'

'Oh yes, but the Dictator is merciful. Darling Dictator.'

'Darling Dictator,' repeated Jael dubiously.

'I'm sure he won't be hard on you . . . But let me go back to what I was just saying about being Beta. It's like when your temperature goes back to normal after an illness —mine was never high like yours, but I was permanently subnormal, and tired, and felt there was something that made people fight shy of me, like bad breath or superfluous hair or something. I felt that they were making allowances for me—or trying not to make allowances . . . But what I meant was, the sense of being apart. You couldn't react with the others, at least I couldn't—I had to make a kind of personal adjustment, before I thought and felt as they did, and it was very tiring and frustrating. Now I don't. When anything happens—well, like the episode at Ely—I automatically think and feel about it like everybody else. It's just like when you're dancing, you feel the rhythm going through you, and you *know*. You don't have to ask yourself: "Am I doing it right?"—because the sense of what the rest are doing keeps you right. And well, too. As you know, before I was betafied I used to have headaches and all sorts of things—I nearly had a gastric ulcer—and all because I was shirking something which I knew I ought to do. I didn't want to do it, when the time came, but I'm so thankful that I did.'

Judith stopped, a little breathless with the effort of saying so many intimate things in a voice too low to reach the others. She needn't really have worried, for the wireless was still filling the ward with its competing voices.

'Thank you for telling me,' said Jael. 'I know that there's a lot in what you say, and I often used to feel the same before . . . before . . . Ely and all that. But now I don't, I'm happier this way. It won't come between us, will it? I still feel towards you as I always felt——'

'I'm glad in a way,' Judith interrupted her, 'but I'm not sure you ought to. You see, I'm just an ordinary human unit—Judith 91—there are thousands of us—and by singling me out you're putting Personal Pressure on me, and I don't know if I can take it. I haven't got the full Beta point of view yet, but what we have to aim at is undiscriminating friendliness that doesn't stress the personal. Cain's a Home Husband——'

'A Home Husband?'

'Yes, a Home Husband or a Halter Husband, as they sometimes call it. Didn't you know? I expect it was while you were still unconscious, but you ought to know, or you might get fined or something. There's been a new Edict.'

'Tell me about it,' Jael said.

'Oh, there are now two sorts of husbands—a Home or

Halter Husband—the old kind, a man who lives in the same house with you—at too close quarters, many women think, and is more or less tied to you; and a Hygienic Husband, one who does the necessary services but isn't tied to the house. He lives in a Husbands' Hostel and you need only see him by arrangement. It's much more civilised, don't you think? And it does away with all that jealousy business.'

'Can he have more than one wife?' Jael asked.

'Oh yes, if he's good at husbandry. He has to pass a test—there have been quite a lot of jokes about it, but I don't suppose they take that sort of paper here. You see, being a husband is a vocation—most men aren't really suited for it.'

'But isn't being a wife a vocation, too?'

'Oh yes, much more, but it's been proved statistically—your brother could tell you the figures—that most wives can do better, as wives, without having a husband all the time around. Husbands get in the way so and make scenes. And if they are away from home the wife is always asking why—we can't help it, it's our nature. But with a Hygienic Husband——'

'Yes?'

'Well, naturally he comes and goes and no questions are asked. It's working out very well. I shouldn't be surprised if in a few years there won't be any Halter Husbands left. And we shall be so much nearer to the Ego's Exit.'

'The Ego's Exit,' repeated Jael, with distaste.

'Well, the Beta Band-waggon is going that way, and isn't it what we all want—to be in on something? No fun in standing aside. The Common Wish for the Common Weal—that's the ideal we should set ourselves.'

'Does the Dictator really want that?'

Judith opened her eyes in surprise.

'Presumably he does, or he wouldn't have made the Edict. I know people say that he's an opportunist, that he doesn't initiate, he only follows, like a dog barking in front of a horse and cart; but I don't believe that. He has his head screwed on. But I didn't mean to lecture you, darling, I only meant to put you wise about what's been happening while you were laid aside, and to tell you it isn't so bad to be a Beta after all. Can you Beta it? as they say. Or can you Beta me to it? That's the latest.'

'There's one thing you haven't told me,' Jael said. 'What has happened about the Expeditions?'

'The Expeditions?' Even for a Beta Judith's face looked wooden.

'Yes, the motor-coach Expeditions.'

'Oh,' said Judith, 'we were told to forget about them, and I'd almost succeeded. You shouldn't really have reminded me. They've been suspended.' Judith frowned. The frown came a shade late: you could tell a Beta by the time-lag between thought and facial expression. 'But we haven't heard the last of them,' she added, and after kissing Jael's still stiff face, she took her leave.

CHAPTER ELEVEN

'I THINK we'll throw that flower away, dear,' the Sister said, 'and give you a nice new one. The Visitor's coming this afternoon and we don't want to have her asking awkward questions, do we?'

Jael's heart turned over.

'Oh please don't!' she cried. 'Please don't throw it away, I'm fond of it.'

'You can't be fond of such a shabby thing,' the Sister said, 'and if the Visitor sees it, she'll raise the Underworld.'

'Oh no,' pleaded Jael. 'I'll explain to her that I love looking at it—it gives me something. I'd like to take it with me when I go, as a memento of——of the Hospital and your kindness.'

'We don't know where you're going to, yet,' said the Sister darkly. She sometimes spoke to Jael as if she was a criminal awaiting trial.

'*I* shan't object if *they* don't. What I'll do is to hide it while she's here, and give you a decent one instead, and when she's gone you shall have the old one back. But I still can't understand why you like it.'

'Because it's mine, I suppose.'

' "Mine" is not a word you ought to use,' the Sister said. 'We only use it because we haven't found a substitute. We can say it's "yours", of course, but yours means everyone's. "In my charge", you ought to say, or "in my care" or "in my keeping", only it takes so much longer.'

'But it isn't quite the same thing, is it?' said Jael. 'When I say "my" face, it is mine, I'm not just in charge of it. I could be in charge of yours, if I was a beauty-specialist.'

'No, because I'm a Beta,' said the Sister, 'and Beta's don't need beautifying.'

'But all the same they do have treatments,' Jael said, 'I know quite a few who do.' She saw she had made a slip, but went on defiantly. 'They want to look *themselves* as well as Betas.'

'I don't know why some of you are so struck on looking yourselves,' the Sister observed good-humouredly. 'I'd just as soon be taken for the next woman. But then I have a job to do, and it's no sinecure, I can tell you, with some of you face-conscious patients. Of course, it doesn't matter what you say to me, Jael, it won't go any further, but you'd better not talk that way to the Visitor.'

'Who is this Visitor?' asked Jael.

'She's one of these nosey-parkers who come round. There are several of them, and you never know which one you're going to get. Between you and me, they're a confounded nuisance. They ask a lot of questions, and we have to think up answers. They ask the patients questions, too. "Are you quite comfortable, dear? Have you any complaints? Has the Matron, or the Sister, or the nurse, or whoever, been quite kind to you? Is there any favouritism? Are you all treated just alike? Can you suggest any improvements, dear, in the running of the hospital? Would you rather be waked at six instead of five? Do you find the food as good as it is in your own home unit, if you have one?" All tommy-rot, of course; but we have to put up with it, as we have to put up with so many things . . . Those snoopers, mass-observers or whatever they are, are all amateurs: they haven't the foggiest idea what it means to run a place like this! It doesn't matter whether Corday 964 or Thompson 91 or Medea 9003 thinks she has a grievance— they really don't come into it—it's the organisation that matters—making them all do the right thing at the right time! If I listened to every moan and groan and squawk and squeak, do you think I should get *anywhere*? Discipline, discipline is what matters, and if they didn't have it they'd simply turn their toes up. I tell you, Jael 97, if I'd listened to all the various croakings I should have needed a Brain Brightener before now and this ward would have been full of corpses—Death Deviators, I should say. There isn't a single one that hasn't wanted something special doing for her—more food or less food or different food, more light or less light or no light, more wireless or less wireless or louder wireless or softer wireless or no wireless, they simply have no idea of collective action, they think that being ill (and it's their own fault they are, in most cases) entitles them to special consideration. They won't go on like that when they get out of here, or they'll have the Inspectors after them. Of course, I don't tell them so—we're not allowed to tell anyone what's coming to them—but I shouldn't be surprised if it wasn't P.S. for all of them when they get out.'

'P.S.?' queried Jael.

'Permanent Sackcloth, and a good thing, too.'

What a prospect! Sackcloth, that dreary uniform! Day after day, every day! When worn as a punishment, sackcloth had to be worn plain: you weren't allowed to embroider it. Jael couldn't think of herself apart from the clothes she wore; her vision of herself was sartorial; she never thought of herself as naked, still less as a formless entity. Without an individual appearance, and appearance meant a vesture, she did not exist for herself. Clad in Permanent Sackcloth, she would not exist for herself, either. She felt herself shrinking, withering away. An overwhelming longing seized her to be reassured by the sight of her own face, to know that she was really there. Desperately she cried:

'Oh, do please give me a looking-glass!'

'I'm afraid I can't,' the Sister said. 'We can't have patients looking at themselves, it isn't good for them. There's plenty else to look at. The whole secret of getting well is not to think about yourself, and the first step to that is not to look at yourself. Thinking about yourself disturbs the gastric juices. If I started thinking about myself, I should get nowhere, but luckily or not, I've got all of you to think about. I don't have time to look in a looking-glass: I take my face for granted, and so will you, when you're my age. But you'll be given a looking-glass all right, the day that you're discharged. Then you can look at yourself till you're blue in the face.'

Only another week, thought Jael, and then I shall see myself, and be myself! Mentally she invented a little dance she could do with the mirror in her hand; she saw herself bowing to it, curtseying to it, holding it at arm's length and gazing into it, sinking on to the floor and (in defiance of the regulations) looking up at it: her dear Failed-Alpha face! She couldn't believe that the Betas round her, poor darlings, would be so excited about seeing their reach-me-down faces. And why should she be? Didn't this face-hunger, this face-starvation argue lack of sense of humour, a quality she had always felt that she possessed? And what would the others say, when they beheld her antics? Would they attack her, fall upon her, smother her with pillows? Beat her to death with the very mirror she was looking at? Or would they, as they had at Ely (dancing is so infectious), join in and stifle her with praise, not pillows? Sing paeans to her glory—worship her?

The vision faded. Suddenly she knew why she wanted so much to see herself—she wanted to see herself as *he* would see her, as she would look through *his* eyes, when he came; was it not what all women wanted, when they took out their little mirrors—to see themselves reflected in some man's eyes?

'You look as if you were seeing things,' the Sister said.

'Well, perhaps I was.'

'You must be more on the spot when the Visitor comes. And here's a tip: just answer the questions that she asks you, don't volunteer anything. It's much the safest way. We don't want any trouble, do we? If you have anything to complain of, complain to me.'

'I haven't,' said Jael. 'You have been most kind, and so has Nurse. Of course, I would like to have a looking——'

'All in good time, all in good time. They've made a very good job of you, if you ask me. Now one thing more——'

She got no further, for at that moment the wireless, which had been crooning to itself in a desultory fashion, suddenly changed its tone, seemed to clear its throat, made several impressive premonitory rumbles, and began its signature tune. Not once but three times did the opening phrase of 'Every Valley' soar through the now silent ward. Foreign, indeed opposed, as its message was to all her present convictions, Jael felt her spirit lifting with it.

'Gracious Dictator!' cried the Sister, awe-struck. 'A triple summons!'

Rather frigidly, and jerkily, like a puppet directed by an unskilful hand, she went through the prescribed motions, while Jael sat up in bed and bowed three times, as did the other patients: it was the recognised routine for hospital use.

'Patients and Delinquents,' said the Voice, whose intonation varied with every announcement, but was always designed to strike at the listeners' nerves and heart as a baby's cry does:

'Our sleepless concern for our people has been much exercised and harassed by an event that happened nearly a month ago. We need not tell you to what we refer: the tragedy that overtook a fortunately small section of our community on the road from Ely. Happily the loss of life was slight: only five of our dear subjects paid the penalty of

Death Deviation, and are now for ever beyond the reach of our most loving care. We need not remind you that in the bad old days thousands of patients and delinquents perished on the roads. They gave their lives, we will not say gladly, but ungrudgingly in the service of that most beastly and insatiable of deities, the God of Speed. Whether it be true, as some have claimed, that the growing disregard for human life that made possible, indeed inevitable, the three world wars was due to that invention, the internal, and infernal, combustion engine, we cannot say. We ourselves have never disguised the horror with which we regarded it, and accordingly we limited the pace at which our subjects could travel to a maximum pace of $7\frac{1}{2}$ miles an hour. During the many years in which it has been our painful duty to rule over you there has not been, until now, one single case of death on the roads.

'Patients and Delinquents!

'It has always been our principle to reduce as far as may be those instincts of yours (alas, too many) that tend to homicide or suidice. It is our mission to save you from yourselves. If you knew how difficult that task was, you would perhaps behave with more consideration. Naturally you regard us as a tyrant, and naturally we behave like one, for even Dictators behave as they are expected to behave. Judging by the complaints that reach us from various sections of the community, bitterly attacking other sections of the community, sometimes even demanding their extinction, it appears that you would like us to behave like a tyrant, and so we have and shall, for it is our principle to give our people what they want.

'Discontent and unrest and murmuring there will always be where you, our dear, dear people, are concerned. For your sakes, much more than for our own, we do not wish to see rebellion raise its ugly head, and this, our statisticians tell us, is bound to happen if so much as 26% of the population feels, or thinks it feels, a grievance. We are not betraying any secret, either ours or yours, when we say that our main concern for you, our chief headache, to use one of your own vulgarisms, is to keep your blood-lust down. And by blood-lust we do not only mean your strange propensity for shedding other people's blood, but your still stranger wish to spill your own.

'Accordingly we devised a system of safety-valves whereby your bloodthirstiness could escape when it had reached boiling-point. One of these was the Motor Expeditions (Country) Service, sometimes known as Rural Rides, a regrettable and ridiculous survival from the Bad Old Times, but one which, we were assured, would release a $3\frac{1}{2}$ per cent pressure of unrest. For several years this service fulfilled its function, and that apparently irreducible element of disobedience in you seemed to be appeased. But not long ago the Discontentometer showed a sudden rise; and it was then, after much painful deliberation, that we decided to make the experiment of the Death and Glory Service, the outcome of which you all know. Five human units lost their lives and twenty-seven were injured. The experiment seemed to be successful; the Discontentometer recorded a sharp drop of $19\frac{1}{2}$ degrees. A cry of horror and indignation went up; everybody criticised everybody else and we ourselves, yes we, were blamed for having allowed the incident to happen. Thankfully we suspended the provision for accidents in the Motor Expeditions (Country) Service and decreed that the Service should be conducted without mishaps as before. We thought that this would be your wish, as it was ours.

'Patients and Delinquents!

'We were mistaken. Again the Discontentometer has risen and it is still rising. Can it be that our subjects have not learnt their lesson? Do they still wish to spill their own blood, or drink the blood of others? Are we on our way back to the Bad Old Times with their unslaked thirst for death? We did not promise you immortality but we did promise that, accidents apart, you should die natural deaths, and it was only in response to your own craving for danger that we revoked our promise. Has that craving not been glutted? Has it in fact grown on what it fed on? We cannot think so; we can only suppose that the Voluntary Principle, that unavoidable but noxious adjunct, has become inflamed at the prospect of what it calls compulsion. Compulsion! Has not the motto of our régime always been "Free Will"? Would any of you, standing, sitting or lying (alas, you are all of you too fond of lying), who hear these words, dare to say that since the time our envoy led you from the Shades, into this unpromising land, you have ever acted under compulsion? That we have ever forced you, our dear subjects, to do anything you did not want to do?

'Patients and Delinquents!

'The Motor Expeditions (Country) Service will be resumed, but with this difference: in future not one but three of the six coaches will meet with an accident. Never since our accession has the Voluntary Principle been stretched so far; and we are confident that when the day comes those chariots of death will stand empty on Progress Square: no drivers, no ticket-collectors, no passengers will be seen; everyone will be on his knees or on hers (please do not laugh, no pleasantry is meant), thanking us for having saved them from themselves.

'Patients and Delinquents! We have spoken.'

Again the valleys were exalted, again the Sister and the nurses made their ritual curtsey, again the bedridden bowed three times. And so strong was the feeling of relief that for a moment no one noticed the small figure in the doorway who made her curtsey not once but several times.

'Gracious Dictator!' exclaimed the Sister, who all this time had been immobilised beside Jael's bed. 'There she is!

And now there's no time to hide the flower! Ten to one she won't spot it, all these old girls are as blind as bats, but if she does, Jael 97, you'd better say an angel sent it! This old thing is not too bad, and she's quite religious. She's a bit ga-ga, too, if you ask me. But mind, don't start any hares. Just answer what she asks.'

The Sister bustled off towards the doorway where the Visitor was still standing, peering round the ward with her near-sighted eyes. Tiny as she was, her trim figure and unbowed shoulders gave her a faintly martial air.

CHAPTER TWELVE

JAEL'S bed was half-way down the ward on the left side. With a mixture of impatience, curiosity and misgiving she watched the Visitor's progress from bed to bed. She did not go straight up the row, she zig-zagged, so she would have seen twelve patients before Jael's turn came. She seemed to stay about five minutes with each. An hour of waiting! Jael wished that it was over. Try as she would, she couldn't think her own thoughts; like an examination candidate she kept imagining questions that the Visitor might put to her. She would see at once, of course, that Jael was a Failed Alpha; that would prejudice her from the start. She couldn't help knowing that Jael was a coach casualty, as every woman in the ward was; but would she know that she had been the ring-leader in the dance round the tower? Would the Sister have told her? Jael didn't think so; she didn't talk much to the Sister, whose chief part in the proceedings seemed to be to accompany her from bed to bed, wheeling a sort of canvas hut, with straight sides and a barrel roof, such as road-men sometimes use, big enough to enclose bed, Visitor and patient. It had the air of a confessional, sight-proof and sound-proof.

Why were her thoughts so self-accusing? Jael wondered. She couldn't think of a single virtue she possessed, or any quality that would pass as a virtue in the eyes of the régime. The Visitor, who was no doubt an emissary of the régime, would look upon her as a hopeless backslider. How did the other patients look, after their ordeal? Shattered, in tears? Jael couldn't see very well, for some of the lights had been turned off, perhaps at the Visitor's request. Wireless and television had been turned off, too. She told herself she was working herself up about nothing. Punishments were notoriously light; many critics of the régime said they were too light. Sometimes they were intended to make the culprit look silly, like the stocks and pillory of olden days; but they were seldom physically painful. If it wasn't a fine, it would be the withdrawal of her entertainment licence. But supposing it was something much, much worse!

The hut was being moved again. Trundled on wheels, it scarcely made a sound. Now there were only four more patients to be examined before she was.

Reviewing her past life, Jael felt herself a stranger to it, almost as if she had died and been re-born. In those days she hadn't felt it empty; she had fulfilled herself in many ways. By dancing chiefly, and by little flirtations, gossip, meeting friends. Gay spirals of femininity had welled up in her, like bubbles in a soda-water siphon. How she had laughed and giggled over nothing. Nothing! Yes, at that time she had been content with nothing. Now she was not content with anything. How had the change come about? What had marked it? That day at the Ministry of Facial Justice, she supposed, when Judith had persuaded her against being betafied. Or earlier, really, with the stirring of conscience, or whatever it was, that told her she ought to look more like her fellows. Till then she had been as frivolous as they were: more frivolous, in fact. Then the blight of seriousness had descended on her; she had discerned a purpose in her life.

The hut was crossing the ward again: only three more patients intervened.

Since then she had lived much more intensely; her life had narrowed down. The Purpose! She had felt she must serve it; it had become a sort of deity that demanded sacrifice, a Voice she must obey, a Voice that spoke with different accents, and a different message, from the Voice she had heard just now. For the first time, almost, she had been aware of opposition, of hostility: she was resisting a surrounding will, the combined wills of other people. At times she had felt guilty, but at other times she took a fierce pleasure in her resistance, because it made her feel herself; the feeling of unlikeness was a positive pleasure, whereas to be like was only a neutral happiness. Yet most of the time she was unhappy, because it was foreign to her to be in opposition, she was a natural conformer, in conforming her being had fulfilled itself.

With the tail of her eye she saw the hut moving across the ward. She did not have to count, she knew that after two more visits it would be her turn.

But at Ely she had turned the tables on them, she had been in opposition then, she had made her will prevail, she had brought them over to her side. She couldn't recapture that sense of triumph now, for now she was among enemies, and going to be 'visited' by an enemy: they were all against her, everyone, and here she was, confined to her bed, unable to make herself felt or her views known, in disgrace, who knew in how much disgrace, or what her punishment would be? Would the Visitor know? The Visitor was a poor old thing, a welfare-worker, no one to pay attention to or be afraid of. A piece of window-dressing, the Sister had said, a splash of eyewash, no one that counted. Besides she was, nominally at any rate, the patients' friend; the purpose of her visits was to hear their complaints. She wasn't an accuser or a judge, she was an ally! Remember that, Jael! She is here to help you. Why had she thought otherwise? But no, any report she made would at once be pigeon-holed: it would never reach Authority; she would leave it with the Sister, perhaps, and the Sister, who wasn't a bad sort really, would forget to forward it to the Matron, or the Matron would forget to pass it on to the Supervisor, or the Supervisor would forget to pass it on to the Inspector

Only one bed now between her and the examination.

The Inspector! And at the word (for it was a word, she breathed it to herself, almost aloud) Jael's thoughts took on another hue, and a more sanguine one. The thought of the Inspector was a talisman which, so long as she did not consider it too closely, supported the tottering fabric of her emotional life. When she considered it closely she realised how insecure it was. Two meetings: and was the second real, or had she dreamed it? It had left her with a memory of rapture, rapture pure and unalloyed, such as only comes in dreams. But common-sense told her that the whole experience was far more likely to have been a result of the accident. Concussion, shock, anything might have mirrored it on her wishful-thinking mind.

But if at times her faith in the experience burned too low to give a light it never quite went out, for always there was the flower. And since the flower was real, must not the experience be real, too? She had no proof that the two were connected; yet in her feelings they were: when she thought of one, automatically she thought of the other: the flower was a symbol of the experience. If the flower had some quality of the forbidden, so had the experience. If the flower was so rare as to be almost fabulous, so was the experience. If other flowers were substitutes for this one, so were other experiences for this experience. And just as the flower was so full of awe and dread that it must not be shown or even named, so was the experience; neither could be shared with anyone, on pain of . . . on pain of . . .

So intense were Jael's thoughts, so far had they taken her outside herself, that she did not hear the light trundle of the wheels or notice the familiar ward-sounds die away, or see the unfamiliar light shine on her eyes.

The Sister's voice recalled her to herself.

'Jael 97,' she was saying in official tones, 'here is the Visitor to see you.'

'Supposing I did,' Jael said, 'supposing it was made possible for me——'

'On whom would it depend?' the Visitor asked.

Mentally Jael drew back. 'Oh, on so many things. Even if they kept my job open for me——'

'You might be handicapped in other ways?'

'Yes,' said Jael, and for a moment had the feeling that the Visitor could read her thoughts. 'I might have to wear . . . to wear . . .'

'Permanent Sackcloth?'

'Yes, or some other sign of disgrace. That's what they say.'

'Don't pay any attention to them. They know no more than you do, and the Dictator is merciful.'

'The Dictator is merciful,' repeated Jael. 'But'—she drew a long breath—'it isn't possible, is it, that *nothing* will happen to us? That we shall go on as we were before?'

'I'm afraid you may,' the Visitor said, and smiled for the first time. 'I'm very much afraid you may.'

Jael smiled, too, in inexpressible relief. But it sounded too good to be true.

'Shan't we even be fined?' she asked.

'Some of you may have to pay a little but not more than you can afford, nothing ruinous . . . You needn't worry about that, I'm sure.'

'They say no man will want to marry us, if we're deep in debt, because he would have to pay it off.'

'My dear, what nonsense.'

'And then no holidays, no games, no cinemas, no amusements—no fun, except just the Litany. If he went out, he would have to go on his own.'

'He?' asked the Visitor.

'A husband, I meant,' Jael said.

'You harp on husbands. Had you thought——?'

Jael saw that the Visitor wore no wedding ring. But

surely all women, married or not, understood about husbands.

'Something happened to me,' she said, 'that made me think—it wasn't an ordinary experience. I may have quite misunderstood it. It wasn't anything to do with daily life—it didn't happen here, really.'

'Where did it happen?' asked the Visitor.

'I don't quite know—in the air, I think. It may have been a dream, but I had such an assurance of something—well, not of this world.'

'Doesn't this world content you?' asked the Visitor. 'Isn't ordinary life good enough for you?'

'It was, it was,' said Jael. 'But since I had this taste of something else—only a taste, perhaps it wasn't real—I don't feel I can go back——'

'You broke a rule,' the Visitor said gently.

'I know, I looked up, I made others look up, too. Surely I was right. Wouldn't you have?'

'I am only an old woman,' said the Visitor, 'whose self-appointed business it is to try to find out how people feel. The Dictator——'

'Darling Dictator,' Jael said.

This time the Visitor didn't rise: she bowed, as Jael did.

'The Dictator, as far as my poor intelligence can understand him, doesn't think that we should sever ourselves, even in thought, from quite a humdrum way of life. What the imagination imposes on it is false and risky to oneself and others. I am not in his confidence—how could I be?—but that has been his policy, to reduce accidents. A war is the greatest of all accidents, and how does it come about?—through the imagination. Only through the imagination can one kill a man.'

'But can one love him except through the imagination?'

'Indeed, one can. One loves what's there, not what the imagination pretends is there. Look at these flowers! You all have them; the Ministry of Health sees to that. No one goes without. They're not the real thing, of course; the real thing perished with the war, and these you sometimes see are just museum pieces, doomed to extinction, so they say; the earth won't nourish them. These plastic flowers are much more satisfactory because they don't depend on anything outside themselves. Now this flower of yours—'

Without looking at her cineraria, Jael said:

'But don't we all rely on things outside ourselves, and people, for what makes life worth living, indeed for life itself?'

The Visitor didn't answer for a moment. She turned her faded eyes upwards, and one blue-veined hand moved restlessly on her knee.

'We did,' she said, 'I did, when I was your age. But now I think the Dictator—no, my dear, you needn't trouble to make the obeisances—I'll excuse you—he means us to draw our nourishment from a common source—a kind of spiritual reservoir to which all of us unconsciously contribute as bees used to contribute honey to the hive. You don't remember that! There are no bees now, because there are no flowers, but every educated person knows about them. The bee didn't eat its own honey, or honey brought it by a friend; it just ate honey. That's what's meant, I think, by replacing intellect by instinct. Now this flower of yours——'

Jael tried to look as if she hadn't heard the Visitor's last words.

'But I don't want to give up my intelligence—such as it is,' she said. 'I would much rather act on my own, even if I made mistakes, than from some mass-suggestion that was stronger than me. I like to have my own thoughts, just as I like to have my own face, simply because they're mine. I shouldn't want to like or dislike something because other people did.'

'And yet you do that very thing,' the Visitor said. 'You

103

believe you are thinking for yourself, but you share the ideas and prejudices of people like-minded with yourself—we all do. And those ideas and prejudices may well be wrong. And even if they're not, diversity of ideas is dangerous. At worst it leads to murder or to war. Better have one idea, to which we all unconsciously subscribe, and leave intelligence and the power of choice to the Inspectors, who are trained not to abuse them. Dancing is a kind of harmony, isn't it? You do what the others do, to make the figure complete, but you do it in your own way. You express yourself, as a means to a larger expression, outside yourself. Uniformity isn't bad, as some people still think, because if the quality is good, it satisfies. People are never happy who want change. Now the design of these flowers is a good design, that is why all hospitals have them. They are cinerarias, as you know. A committee decided that, of the few flowers left, they are the loveliest, and earmarked them for hospital use. Think if you all had different flowers, your own special flower! What opportunities for Envy—no, my dear, you needn't move—there'd be Everyone thinking her own flower the best, or green with Bad Egg, as they call it! The whole ward would soon be in an uproar, and no one would get well. Whereas, by this plan, each of you gets from the flower its special quality—all that the word flower implies—the same reaction, the same pleasure, and nobody is hurt or discontented. Now that flower of yours—'

'Yes,' said Jael, feeling as though the cineraria was scorching her face and setting her on fire. 'My cineraria——'

'You say "my cineraria",' said the Visitor kindly, 'but it isn't really yours, is it? It really belongs to the Health Service. When you leave next week, it will stay behind to be a pleasure to the next patient who occupies your bed and you won't mind leaving it, you'll be glad, whereas if it was yours——'

'But it *is* mine!' Jael cried.

'Yours, my dear child? How can it be? We none of us have flowers of our own—they are far too precious.'

'But it *is* mine!' Jael repeated. 'I know it is, for someone gave it me.'

'Someone gave it you?' echoed the Visitor. 'But that's impossible—you must be dreaming. Shock and concussion—Will you let me see it?'

Torn between terror and triumph, Jael cried, 'Please look!'

The Visitor rose and stood over the flower. She bent her head down till the petals cast a bluish shadow on her face. Then she fingered the leaves, and touched the mould in which the flower grew. It left a brown stain on her finger. A look of bewilderment crossed her face. She looked round for her chair and dropped into it.

'You're right,' she said. 'It is a real flower. I thought it might be, when I first saw it, but couldn't believe my eyes——Do you know what made me think it might be real?'

'No,' said Jael.

'It is beginning to fade——The other flowers don't fade, they cannot.'

'Are you angry with me?' asked Jael.

'My dear, why should I be? It is a——a miracle, and you are not to blame.'

'Will they let me take it away with me?'

'Oh yes.'

'And keep it at home?'

'Yes, why do you doubt it?'

Like a hypochondriac seeking reassurance from a doctor, Jael wanted her immunity confirmed.

'I thought I might be punished. I thought that when I got away from here they would——would make an example of me.'

'They?'

'The authorities.'

The Visitor shook her head. 'The Dictator is not vindictive,' she said.

'Will everything be as it was before?'

'Yes, I believe so.'

'Shall I be fined?'

'Oh no.'

'Shall I be allowed to come and go as I please?'

'Of course.'

'Shall I——shall I have to wear Permanent Sackcloth?'

'I don't think so.'

Jael searched her mind for further fears to allay. The Visitor had quite won her confidence; sweet, gentle old thing. But she couldn't in a moment lose the terrors of several weeks; she couldn't quite believe she would get off scot-free. The Visitor was rising to her feet, pulling her cape about her; the ordeal was over.

'I should like to kiss you,' she said, bending down, 'although it's against the regulations. I might catch something—not from you, my dear—you're harmless, or at least, I think you are.'

'Then I'm not to be punished?'

'No.'

'Why not?'

'My dear child,' said the Visitor, 'you *have* been punished.'

At this an extraordinary sense of peace descended on Jael; she felt she had been absolved from all her sins. For of course she had been punished; she had been a victim of the accident; she had suffered a great deal of pain; she had been operated on; she had been detained in hospital for three, or was it four weeks. A sufficient expiation!—and now she could start again with a clean sheet, or perhaps with one or two minor disabilities, the loss of a few civic privileges, which she could laugh at, just as everyone else did. 'The Dictator is not vindictive.' Darling Dictator, of course he

106

wasn't. People made fun of him, and grumbled at him, and sometimes, as Jael had, they dreaded him. But he was all right, really: by and large, as he himself had often told them, they were lucky to have him. He wasn't out to make trouble; he hadn't made trouble for her . . .

Jael's spirits soared, and so intent was she on relishing her sensations that she forgot to say goodbye to the Visitor; forgot her existence for the moment, until she realised that the sights and sounds of the ward were all about her, and saw the hut, with the Visitor walking beside it, being trundled to a bed on the opposite side. Then she sat up and tried to say something but the Visitor didn't hear. No doubt she was busy thinking up questions for the next interview.

Had she really kissed her? Jael wasn't sure. She hadn't been kissed a great many times in her short life, and only once in a way that counted; her mind and her flesh would remember it for ever, that embrace among the stars. But even an ordinary kiss, even the peck that Joab sometimes gave her, even the routine kisses that her women friends gave her, at meetings and partings, left an imprint on her psycho-physical memory—one didn't, for a brief instant, feel the same afterwards as before. Virtue had gone out of her, and come in; however seemingly insignificant the contact, it left a momentary sense of heightened being. Her being was heightened now, but from the pardon, not, she felt sure, from the touch of the Visitor's lips. Poor old lady, she would have so much kissing to do if she kissed everyone, no wonder she said it was against the regulations, had adopted the stage technique of kissing not the face but the adjacent air. Still it was a kind gesture.

Blissfully relaxed, unaware of time, Jael watched the hut with its attendant ministers pursuing its zig-zag course. Did everyone to whom the Visitor had talked feel as happy as she did? The answer seemed to be yes; she noticed that the faces which had undergone the ordeal, and presumably

107

received the kiss, looked as carefree as she supposed hers did; whereas those, rapidly growing fewer now, which had not, looked tense and strained. Of course you couldn't always tell with Betas; their features didn't change much. But their eyes betrayed them, and their voices too, or rather their lack of voice. Ever since the Visitor appeared at the door, a hush had fallen; but those who had been visited were now talking a little, although with some constraint; while not a sound was heard from those whose turn was still to come.

Jael was too happy to want to talk. But idly she asked herself, How was it that she, and apparently the others, set so much store by what was said to them by an elderly civil servant, a State employee like themselves, whose word could have no more weight than theirs had? What reason had she, Jael, to believe that she had been punished and was now in the clear, just because an old welfare-worker, who went about trying to be nice to people, had said so? None; and for a moment a doubt crept into her mind, but the current of suggestion, to which she was so susceptible, flowing through the ward, soon banished it.

An hour had passed. Now the last delinquent was receiving absolution, had received it, was sitting up and stretching herself and rubbing her eyes; the hut had been folded up and whisked away; and the Visitor and the Sister were coming back down the central aisle, the Sister's tall figure bending protectively towards the Visitor's short one, her face wearing a smile which was affectionate but also amused and patronising. As they passed Jael's bed she heard the Visitor say: 'Very satisfactory, I must congratulate you,' and the Sister answered: 'They're a good crowd on the whole, very little trouble.'

But when she came back into the ward her demeanour was very different; the starchiness had gone out of her bearing and she seemed as relieved as anyone. Discipline was relaxed, and she went chatting among the patients. When she got to Jael's bed she heaved a sigh and said:

'Well, that's over for a month at any rate. Not a bad old thing, is she? One of the best of them. How did you get on?'

'Quite all right, I think,' said Jael.

'She didn't spot the flower, did she?'

'Well, as a matter of fact, she did.'

'Gracious Dictator! (no, don't bother). What did she say?'

'She seemed a bit taken aback. She said it must have been a miracle. But she didn't really seem to mind. She told me I could keep it and take it away with me.'

'What cheek! It isn't for her to say, but I suppose you can. As long as she doesn't report it to anyone who matters! If she does, we might have the whole place closed down. What else did she say?'

'She said I had been punished.'

'Punished—I like that! Poor old thing, she's obviously losing grip. I should say you'd got off very lightly.'

'I think so, too,' said Jael, happily.

CHAPTER FOURTEEN

As the date of Jael's discharge drew nearer, her visitors began to fall off. 'Be seeing you outside next time,' they said; 'goodbye for now.'

Outside! The word had lost its terrors for Jael; since the Visitor had reassured her, she began to feel she would be welcomed as a heroine. The régime was not so popular that no one could give it little digs; she might find herself the centre of a cult for poking fun at the Dictator. She devised the choreography of a ballet in which the finale would represent the Dictator, on bended knee, offering her, Jael, a flower far more beautiful than the blue cineraria by her bed. At first Jael would not accept it; she waved it away with negligent gestures and raised eyebrows. Ultimately, of course, she would be prevailed on to accept the proffered flower, after which the Dictator would salaam three times. (Ballets satirising the Dictator were not uncommon: generally they were held in secrecy or semi-secrecy; sometimes they were rather improper.) Nobody knew what the Dictator looked like or how old he was. The representations of him were many and various, but he could always be identified by a balloon coming out of his mouth enclosing the words, 'Patients and Delinquents!' Sometimes he was represented as the Man in the Moon, with a gamut of expressions ranging from sickening benignity to appalling ferocity; sometimes as the Old Man of the Sea, an incubus, vast, shapeless and corpulent, supported on the straining, sweating backs of as many citizens as could be got into the picture; on one occasion he had been presented as an androgynous, not to say, epicene figure, pointing vindictively to a crowd of women—suppliants who were stretching up their arms and outspread fingers, begging vainly for some boon. This was, of course, an allusion to the Dictator's often-remarked prejudice against women, and it received a severe punishment. The cartoonist, the editor and the publisher were fined and sent to prison, and on their release were denied many civic privileges, obliged to go barefoot and condemned to wear Permanent Sackcloth. On the whole this sentence was regarded as just; the community thought the joke had gone too far: 'We must have law and order.' Jael was of the same opinion; she had no clearer idea of the Dictator than anyone else had, he was beyond thought; she neither liked nor disliked him, she accepted him. In her old care-free days she scarcely thought of him at all. Now she felt she had definitely scored off him, and meant to cash in on her success, but in the friendliest way, without lèse-majesté, for she had to admit that, as the Sister said, he had let her off quite lightly: she had only to remember her haunted, miserable state of mind before the Visitor calmed her fears, to realize that. Just a little fun at the Dictator's expense!

So her friends had given up coming to see her, all but one, the doctor. She counted him as a friend, because he had always been especially nice to her. She fancied that he gave her more time and attention than he gave the others—and the others thought so too, and teased her about it. 'Yes, 97!' (Where there was no ambiguity it was becoming fashionable to address someone by number rather than by name or name and number: to do so was a sign of familiarity, affection and facetiousness; and it was encouraged by the authorities as leading to depersonalisation.) 'Yes, 97! We all watched the clock, and do you know how long he stayed with you this morning? Five and a half minutes, and the most he gave anybody else was four! And he went so close to you! He has to come close to some of us, because we were injured in our legs and arms and so on! But all he needs to see of you he could see quite well from the end of the bed, and further off than that! We don't come crowding round your bed, do we? But he goes right up to you, and takes your pulse for much longer than necessary, and pats your hair and strokes your face and—are you blushing? You damned well ought to be!'

Jael was surprised: couldn't they see the blood rushing to her cheeks?

'Yes, and the look that comes into his eyes when he knows it's your turn! Just like an animal, it isn't decent! And when at last he drags himself away he shakes his head and looks so disappointed, just like a——just like a——'

Jael stopped her ears, and the next time Dr. Wainewright came to see her she could hardly look him in the face. All the same she did look at him, as she had never looked before. He was a square-built man, just over middle height, and under middle age, with a square-cut face, dark hair, and steady, grey-blue eyes, which were his best feature. His nose was Roman and a little askew (surely, being a plastic surgeon, he could have had it straightened?), his mouth was wide and his teeth were irregular. A Beta-plus appearance, or just Beta, though, of course, men's looks weren't reckoned that way. He had a confident bedside manner, or so she had always thought; but today he seemed a little jumpy; or was it that she herself was ill at ease? She couldn't help watching the clock while he took her pulse; he was certainly a full minute over it, and he looked at it as fixedly as a dog looks at a bone. When he parted her hair to find the scar on her head, he couldn't find it at first; his fingers groped about; were the other women all looking?

'It's healed up nicely,' he said, a little breathlessly, 'and your hair's grown over it, no one will be the wiser, unless you tell them.'

'Oh, I shan't do that,' said Jael, mechanically.

'Now for the face,' he said, so seriously that Jael had to

112

restrain a nervous giggle. He passed his finger over it. 'Can you feel that?' he asked.

'Well, only just,' said Jael.

He stroked the other cheek.

'Can you feel that?'

'Well, only just,' repeated Jael.

'Now the forehead and the chin, to make sure . . . Any soreness there?'

'None,' said Jael, and couldn't help adding: 'Your finger feels as light as a feather.'

'Splendid, splendid,' he said, giving her a nervous smile. 'You've made an excellent recovery, and from what Sister . . . er . . . Electra 94 tells me, you've been an exemplary patient. Exemplary—good word, that,' he said, half catching her eye in an experimental manner. 'It's been a pleasure, a pleasure to . . .' His voice died away. 'Well, anyhow it's been a pleasure,' he concluded.

'And to me, too,' said Jael. 'I'm very grateful to you.'

'Well, yes. We do our best, of course, but in some cases it's more . . . more rewarding than in others. I oughtn't to say that, ought I?' he added, 'it's highly unprofessional, and besides we're all alike, or we're supposed to be.'

He raised a questioning eyebrow.

'I'm very glad to have you as my doctor,' Jael said, feeling his eyes trained like machine-guns on her.

'Yes, well, nice of you to say so. This will be my last visit, I'm—I was going to say, "I'm afraid", but really it's a good thing, isn't it?'

'I . . . I suppose it is,' said Jael.

'Yes, of course it is. You're going out tomorrow, aren't you?'

Jael said she was.

'Well, the best of luck. You'll be all right, you know, only take it easy, don't get tired or . . . or over-excited.'

'No fear of that,' smiled Jael.

'And no more Country Expeditions,' he said, forcing a laugh. 'At least I don't advise them, not as part of the cure. But if you do go, and come back here, we'll do our best to look after you.'

Jael thanked him.

'I think that the Dictator—no, my dear, don't bother, remember we're still in hospital—should have suppressed them. They'll give us so much work! But in this case . . . There was something I wanted to say—what was it?'

Jael's eyes searched his face in sympathy, trying to draw the question out of him.

'Oh, I know,' he said, as if suddenly remembering. 'If you shouldn't be quite well . . . though I'm sure you will be, or if you should find yourself at a loose end, which I'm sure you won't, here——here's my address.'

He thought a moment, and added: 'In any case, I've got to drop in and have a look at you, to see you are following my instructions.'

Before she had time to answer he was gone.

Why had what had been so clear to everyone else, Jael asked herself, been hidden from her? Before her mind had time to answer, her heart told her. She heard her rescuer's voice: 'I'll get you out of here,' felt herself soaring upwards, the sense of time and place dissolving, her mental landscape disappearing, in the glory of his presence. So radiant was it that it eclipsed, for a brief moment, Dr. Wainewright's physical presence far more effectively than a cloud of darkness would have. Beside the other, brighter flame, his flicker didn't show.

When she had regained her thinking self, it told her this: even had Dr. Wainewright gone down on his knees by her bedside and felt her pulse with his head buried in her breast, she might well have seen nothing odd in his behaviour, so completely was her mind occupied by the vision of another man. Another man!—for she supposed he must have been one; he must have been the Inspector who had challenged her about the current epithet for—Alpha. Inspectors were more than men, of course, but they were men.

He hadn't come to see her, and now she had only twenty-four hours left in hospital. Yet she was certain he would come; and strangely enough every moment that he didn't come increased her certainty. With a gambler's faulty logic she believed that luck would somehow be localised within a time-limit; he was the winning number that must turn up because, so far, it hadn't. Every minute that was empty of him seemed to fill the next one with his presence.

It hadn't always been so. Before the Visitor came her hope had burnt so low that only by looking at the flower, that tangible token of his existence, could she keep it alive. Punishment was in store for her, a punishment was due; it was a black cloud blotting out the horizon, sometimes blotting out the sky; and always at the heart of it—a deeper shadow within the shadow—had been the fear that he, whoever he was, was lost to her. She never quite succumbed to it, the flower prevented that; but as a light to her life it was as unhelpful as a will-o'-the-wisp; and as a fire on her hearth, a focal centre for her spirit, a vehicle of warmth, it counted as little as a candle in a church—the candles by whose meagre light she sometimes listened to the Litany.

The Visitor had changed all that—dispersed the cloud, banished the fear, restored the hope. Jael had been punished, and therefore she was absolved. As little did she know of what the future held for her as she had known before; she only knew that instead of dreading it she looked forward to it, that instead of a frost numbing her faculties, it was a soft spring morning, pregnant with promise. So indeed she thought of it, in metaphors drawn from long ago. Mental habit dies hard; the survivors of the Third World War helped out their thoughts with pre-war images. In the New World there was no frost, no soft spring mornings—the war had swept them away, along with all the other changes of climate, temperature and season; they had this uniform, perpetual March, with an east wind that did indeed grow keener towards evening and a grey sky which the sun never quite pierced. But the language hadn't adapted itself to the new meteorological conditions; it was still, as ours is now, a storehouse of dead metaphors, still retained phrases like 'at daggers drawn', though no one in the New State had a dagger.

How far could the past be said to have survived into the present? Some writers said that history had come to an end with the Second World War; how little they knew! She herself could not remember that time; but this was like another incarnation and needed a new language. Why, in those days a meal had courses. Nominally it still had: luncheon, which she was now having, consisted of three courses, the soup, the meat, the pudding; but they were contained in three capsules, of many flavours, true, and varying size to suit the taste and fancy of the eater; one was supposed to suck them (though no great harm came from swallowing them), and allow an interval of at least five minutes between each. But capsules they were, and round, and the metaphors drawn from eating in the old days, such as a square meal, were totally undescriptive of them.

Jael was dutifully sucking her third course and wondering what Pêche Melba really tasted like and looked like, when she was aware of a commotion at the end of the ward, as though someone had broken in. The Sister had gone to the door, and two of the nurses with her—apparently to bar the way; but there seemed to be more of them; someone else was there, and something like a lantern swinging in the doorway, streaking the air with gleams and flashes. Then the nurses fell back, and the stranger came forward, the tall

Sister looking up at him with a dazzle in her eyes, and prancing a little as though she trod on air. Jael swallowed down the remains of her Pêche Melba; she knew who it was before the Sister, stopping at a respectful distance, announced:

'The Inspector to see you, Jael 97.'

CHAPTER FIFTEEN

AFTERWARDS she remembered that he looked puzzled, so far as an Inspector could look puzzled, and drew back to look at her before he took her hand.

'You remember me?' he said.

Now indeed they would all be looking at her.

'Yes,' she breathed.

His smile came back, but uncertainly and with an intrusion of discomfort in it, like an alien flavour in a well-known taste. But she couldn't really look at him; she had never been able to.

'And you're better?'

'Quite well,' she said. 'I'm going out tomorrow.'

He nodded thoughtfully.

'I couldn't come before,' he said. 'We had all sorts of things to do, top-secret, of course.' His eyes twinkled. 'But I see you got the flower.'

'So it was from you?'

'I thought you'd guess.'

She tried to speak, but her voice failed her, and for a brief instant she wondered if she had been struck dumb. Finding her voice, she said:

'It's wilting, I'm afraid. But I shall have it with me, and take great care of it.'

He looked at the dark blue stamens, which had begun to shrivel and turn inwards at the edges.

'I'll get expert advice on it,' he said. 'It seems a pity——'

'Oh, much more than a pity!' Jael broke in.

His troubled look returned; his gaze did not search her face as it once had, but seemed to stop short before it reached her.

'But then I should have to part with it,' she said, 'and I do love it so! It maddens me that all these plastic flowers should last, and mine, which is a real one, shouldn't! You can do so much: can't you *order* it to live?'

'It's only an annual, you know,' he said.

Something in his tone troubled Jael. Again she tried to look at him, sitting with his helmet on his knees, his white uniform aglow with cords and epaulettes, the silver and gold insignia of his office; without his helmet he looked more youthful, and the sternness in his eyes seemed half assumed. But still there was a glitter coming from him, the prestige of his position and good looks, which dazzled her and made a barrier between them.

'Well, promise me,' she said, 'that if you take it away, you will bring it back yourself. My address is——'

'I know what your address is,' he said sombrely. 'We—er—know people's addresses. Besides, you gave it me. But I can't promise you to bring it back myself, because, you see, we never know where we shall be.'

Jael tried to hide her disappointment.

'Oh well,' she said, 'let me keep it, then. I'll—I'll look after it. It isn't dead. It's natural, isn't it, for flowers to fade? It isn't withered yet, and when the spring comes, or what they used to call the spring, it may flower again, with any luck. But you'll come back sometime, won't you?'

He looked down at his helmet. Some strands of the white plume had got tangled, and he smoothed them out with his long fingers.

'Of course I'll come,' he said.

If only words could be the same as deeds! If only his saying he would come could be the same as coming! For a moment she persuaded herself that it was, and her slither down the slope of happiness seemed to be arrested; but she had travelled a long way from the summit.

'It was real, wasn't it?' she asked suddenly. 'I mean—you

are the man who let me off the fine, and then rescued me when I was pinned down in the coach? You are the same man, aren't you?'

It seemed strange, almost irreverent, to be calling him a man, but after all he was one.

'Yes, I'm the same man,' he said.

'You never told me your name.'

'We're not supposed to.'

His answer chilled her. Had she begun to slip again? 'But,' he added suddenly, 'I'll tell you. It's Michael 21.'

Could there be other Michaels? But the fact of knowing his name brought him nearer to her.

'Well, I'm the same woman,' she said; 'there's no doubt about that, is there?'

He looked at her uncertainly, between pain and doubt, shorn of his self-confidence, his super-policeman look.

'You're not quite the same, you know,' he brought out, as gently as he could.

'Not the same?' She wouldn't let herself take in the meaning of his words, it was too wounding; she tried to think of something else he might mean.

'I suppose nobody's quite the same after an accident,' she said. 'It—it shakes one up so. You're right in a way: I haven't felt the same. I've had to think of a lot of things I never used to think of. Think for myself, I suppose you could say, though we're not supposed to do that. In that way I am different, I'm more serious than I used to be. Once I never took anything seriously: it was all this face-saving business, as it's called, that started me off.'

He nodded, gravely.

Surprised that she could speak freely to him, for hitherto he had imposed himself on her so much that her thoughts could only follow a certain track with him—a lane of light with darkness on both sides—she added, feigning gaiety:

'But it's only temporary, my seriousness! I shall go back

to being like I was, I hope, if that doesn't sound too conceited! I've won my battle, whatever it was, and I've been punished—at least,' she laughed, 'an old welfare-worker who sometimes comes nosing round here told me I had.'

Jael gave the Inspector a questioning look, for he must know better than the Visitor what her fate was going to be; but he made no comment.

'So having made my sort of protest, which I felt in duty bound to make, both for myself and others, I shall forget about it, and be as carefree as I used to be, for I'm not a natural rebel and people with a grievance are so unattractive, aren't they?—you must know that better than anyone, since it's your job to keep us all in order.'

Jael felt very happy saying all this to the Inspector, which she had long had it in her mind to say, and the wireless was making such a din, cooing, crooning and sighing, that there was no danger of being overheard. Nor much of being seen; for each patient had a television screen at the end of her bed, and what happened on it was to her more real than what was happening in the ward. She wasn't too much discouraged by Michael's silence, but she began to feel that she had held the floor too long, and said more diffidently:

'What I meant was, that I may seem different to—to talk to, but I'm just the same underneath.'

'I'm sure you are,' he said. 'But you are changed, none the less.'

Again the sensation of slipping . . . Jael struggled to arrest it, and said brightly:

'I know you didn't mean to hurt me, but why is it one *minds* being told one has changed? It might so easily be a change for the better! But people always mean it's a change for the worse! I hope you don't?'

'Oh no, of course not,' he said mechanically. 'Most people would say it *was* a change for the better. But I, as

121

you were, am a bit of a rebel, although I have to keep the rebels down . . . Now, Great Dictator (no don't bother, nobody has heard us), is it really as late as that?'

He looked at the ward clock.

'I'm afraid it is,' she answered sadly. 'But I thought that you Inspectors paid no heed to time.'

'Well, sometimes we can steal a march on it, but that depends on where we're going, and how. Now I want you to be very happy, Jael——'

'I am, I am,' she murmured.

'And will you promise me to go on being very happy?'

'How can I promise that?'

'Then I'll make it an order . . . We Inspectors can, you know. And if you don't obey——'

'What will happen?'

'Oh, the most thundering fine.'

'Will you come and collect it?'

'Yes, no, I have to be in so many places.'

'But how can you tell whether I'm happy,' Jael asked, 'unless you see me?'

'Oh, there are ways of telling.'

'But isn't seeing me the best way?'

A look of sadness came behind his eyes and dimmed their brightness.

'It's one way,' he said, 'and used to be the best way. But now I'm not so sure. I might have to ask you, or even use the Contentometer——'

'But surely you can tell,' cried Jael, 'just by looking at me? If you can't, who can?'

He didn't answer, but all in one movement he got up and bent over her. In the crook of his arm between his shoulder and his chest, his helmet nestled. Level with his face, the white plume came towards her. Was it his lips that touched hers, or did the horsehair brush them? It was a ravishing moment, a moment not in time or place, the longed-for moment, the moment of moments; and yet she could not afterwards, tell how it came to her.

'Now, 97,' said the Sister briskly, 'it's time for you to go.'
Jael was sitting on the chair beside her bed, which had been made up for the next occupant. She had done a little tour of the ward: with some, her farewells had been brief, with others she had sworn eternal friendship; with all she felt on better terms than she had ever thought she would be. How kind they were, and how sorely she would miss them! Nearly everyone had thought of something nice to say to her, something that made her feel they really liked her. Yes, they had accepted her as one of themselves. Many of them she had known only for a short time, for she was almost the doyenne of the patients! Sometimes the ward had seemed like a prison, sometimes like a fortress; which was it now? The outside world pressed heavily against the windows. Beyond the broad border of macadam which formed the garden of the hospital, rose a low wall (all walls in the New State were low: it was forbidden to build a wall too high for the average person to look over), and on the far side you could see torsos moving by with the slightly dragging gait which the regulation speed-limit of three miles an hour imposed on pedestrians; sometimes a horse and cart rumbled by; sometimes a ritual dance brought traffic to a standstill. Slow motion, slow motion was the rule, and Jael's thoughts, losing their urgency, began to catch the rhythm and slow down. Thinking at the same pace as the rest, she began to think what they did; she felt the tug, the attraction of a common thought, outside her own and greater than her own; it drew hers like a magnet. She remembered people telling her that under the influence of this telepathy they could think the generalised, universal thought for hours at a stretch: instinct replacing intellect! How comforting it was! —and then suddenly she remembered those blissful,

agonising moments with Michael, and the hope that had kept flaming up and dying down in her, setting her heart racing and her thoughts racing, too, hopes she could share with no one, fears that no infusion of collective sympathy could allay. These were to be the companions of her life, not those others.

'Now come on, 97! Don't sit there wool-gathering! You've something else to do before you leave, remember.'

'Something else?' asked Jael, startled out of her reverie.

'Why yes! You can't go out into the world looking like that! What would people say?'

'I don't quite understand,' said Jael. 'I thought I'd done everything. I was just waiting for——'

'Your conveyance? Well, it's at the door, a nice one, too. A white horse, think of that! Buck up, you musn't keep it waiting!'

'But what am I to do?'

'Take a look at yourself, silly, and make sure you're tidy.'

'Oh,' exclaimed Jael, 'I had quite forgotten my face!' She burst into shouts of uncontrollable laughter—somehow it seemed so funny.

'You've changed, I must say,' the Sister said. 'When you first came round, you were always asking to have a look at yourself.'

'Well, I do want to now,' said Jael, seized by an overwhelming appetite for the sight of her own face. 'Where's a looking-glass?'

'It's here, your own,' the Sister said. 'Don't you remember we took it from you when you came in? We can't have patients staring at themselves, it isn't good for them. But you're not a patient now, so here you are.'

She handed Jael her compact, and watched her open it.

'Oh!' cried Jael. Her eyes grew round with horror and dismay. She stared transfixed; put the little glass face downwards on the bed; picked it up but didn't look at it, picked it up again and looked in it with her mouth open and her breath coming gustily.

'Why, what's the matter?' asked the Sister.

'You've—you've betafied me!' Jael gasped.

'Well, yes, we did.'

'But you never asked me!'

'How could we ask you?' said the Sister. 'You weren't conscious.'

'But it isn't *my* face,' Jael almost screamed. 'It's someone else's.'

'It's quite a nice face,' the Sister said, 'and we took some trouble, believe me, to match your colouring and your hair.'

'But it isn't me,' said Jael. 'It's someone else.' The horror of nightmare overcame her; she seemed to be sinking through layers of realisation, each more appalling than the last.

'Don't take on so,' the Sister said, 'or you'll disturb the ward. I tell you it's quite a good face: Dr. Wainewright said it was the best he'd ever made. He fell in love with it, if you ask me. You'll soon get used to it and grow to like it.'

'I shan't, I shan't,' sobbed Jael.

'And luckily for you it's tear-proof. Now if you had your old Failed Alpha face, you'd be in a frightful mess—you wouldn't be fit to be seen.'

Jael snatched the looking-glass up again. It was true: the tears were running off her face like water off an oilskin; when she wiped them away no trace was left; no puffy eyelids, no streaks and blotches, nothing. No one but herself could have known that she'd been crying. At the thought of this her tears started afresh.

'But now nobody will know how I feel!'

'But do you want them to?'

'Oh yes, oh yes!' Again she wiped the tears away: it was like mopping up water from linoleum. She rubbed and scrubbed, trying to hurt herself; but all she got was a dead sensation, as though her skin was no real part of her.

'Don't do that,' said the Sister sharply. 'You can't play about like that with a Beta skin. You might rub it off.'

'I want to rub it off,' said Jael. 'I want my old face back. Where is it?' she demanded. 'Have you got it?'

The Sister couldn't help laughing.

'No, my dear, it went down the drain long ago.'

'You mean it's *lost*?'

'Well, what do you think? We can't keep pieces of old skin hanging about.'

Jael went stiff with fury.

'But was my—my old face so damaged . . . that nothing could be done with it?'

'Oh, Dr. Wainewright could have patched it up, but the orders are: if in doubt, betafy.'

'Whose orders?' demanded Jael.

'Well, dear, the Dictator's (no, please don't, when you're so upset)—if you go back far enough.'

'But how could the Dictator know about me?'

The Sister shrugged her shoulders.

'I think he knows about us all,' she said.

'Then he must have known I didn't want to be betafied.'

'Perhaps it was a punishment—you hadn't been a good girl, you know.'

Jael remembered the Visitor's words: 'You have been punished already.' So that was it. It explained everything; it explained why the other patients had been so chummy with her, a Beta like themselves; it explained why she hadn't felt, or hadn't properly felt, the kisses. It explained——a spasm of hate shot through her, zig-zagging like lightning through the darkness in her mind. And the same flash brought another realisation: losing her face, she had also lost him, Michael. He had loved her Failed Alpha face; he did not love her Beta face, he had as good as told her so. She would never see him again, never.

Darling Dictator!

The little mirror was lying on the bed, face downwards, close to her hand. She snatched it up, flung it on the floor, heard the crash but didn't see the splinters, and ran crying down the ward.

The Sister called after her: '97, 97, you've forgotten something.'

'I don't care,' she sobbed, but all the same she stopped.

'Your flower! You left it by your bed.'

Dazed, Jael walked slowly back between the rows of beds. One or two of the patients stared at her curiously, as if she was someone they hadn't seen before, but most of them were too intent on their television sets to have noticed her private drama. Picking her way through the broken glass glittering by her bedside, she reached the cineraria. Someone had wrapped the flower-pot in a swathe of paper, which somehow comforted her. Putting it under her arm, she felt she still had something left to face the world with.

PART II

Take but degree away, untune that string,
And, hark, what discord follows!

Troilus and Cressida

CHAPTER SIXTEEN

THE conspirators did not advertise the fact that they were such. They called themselves the Dancing Class. They met in a hollow in the ground, a mile or so from the town, and came not in a bunch but singly, with carefree looks as though to take an airing; and sometimes they would break off their deliberations and perform an impromptu ballet, which started idyllically but ended with a murder. They used no violence; sometimes their fluttering fingers hardly touched the victim; yet more than once he or she had fallen into a faint and taken some minutes to come round. The Assassin's Dance was Jael's idea; it would make killing easier, she said.

But this time Jael was absent.

'Shall we wait for her?' said one of the three men.

'She's our secretary,' said a woman, a Beta like the other of the two. 'What does the Chairman think?'

The Chairman, a man of medium height, with dark eyes, a sallow face and a broad jaw, answered:

'Well, we don't keep any records. We agreed it was too risky. What's the time?'

'Ten minutes past eleven,' someone said.

'Let's give her another five minutes,' said the Chairman. 'She's not been late before. She's generally the first.'

'Well, the whole thing was her idea,' observed one of the Betas. Without a trained eye, or unless one knew their voices, it was difficult to tell them apart.

'No, that's not true,' the other said. 'We all thought of it together—I mean, at the same moment.'

'You shouldn't say that, even if it was so,' one of the men remarked. 'You're talking like a Beta. It's one of the things we've got to fight against—the Beta conscious-ness.'

'It's easier for you,' the woman retorted. 'You have your own faces.'

Compared with the women, the three men did look extraordinarily unalike, almost as if each belonged to a different species.

'Never mind,' the man said. 'When we've done the job, we'll have every one of you looking absolutely Alpha.'

'When we've done the job,' the woman said. 'When we've done the job . . . We've been at it for six weeks, and we're no nearer now than when we started.'

'Order, order,' said the Chairman.

'I'm all in favour of it,' the woman said. 'I want it just as much as 97 does, though I don't throw my weight about as she does. How she loves the sound of her own voice!'

'Now, now,' the Chairman said. 'This sort of talk won't get us anywhere.'

'What will get us anywhere?' one of the men said. 'We're in the dark, we haven't a clue. When the meeting starts I'm going to move that we drop the whole con-founded business.'

Both the women made sounds of violent protest, and one of them spluttered:

'I knew that one of you was going to say that! It's all sex solidarity. You haven't been betafied, that's why you have a soft spot for the Dictator——'

'Darling Dictator,' began someone.

'And for goodness' sake, man, don't say that.'

When the breeze had died down one of the men said:

'After all, you weren't obliged to accept betafication—it's only compulsory for Failed Alphas. You were just following the fashion, as most women do. And you can still be as ugly as you like—Gammas aren't interfered with, unless they want to be.'

'That's to come.'

'Well, it hasn't yet.'

'No . . . Are you really running out, Ehud 98? Traitor isn't a nice word, you know. Why did you bother to join, if——'

'Well, for the principle of the thing—we did feel that standardisation was going too far. And also because some of us, quite a lot of us in point of fact, don't really *like* Beta women.'

'Thank you.'

'Don't take it personally. But all those cartoons, you know, about chaps finding themselves with the wrong women——'

'You needn't be coarse.'

'They're in all the papers. "My darling Jezebel 908! Gracious Dictator, it's Jezebel 909! Hop out of bed, my girl, we've made a muddle and you've come to the wrong place."'

'It isn't our fault if there were more men murderers than women.'

'No, but as I said, it is confusing, and we don't altogether like it. Every man has his type, of course——'

'I wouldn't know about that.'

'But the Beta type doesn't suit every man, if you understand me.'

'Perfectly.'

Another man said: 'When they made the blue-prints for the type, they consulted the psychiatrists, who got together a representative body of men, a panel of twelve it was, I think, a sort of cross-section of masculine susceptibility, if you follow me——'

'You're not hard to follow.'

'And watched their reactions.'

'And *watched* their reactions?'

'You know what I mean, got some idea of their responses.'

'It sounds rather cold-blooded,' said a woman, trying to wrinkle her nose, though Beta noses didn't wrinkle easily.

'In some cases it was, but not in all, I can assure you. Then they made certain modifications in the prints designed to raise . . . to rouse . . . desire, and in the end the proofs were passed, with only three dissentients.'

'I didn't know that men agreed about such things,' a woman said. 'They are even more sheep-like than I thought.'

'In the old days, I'm told, when there were film-stars, the men were *quite* unanimous.'

'Yes, but presumably those women were all Alphas. Now those of us with claims to looks are police-women and Misses. Uniforms suit men, they don't suit women.'

'Not all men would agree with you.'

'Now then, now then,' the Chairman said. 'The immediate question is: shall we wait for 97?'

'She's probably arranging her veil.'

'Her veil?'

'Yes, didn't you know she'd taken the veil?'

'But—is it legal?'

'There's no law against it. She's so ashamed of being a Beta that she can't bear the sight of herself, she says.'

'Since when has she worn it?'

'Oh, not long. It's been growing on her.'

'The veil has?'

'No, the habit.'

'Does she wear the veil indoors?'

'I fancy so. In bed, probably. She'd like us all to wear it.'

'Does she think it makes her more attractive?'

'I don't think she worries about that. She's so possessed by her idea of getting rid of the Dictator.'

'It will never be more than an idea, if you ask me.'

'I think,' the Chairman said, 'we'd better start now. I'm sure that 97 would wish us to. Let me see: you've all got the agenda?'

134

'I've forgotten mine,' one of the men said. 'But I can share with 913.'

'Then let's begin,' the Chairman said. 'The first item is to summarise the progress made so far.'

There was a long pause. The Chairman looked hopefully from face to face, but nobody spoke.

'Are we any nearer to finding out who the Voice belongs to?' he asked.

'The Dictator, presumably,' someone said.

'He might have a mouthpiece,' said the Chairman.

'That would only make our task more difficult.'

'I suppose so. He might be any of us three.'

'Except that his voice isn't like any of ours,' said one of the men.

'No, none of us has got a golden voice. Do any of you know someone with a voice like his?'

They shook their heads.

'Need it be *anybody*?' asked one of the women. 'Many people say that it's a spirit. They say that only a spirit could know all the Dictator knows.'

The Chairman sighed.

'If it's a spirit—— The trouble is, you know, that except for ourselves, nobody *wants* to know who the Dictator is. They've lost all curiosity. They take him for granted. I wouldn't mind betting that ninety-nine out of a hundred people think of him as a Voice.'

'A spirit, in fact.'

'Nothing as definite as that, something more like the wind when you can hear it.'

They listened to the wind moaning across the fen.

One of the women shivered.

'It does seem a hopeless business,' she blurted out.

'Now, now,' the Chairman said. 'We're still at item one, and we've got six on the agenda. Are we all agreed that we have no progress to report?'

While he was looking interrogatively from face to face, the latecomer arrived. For some of those who saw her Jael needed, as she needs for us, an introduction. Indeed to us she is a greater stranger than she was to them; for since her hospital days her figure seems to have grown tighter and trimmer, her walk and all her movements more decided, and then, of course, there is the veil. Quite a short veil, hardly reaching further down than the tip of her Beta nose; with a wide mesh and a few spots on it: not so much a disguise as a challenge to recognition. In any case, we shouldn't have recognised her, for what we can see of it is not Jael's face, or the face of anyone remotely like her: it is someone else's face, a face you wouldn't look at twice, certainly a face that no patient and delinquent would look at twice, for it is exactly like the faces of four-fifths of the other women: a face you take for granted. The remaining fifth, the Gammas, are plain, if not ugly, by comparison; one looks at them with tolerance, of course, but with the same kind of irritation one feels for people who have not made the best of themselves. One would have passed Jael in the street without noticing her, as one passes a lamp-post or a pillar-box; they differ from each other, perhaps, in detail; but one knows them by their function, not by anything particular in their appearance. Some pillar-boxes and some lamp-posts, from their context, stand out more than others; Jael would not have stood out, but now she does, by reason of her veil. Behind the veil her eyes, the only part of her face which she can call her own, gleam darkly with a fanatical fire; but they, too, are new eyes, they have lost their gentle, deprecating look, their sympathy and softness. They seem to be used for thinking with, not seeing; but what thoughts are going on behind them it would be hard to say.

The others rose when she joined them, even the Chairman rose, a compliment seldom paid by members of a Committee to a latecomer. But Jael's dedicated look seemed to demand this sign of deference. When she was seated on the ground, the Chairman said:

'Excuse us for beginning, 97. Time presses and some of us have other engagements——'

'Other engagements?' repeated Jael. Her voice had altered, too; it was deeper, and no longer reflected the changes of her mood; it was hard, dry and monotonous. 'Yes,' she said, her veil swinging a little as it brushed, so to speak (for each had the feeling that it had come very close to them), the faces of her fellow-conspirators; 'I suppose you have other engagements. I have only one.'

'You were a little late for it,' said the Chairman, gently.

'I was. I am sorry. I apologise,' said Jael, all in one level breath. 'But I was working for us and have found out something.'

'And may we know what it is?' the Chairman asked.

'Of course,' said Jael almost scornfully. 'We pool our information, don't we? We have no secrets from each other, have we?'

'And may we know the source?' the Chairman asked.

Jael hesitated. Her complexion kept its colour, for Betas could not blush; but at the roots of her hair above her veil a pinkish tinge began to spread.

'It was Wainewright 913,' she told them. 'Dr. Wainewright.'

'The plastic surgeon who looked after you in hospital?' asked one of the women.

'Yes.'

'The one who betafied you?'

'Yes.'

'The one you . . . er . . . said you didn't like?'

'Yes.'

'I don't think 97's personal affairs are our concern,' the Chairman interrupted.

137

'But I have always understood,' said one of the women, without looking directly at Jael, 'that Dr. Wainewright was a particularly convinced supporter of the régime.'

'He is,' said Jael.

'Then how did you——?'

'I made him talk,' said Jael.

Her tone discouraged further comment and the Chairman, eyeing the agenda, said: 'We had been discussing the first item, 97, when you came. You have it before you: to summarise our progress until now. We did not . . . er . . . find much progress to report. I mean, in our attempts to establish the identity, whereabouts, or even the existence of the . . . the Dictator. No, no, please don't darling him.' (Somebody was always slipping up.) 'We had in fact almost decided—that no progress whatever had been made. Now I will ask you, 97, to give us your report.'

Jael threw her head back, so that for a moment the veil swung clear of her eyes.

'I can tell you this,' she said. 'The Dictator *does* exist.'

For some time no one spoke. At last the Chairman said, in his rather courtly way: 'I think it's time we had a dance. Jael, will you be the assassin?'

CHAPTER SEVENTEEN

ON leaving the hospital Jael had tried to resume her pre-accident life.

Her work with Joab, and the various sedative entertainments and amusements that the New State offered: she threw herself into them, hoping to find an outlet for the feelings that were surging in her, feelings that made her strange to herself. Her instinctive resolve, on discovering that her outside had been altered, was to remain, inwardly, exactly her old self. She tried to reproduce the pattern and routine of her Failed Alpha days; to do things at the same time as she used to do them, think the same thoughts and say the same things. 'I won't let myself be different,' she kept telling herself: 'I won't!' To repeat herself became almost a religion with her; the smallest deviation from her remembered routine, she tried to curb; she walked to and from work on the same side of the pavement, she even tried to make her footmarks tally. These efforts to recover her lost self were a great strain, for all the time, partly unknown to her, she was developing a new personality quite unlike her old one. Sometimes in her attempts to force herself into the old grooves she felt herself going physically rigid. Still, she persisted, imagining she was giving other people the same impression of the old Jael that she was giving herself, when one day Joab surprised her by saying:

'Do you know what everyone's been telling me about you?'

'No,' said Jael, surprised again, for people seldom gossiped with her brother, and still more seldom did he retail what they said.

'They've been saying how much you have changed.'

'Changed?' repeated Jael, and the word stabbed her as if it had been a charge of disloyalty or even treason. 'I know my face has changed, I can't help that, but I thought that I myself——'

'It's the change in you yourself that people notice,' Joab said, 'much more than the change in your face. I hadn't noticed it, of course.'

'But you had noticed that my face was changed!' cried Jael.

'Naturally, and in spite of what you say, I have always thought it was a change for the better. Beta is better, as you know.'

At this well-worn pleasantry Jael clenched her teeth.

'Everyone but you,' proceeded Joab, 'prefers your new face. I should say that $99\frac{1}{2}\%$ of delinquents regard it as an improvement. Only yesterday Corday 900 said: "It's so nice to have dear 97 looking just like everyone else."'

'I loathe that woman,' Jael said. 'I believe she has designs on you.'

'Designs?'

'I don't mean drawings,' Jael said. 'I mean matrimonial or just sexual intentions.'

'Jael!'

Joab took a moment to recover, then he said:

'Now I see what they mean when they say you've changed. You wouldn't have said that once.'

'I've often thought it,' Jael said.

After a moment Joab said, seriously:

'Some observers put the change in you as high as 51%, which amounts to a reversal of personality. They say the switch from intellect to instinct sometimes has this effect. It's like er . . . er . . . a change of life. It's the effort to live up to your new face that brings out these reactions. You should have medical attention. Dr. Wainewright——'

'I've seen him,' Jael said.

'See him again, then.'

'I have seen him again. He forces himself on me.'

'You're lucky, Jael. He is a very busy man.'

So that was what was happening. In a flash Jael realised that the strain under which she was living came from the conscious and desperate efforts of her personality to keep at bay the psychic forces that were threatening it. Inside as well as outside she was being tampered with. It was too much. Others must feel as she did; others must feel that life wasn't worth living if you couldn't rely, in the most literal sense, on yourself.

In one way it turned out to be more difficult than she thought it would; in another, less. It wasn't difficult to find people who criticised the Dictator, for nearly everyone ($83\frac{1}{3}$% of the population, Joab told her with a shocked face) criticised him. The newspapers vied with each other in printing irreverent cartoons of him. Certain radio personalities had achieved fame by making jokes at his expense. His chosen epithet, 'Darling', was used with every shade of irony. Apart from ritual lip-service, and bowings and genuflexions, it was considered exceedingly bad form to speak well of him; hardly anyone, even the least sophisticated, would have committed such a social solecism, any more than they would have given out, in public, that they were fond of their husbands or their wives. There was even one society, called by its initiates the Anti-D Society, in which merely to name the Dictator, however disparagingly, incurred the payment of a fine.

There were also the Sceptics who maintained that the Dictator didn't really exist, he was just a Voice, a voice that was the materialisation of their common guilt-complexes, not exactly the Voice of Conscience, but something allied to it, that represented the longing for self-punishment that many people feel. With the Voice telling them what was the matter with them, and demanding forfeits for it, they were all much happier, so they said, than if they had been obliged to work these things out for themselves; their resentment was diverted from themselves and fixed on the Voice, as on a scapegoat. The idea that the Voice was really their own voice, or the sum of their own voices, the highest common factor or lowest common multiple of their own voices, appealed strongly to such metaphysicians as were left in the New State.

Even Judith joined in the chorus of criticism.

'No wonder you're disgusted with him, 97,' she said affectionately. 'We all are. We all think the same about him, though some of us express it differently. I'm not clever, as you know, I just think he's a pain in the neck, but, of course, there are worse pains, as everyone knows who can remember what it was like Below. He's beastly to women—most people say he's a bachelor, and some say he's homosexual—that is, if he exists at all. Still, we have to thank him for some things. I've been much happier since I was betafied—I hated those pitying looks I used to get, and people crossing the road sometimes to avoid me, because they said my face made them feel sick. As Betas we don't have to compete, do we?—which is such a blessing. Feminine competitiveness used up so much energy, and what came of it? Only Bad Egg,' (Judith performed the ritual spit) 'and I'm sure you must be glad not to be causing it, as you used to.'

'I don't know that I am glad,' Jael said.

'I'm sorry for that, but you will, in time. It's a great relief to be taken for granted, and not have to impose yourself, or express your personality by what you wear. I haven't spent half as much on clothes since I was betafied; nor, I suppose, have you.'

'I rather enjoyed spending money on clothes,' said Jael.

'Well, so did we all. Damn the Dictator! Still, I suppose we might do worse. Anyhow it's a relief to be able to say what we think of him. They are nothing like so hot on sedition as they used to be. Now, 97, what news of Dr. Wainewright?'

At first Jael could make no headway, for every door she kicked against seemed to be already open. She grew discouraged: how could she, her single self, hope to prevail against an enemy who, even if he existed, was defended by a rampart of criticism and ridicule far more impenetrable than a cordon of secret police? And it occurred to her, has he been too clever for us again? Does he himself foster these criticisms, perhaps even put them about, to make his position the more unassailable?

It was no use looking for malcontents, when everybody was a malcontent, and pleased to be one; she must try another tack.

So when she spoke of the régime her mouth was full of praises. Dear, darling Dictator! Most people smiled at her enthusiasm; some laughed outright; she heard on all sides what a fool she was. Even her brother, who had caught the habit of making fun of the Dictator, said in his ponderous way:

'Do you know, Jael, you're getting out of step? I'm glad you realise what a blessing betafication is (you didn't at first, you know), but there's no need to harp on it as you do. And it's a little pointless, when nobody can really see what you look like.'

'I should have thought praise of the régime would carry more weight,' retorted Jael, 'coming from someone the régime had punished.'

'Kissing the hand that hurt you?' Joab said. 'Yes, but you mustn't be too serious about it. The Dictator wants us all to be light-hearted. You heard the Edict?'

'Yes,' said Jael. 'But that kind of flippancy goes against the grain with me. Think what we all owe him.'

'There you go again,' said Joab, 'thinking you know better. You must try to move with the times. Remember the Edict's closing words: "The Dictator enjoys a joke as well as anyone, particularly a joke against himself."'

'I know,' said Jael, 'but it seems irreverent to me. I can't so easily——'

'No, that's just it. Your mind isn't flexible. You ought to change it as easily as you change your face. You see that I have. Hardly had I heard the Edict when I found myself making jokes about the Dictator, just like everyone else. Have you entered for the competition?'

'No,' said Jael.

'You ought to,' said her brother. 'I've sent in half a dozen entries. Would you like to hear one?'

'Please.'

'Well, it's in Latin. Should you understand?'

'I might.'

'*Vox et praeterea nihil.* Have you got it?'

'I think I have,' said Jael. 'A Voice with nothing behind it. But can't it also mean something rather coarse?'

'Rather coarse? If so, all the better. The Edict said: "Extra marks will be given for ingenious indecency!" Will you explain——?'

'No,' said Jael, 'I won't, and you wouldn't like it, Joab, if I did. Has the Dictator gone mad?'

'Of course not, Jael. You don't seem to realise we're living in the Fun Age.'

So that was what Jael was up against: Fun. Fun was an impalpable enemy. How could she organise a revolution against Fun? How could she strike at the heart of humour with the blade of a pocket-knife two inches long—which was the only weapon that the New State allowed to its delinquents?

Behind the dark veil her thoughts grew darker; they almost frightened her, these flitting shadows which now were her familiar company. Because of the lack of sunshine in the New State, shadows were always pale; like a pale shadow herself, she wove in and out of the resolutely laughing throng, trying one method of approach with this one, another with that; and it was not long before she got the reaction she was hoping for; a man who didn't laugh when Jael told him how wonderful the Dictator was, whose eyes narrowed and whose mouth showed his teeth in a grin that was not a smile. 'You don't admire the Dictator?' Jael said, apparently astonished; 'you make fun of him like all the others do? I think it's a shame, after all he's done for us— even to the point of making himself into a sort of clown, to give us a good laugh. Can you think of any woman, let alone a man, who would have done that? Men are so sensitive to ridicule. Why, it's the greatest sacrifice most men can make—to let themselves be laughed at.'

'Are you so sure he isn't laughing at us?' the man said.

'How could one man laugh at two million? No, the laugh's on him all right.'

'It wouldn't be the first time he's made fools of us,' the man said.

'Now you are talking as they all do.'

'Perhaps, but not in fun, as they do.'

'Not in fun?'

The man shrugged his shoulders.

'What's the use? He gets the better of us every time.'

'Come with me,' said Jael, and they walked down a side street. Her veil stirred softly in the searching, continuous March wind: sometimes she had to warn herself that it was not a cloak of invisibility.

'If we could think of a way——' she began.

'Of getting rid of him?'

She nodded.

145

'By revolution?'

Jael shrugged in her turn.

'That's one way, but there's a quicker way.'

The man said nothing for a moment.

'If you mean direct action involving the D.D.——' he began.

'I do, and then the revolution would follow automatically.'

'But nobody knows who he is, or if he is.'

'Somebody *must* know.'

So Jael made her first contact and her first convert, soon the others followed.

As she was getting ready for the rendez-vous, there came a knock on the door and Dr. Wainewright stood upon the threshold.

'Oh,' said Jael, her eyes glittering behind her veil. She did not ask him to come in.

'I thought it was time I had another look at you,' he said, shifting on his feet.

'I'm quite well, thank you.'

'No, you're not, you need a check-up.'

'I'm quite well, thank you,' repeated Jael, more forbiddingly than before.

'You may think you are, but you're not. You're thinner, for one thing.'

'I prefer myself that way,' said Jael. 'And thanks to the Dictator's clemency, the New State doesn't interfere with our figures, only with our faces.'

Wincing, he grimaced. Every man you talked to seemed to have too much facial expression.

'I'm not going to let you come in,' she said.

'You'll have to,' he answered cheerfully. 'The rule is a check-up every three weeks, and today's the day. You have to sign for it in my book, as you know. Otherwise you'll get me into trouble.'

'And little should I mind,' said Jael, retreating, however, from the door.

Dr. Wainewright came in.

'It's only a routine examination, of course,' he maddeningly said. 'But you'll have to take that veil off. I can't think why you wear it.'

'You should know better than anybody,' Jael retorted.

He ignored this and passed his fingers on to her face.

'It's doing very nicely,' he said. 'I wish you could reconcile yourself to it, Jael.'

'You know I never shall.'

'And to me, too,' he went on.

'That——' began Jael, but then her fury choked her. But to her increasing fury, he didn't seem to mind.

'Your face is all right,' he said, 'and it's one of the best Beta faces, if only you could think so. I fell in love with it, I suppose, because I made it.'

'If you could unmake it, I might fall in love with you.'

'I can't, and if I could I wouldn't. I love you as you are, but I do wish you were happier. I have to report on that as well, you know. Why don't you go about more, instead of shutting yourself up?'

'I do go about,' said Jael, shaking with rage. 'I was just going out when you came in.'

'What do you do when you go out?'

'Is that your business?'

'As your doctor, it is. Why not come out with me?'

'I'd rather die.'

'If you hate me so much,' he said, 'you might come to love me.'

Jael stared at him speechless.

'The Dictator,' he said, awkwardly, 'doesn't want anyone to be unhappy.'

'Doesn't want anyone to be unhappy? How do you know?'

'Well, I do know.'

A thought began to move in Jael's mind; she felt its birth-pangs, but did not know what it was.

'The Dictator doesn't exist!' she exclaimed.

'Oh yes, he does.'

She turned away from him, and spoke more gently:

'What proof have you?'

He heard what he thought was the sound of relenting in her voice, and said, trying to keep his own voice steady:

'I know someone who's seen him.'

Jael didn't turn round, but moved a little further into the middle of the room. Feeling naked and uneasy without her veil, she looked down on the floor and said:

'But how did he know?'

'He recognised the Sign.'

Then she turned to him and said, with most of the hardness gone out of her voice and manner:

'Let's sit down a moment.'

He obeyed and they sat down at right angles to each other, like people in an advertisement for armchair comfort. Jael let her left hand droop in his direction.

'This Sign,' she said, 'what is it?'

'He didn't tell me.'

'Could you find out for me?' Jael asked.

'Why do you want to know?'

'It's not just curiosity. My faith needs strengthening. I can't quite believe in him, you know. If I knew the Sign——'

'Yes?'

'It would make a great difference to me.'

He thought a moment and then said:

'What sort of difference?'

'Well, to all my feelings.'

'Including your feelings towards me?' he asked.

She made a movement to put on her veil, which she was

holding in her fingers like a black lace handkerchief. She couldn't bear to be without it, especially at that moment. It fluttered to the floor, and stretching down to pick it up, she said:

'Perhaps it might. I can't tell, yet.'

Rising, she put the veil on the arm of the chair. He got up, too, and held his hand out, which she took for the first time.

'Then when I pay you my next visit——' he said.

'When will that be?'

'In three weeks' time.'

'Don't let it be so long,' said Jael.

When he had gone, she snatched her veil up. But too late. By an awkward movement, which she was aware of, as one is when turning one's ankle, almost before she had made it, she came face to face with herself in the looking-glass. She had to see herself at times, of course, and for those occasions she prepared herself, as for a small ordeal. She dreaded most what other people, who have no special reason to be ashamed of their faces, also dread—an unexpected, unsolicited glimpse of her reflection. It upset her fundamentally. She could not have reconciled herself to it, even if she had wanted to. It was equally painful as a reminder of the self she had lost, the carefree, easy-going self, as of the self she had become. That self she hated; and though she had transferred some of her hatred to the Dictator, she had plenty left for herself.

Instinctively she looked away and her glance fell on the cineraria standing on the window-ledge. The flower had long since withered; was the plant alive or dead? Its leaves were brown and crinkled at the edges and it seemed to have no sap in it. The few plants that survived in the New State were liable to die at any minute, from delayed shock or radioactivity or under-nourishment; and their reproductive power was even lower than that of human beings. Was she going to lose it, as she had lost the favour of the giver? At the thought of that her tears flowed and she felt happier; better to melt than to freeze or burn, as was her lot now. But as she wiped the tears from her shower-proof cheeks the old feeling of bitterness came back. Once she had had no purpose in life and how happy she had been; now she was all purpose, and miserable with it.

Hastily adjusting her veil, for which she needed now no visual aid, she set off for the meeting.

CHAPTER EIGHTEEN

WHEN the dance was over, and Jael had despatched her man, the conference was resumed.

'Now what about this Sign?' the Chairman asked. 'How do we know there is one? It may just be something the Dictator's put about. He's up to every kind of trick.'

'I think there is,' said Jael.

'Can you find out *what* it is?'

'I'll try.'

'Now the next item,' said the Chairman. 'Are there any other signs—signs of discontent—which we could work on?'

After a pause, one of the men said: 'Yes, there are.'

'What, for instance?'

'Well, this stunt of criticising the Dictator. It caught on, as you all know, because of the novelty. We all wanted to say what we thought about him. But now the joke's beginning to wear thin. It's not much fun saying what you are told to say, and laughing when you are told to laugh.'

'Most people think it is,' objected someone. 'I've heard the same jokes about him repeated scores of times, and I've heard people repeat them back to each other half a minute later.'

'Yes, the chatter of starlings. But now they're beginning to grow tired of it: they want to say something different, as 97 realised.'

'It must be something they can all say.'

'Yes, alas.'

'Has anyone any suggestions?' the Chairman asked.

'Well,' said one of the women; 'how about having men's looks betafied?'

All the men present, including the Chairman, registered horror and dismay. To the women, and not least to Jael, their faces were almost unbearably expressive: it was as though, in the course of an ordinary conversation, some of the participants had begun to shout and scream. The little gathering was devastated by the male countenance, as by a tornado. The women didn't know which way to look, they felt they were being bludgeoned, blinded; even the men themselves were surprised at the violence of each other's facial reactions. When the little storm had spent itself, and the men's faces had resumed their wary, non-committal, masculine look, one of them said:

'I don't think you'd find much support for that.'

'Oh, don't you?' said a woman; 'I should have thought you would. At any rate, then you couldn't give us the shock you gave us just now.'

'We don't all like that nasty natural look,' another woman said. 'We sometimes dream about it, not pleasantly, you know. If only you made up your faces sometimes——'

'Or shaved better——'

'Or didn't clear your throats——'

'Or smoke in one's face——'

'Besides it isn't *fair*,' put in another woman. 'And the régime is supposed to be based on fairness. Fairness to all, favour to none. I know that men don't envy each other's looks—why should they?'

Involuntarily one of the men spat.

'There you go—it's disgusting, and superstitious, too. I meant to say, I know you don't envy each other's looks, as we women are supposed to, according to that misogynist Dictator, but all the same it isn't fair that you should have your own faces, and we not. Besides, on aesthetic grounds, it's terrible for us to have to look at some of you. I know a woman who couldn't eat for days after she had seen a certain man, and through glass, mind you——'

'Now then, now then, we mustn't quarrel, must? we' said the Chairman.

'But that's just what we want, to start people quarrelling. If we can do outside what we've done in here——'

'We shan't get anywhere if we're not unanimous,' the Chairman said.

'Unanimous? But that's just what we don't want to be—it's what we're up against—thinking alike, talking alike, looking alike, being alike—we want to spread dissension——'

'Perhaps,' the Chairman said, 'but don't spread it here. Here we want agreement. Now the proposition is, I understand, to . . . er . . . foment discontent within the régime by putting it about that men's faces should be betafied. Am I right?'

Jael nodded.

'Those in favour?'

The women put their hands up.

'Those against?'

Sheepishly, but with much determination, the Chairman and his two male associates raised their hands.

'We are divided,' the Chairman said, 'but I have the casting vote. The proposition is not carried.'

The women looked as sulky as their straightened faces would allow, but the men's expressions of relief were so vivid that they seemed almost audible.

'So much for our unanimity,' Jael observed.

'You couldn't hope for it on that issue,' the Chairman said. 'All we should do would be to throw the whole male sex, so to speak, into the arms of the Dictator.'

'He'd like that if he's what some people say he is,' a woman remarked.

'Well, doesn't it stick out a mile?' another said. 'All this favouritism, such as keeping you in countenance.'

At this the three men looked unbearably smug.

'It doesn't follow,' one of them said. 'He just knows

that men don't Bad Egg each other's looks, as women do.'

'Oh, do say envy,' said Jael wearily. 'I get so tired of this facetiousness. He treats us as if we were children. Some of us are, of course.'

'Speak for yourself,' the man retorted.

'I don't have to,' Jael answered. 'Everyone knows that most men don't grow up. Think of all the things you do to keep the child alive in you. Football, cricket, tennis . . . You're never happy until you've made mudlarks of yourselves.'

'How can we help it, when there's mud all round us? I wonder what the world looked like when it was green? And anyhow you copy us. I've seen you looking pretty mud-stained, 97, when you came in from playing hockey.'

'I only played because hockey was compulsory for my age-group,' Jael said. 'There was all that outcry, when the girls who couldn't get a game said it was unfair, and that those who played were privileged. I didn't think it a privilege, I can tell you——'

'It was all in the interests of Good Egg,' persisted the man.

'Oh, say equality, and have done with it. We don't have to go through the motions, we're long past that.'

'Order, order,' said the Chairman. 'But the Secretary has raised a point which was actually Item 3 of the Agenda.' He put on his spectacles. 'To find a slogan which will express the opposite idea and ideal of fairness in a word or words that will be acceptable to the average delinquent.'

'I object to the term "delinquent",' one of the men said. 'Indeed I violently resent it. The fact that the Dictator has called us delinquents does not make us so. Is any one of us here a delinquent? I don't think so. It is an abuse of language. I move that the word be deleted from the agenda.'

The Chairman looked at Jael.

'What do you say, 97?'

Jael felt uncomfortable, and, as far as a Beta could, she showed it.

'The word is common currency,' she said defensively. 'I don't think it has any derogatory meaning attached to it. The phrase "old man", which you men use among yourselves, is, I believe, a term of affection, it does not mean, or even suggest, that the person so addressed is old.'

'There is no moral smear,' answered her critic, 'attached to being old. We shall all be old one day, if the Dictator lets us be. I know that the phrase "You old delinquent!" is sometimes used among friends without giving offence. But I still maintain that it's an abuse of language, and the Dictator, when he fastened it on us, intended it as a reproach, to make us all feel guilty and therefore readier to accept his abominable decrees. It helped the softening-up process by which, in one way or another, he has been undermining us as human beings all this time. Patients and delinquents! By making us feel we are delinquents he puts us automatically in the wrong, we can't stand up for ourselves, we have to do what he tells us. That's one of the things we are fighting against, this imputation of delinquency. We are no more delinquents than he is, and not half as much!'

Jael was vexed with herself for allowing her thunder to be stolen from her by this upstart man. Men!—she hated the whole tribe of them, from the Dictator downwards—all except one, and him she mustn't even think of.

'All right, all right,' she said, 'it was just a slip of the pen. With your approval, Mr. Chairman, we'll erase "delinquents".'

The Chairman nodded. 'Now,' he said, 'the proposition reads: "To find a slogan expressing the opposite of the idea and ideal of fairness in a form of words which shall be acceptable to——?"'

He looked about him with raised, questioning eyebrows.

'The man in the street,' suggested one of the male members of the Committee.

'The man in the street!' protested Jael. 'What about the woman?'

'The phrase is generally taken to include both men and women,' said the Chairman.

'I thought a woman of the street meant something different.'

The Chairman sighed.

'Let us say, "to normal men and women".'

'That might leave out some of us,' said Jael.

One of the men turned red, but the women, being unable to blush, kept their shame, if they felt it, to themselves.

'I think that remark most uncalled for,' the Chairman said severely. 'If I did not know you as well as I do, Jael 97, I might think your interest in our cause had its origin in a private grievance.'

'You would be right,' said Jael, 'I've made no secret of it. The people who govern us—the Dictator's spies—took advantage of the fact that I was helpless to change my face to what they thought a better one. In doing so they changed my nature. Before, I was——' Jael stopped, acutely embarrassed. Her fellow-conspirators tried to help her out.

'A conformer.'

'A Failed Alpha.'

'A State slave.'

'A gentle creature, harbouring no malice.'

'A popular girl, adored by everyone.'

'A sweet, nice person, with not a single political idea in her head.'

'Butter wouldn't have melted in her mouth.'

'She couldn't have said boh to a goose.'

'Everyone had a good word for her.'

'Stop! Stop!' cried Jael. 'That's what you say I was, but what am I now?'

All the other members of the Committee who had been vying with each other to sing the former Jael's praises, suddenly found not a word to say.

'The spearhead of revolt,' said one of them, a woman, at last. But nobody added another word.

Hating herself, Jael also hated them. Tears started to her eyes and trickled down her rain-proof cheeks. She wept for her lost self, the self she knew, for she associated it with her old-time face; she wept for her present self, the self she did not know, for her new self was faceless: she did not know, and would not permit herself to know, what she looked like. She had denied herself that assurance of identity; sometimes she mentally groped for her own image, as someone might who has long been blind. From under her black veil the tears poured down, painful to see and not relieving her, for her sense of contact with her tears, their healing touch, to which, in part at any rate, they owe their power to lessen unhappiness, was not for her: she might almost have been another person crying.

'Has anyone any suggestions,' the Chairman said at length, 'for an attractive-sounding synonym for unfairness?'

'Opportunity,' put in someone. 'The party of unlimited opportunity.'

The Chairman shrugged his shoulders. 'I don't like that much,' he said. 'Too clumsy.'

'Couldn't we bring in the idea of merit?' said another. 'Or is merit now too blown upon?'

'I don't think you'll get very far with merit,' Jael said. 'Merit has always been at a discount with the Dictator. Merit needs effort and we aren't supposed to make an effort. Let the worst man win.'

'I'm afraid you're right,' the Chairman said. 'Merit has been soft-pedalled for a long time, because it leads to Bad Egg—I beg your pardon, Jael, to envy. We mustn't be better at anything than our neighbours. Or if we are, and it sticks out a mile, we must remember that they are better at something else than we are—even if they aren't. The word may have dropped out of the language—it's ages since I saw or heard it used.'

'All the same,' persisted the first speaker, 'it hasn't been officially banned. One can still use it. "The merit of fairness is that there's no merit in it," or something like that.'

The men smiled like ogres, and even the women's faces broadened appreciably.

'Can anyone think of something with "merit" in it?' the Chairman asked, and again there was a smile, but no one spoke.

'I'm afraid that all this suspiciousness of merit hasn't sharpened our wits,' the Chairman said. 'We're all afraid of seeming cleverer than our neighbours. Now let's forget all that, and try to think up something. If anybody has a bright idea, I for one won't grudge it him—or her,' he added as an afterthought. 'We mustn't forget,' he said, when no one spoke, 'that we're all equal here.'

'Oh no, we aren't!' said Jael.

'Not equal?'

'No, isn't that what we're fighting for, the right not to be equal?'

'I suppose it is, in theory,' the Chairman rather testily admitted. 'Outside this circle, in our different walks of life, we are, of course, unequal. Nobody—nobody here that is—would deny that. But here——'

'Even here, I take it,' Jael said, 'the best suggestion wins.'

'Perhaps,' the Chairman said. 'But so far we haven't had any suggestions with much merit in them.'

'The word keeps tripping us up,' said somebody.

'Try not to let it cloud your minds,' the Chairman said. 'Don't be afraid of being competitive. Don't hang back.'

'Doesn't merit speak for itself?' the man asked.

'It used to,' said the Chairman. 'But nowadays it's

silenced. That is one of the things that we complain of. Somebody must speak up for it.'

'Isn't that your job, Mr. Chairman? We chose you for your merit. Are you going to tell us that you haven't got any—that we're as good as you?'

'What do you mean by good?' the Chairman retorted. 'If you mean good at being a chairman——'

'The only good we recognise,' said someone, 'is getting the Dictator down. If you——'

'You nominated me,' the Chairman said. 'I'm not mad about the assignment. If you want to appoint another Chairman, I'll resign at once.' His tone showed that he meant it.

'No, please,' said Jael. 'Don't let us make ourselves a laughing-stock. I'm told it's difficult to find subjects for Five Minutes' Laughter. If they heard of us——'

'Perhaps they have,' said one of the men. He looked round at the muddy landscape, drew his overcoat about him and shivered slightly. 'No one knows how the Dictator gets his information. A bird of the air——'

'He's sometimes misinformed,' said somebody.

'How do you know?'

'Well, he acts as if he was.'

'I don't believe it. He's always a move or two ahead of us.'

'Let's get back to the Agenda,' said the Chairman. 'We want a slogan presenting the notion of unfairness as an ideal acceptable, or indeed inspiring, to the man in the street. If no suggestions are forthcoming, we must go on to the next item. I propose "Careers for the Courageous".'

All the members of the Committee put on their thinking-caps. The men scowled; the women looked perforce but mildly interested.

'I doubt if the public are ready for it,' one of the men said. 'Courage is at a discount and careers are blown upon. I doubt if many people would understand what you mean,

159

and if they did they wouldn't approve. What use is courage, unless you have need of it? By eliminating danger the Dictator has eliminated courage. It's about as much use now as the muscles of a navvy would be to a stenographer.'

'You still need it for an illness,' said the Chairman.

'No, begging your pardon, you need endurance not courage for an illness. Passive courage, yes, but not the active, go-getting courage that you mean. The man in the street wouldn't thank you for courage, any more than he would thank you for inviting him to climb Mount Everest or go to the North Pole, if they still exist. And careers are finished—you might as well ask a man to make a fire by rubbing two sticks together, as make a career for himself. Our lives are laid on for us, from the incubator to the crematorium. Three world wars have drained our energy; the capacity for effort has gone out of us. We want to be directed; we want to stand in a queue.'

'Are you speaking for yourself?' the Chairman asked. 'I imagine not, or you wouldn't be on this Committee. And if you're speaking for others, I think you are unduly pessimistic.'

'How about "Advancement for the Able"?' someone suggested.

'Too challenging. Why should you be abler than me? Ability is for the Inspectors, not for us. It's their prerogative.'

'Yes, but people like to think of themselves as abler than others. Men certainly do,' a woman said.

'Perhaps, but even more they dislike thinking of others as abler than they are. You can't have the one without the other.'

'Oh, I don't know. Some men are quite conceited enough.'

The male members of the Committee darted angry glances at their opposite numbers of the female sex who returned them with unshaken imperturbability. One of the advantages of being Beta was that you couldn't register a hit.

'What about "Advancement for the Ambitious"?'

'You can't be ambitious on bromide.'

'The first thing we shall do when we get control is to stop that silly practice.'

'Yes, but meanwhile.'

' "Advancement for the Adventurous" might do,' someone put in. 'Adventurousness isn't so personal as ambition. It doesn't involve other people taking a back seat. You might mind my ambition, but you couldn't object to my adventurousness. After all, we're allowed to bet.'

'Yes, but not on ourselves.'

'How about "Bet on yourself"? Doesn't that put it all in a nutshell? "Back your fancy", well, I fancy myself—we all fancy ourselves. Yes, why not have "Bet on yourself"?' the speaker repeated, warming to his idea. 'There's no merit in a win by betting—if that's what we're afraid of. Why, in the old days——'

'The Bad Old Days,' put in somebody.

'—the Bad Old Days,' the speaker repeated, 'people made fortunes by betting, and no one minded, because they knew it was just luck. It hadn't been earned, it hadn't even been stolen—it was just luck. Bet on yourself!'

'Are we agreed?' the Chairman asked.

All signified assent.

'Then let's have a dance on it.'

'Bet on yourself! Bet on yourself!' they chanted, in undertones, though nobody could hear them. Into the air they flung themselves, disregarding each other, colliding with each other. Lacking team-work, the ballet didn't go with a swing. 'Bet on yourself! Bet on yourself!' Somebody slipped and fell; the whole pack set on him, the assassin's fingers closed about his throat, he died a ritual death.

CHAPTER NINETEEN

NEXT morning, as Jael was walking to her work, a Beta woman hailed her.

'Hullo, Jael.'

Jael stared. Though her veil was not opaque it blurred her vision, a fact she did not greatly mind, for she had lost a good deal of her interest in the visual aspect of things. Still, it could be inconvenient. If only Betas were not so much alike!

Jael said: 'Sorry, I don't quite remember——'

'No wonder, if you will wear that extraordinary veil. Why, it's Judith!'

When the two old friends had shaken hands with due enthusiasm, and Jael had made her apologies, she said:

'But how did you recognise me? Hardly anyone does.'

'By the veil, of course. You're getting to be known by it.'

Jael didn't like this, and her spirit, which had expanded on meeting Judith, shrank again into its hard core.

'As long as they don't connect the veil with me!' she said, lightly.

'Oh, some of them do. To most you are just the Black Beta.'

They talked of other things, and then Judith, pointing, said:

'Do you see what's written on that poster?'

Jael switched her veil in the direction indicated by Judith's finger. The poster was stuck on to a wall, and level with a grown-up person's eye. Pretending she couldn't read it, Jael asked:

'What does it say?'

'Of course, if you will wear that veil!——It says, "Bet on yourself."'

'Oh,' said Jael, 'what does that mean?'

'Beta'd if I know.' Judith wrinkled her face. ' "Bet on yourself." It must be some kind of joke. How can you bet on yourself?'

'I suppose you *could*,' said Jael cautiously.

'But how? You can bet on a number—we do that every week because it's V.C.—Voluntary-Compulsory, to use the new phrase. But how can you bet on yourself? Yourself isn't a number.'

'We each have a number,' Jael said.

'Yes, yes, but that's only to distinguish us from the other Jaels and Judiths. You can bet on your own number, in the tombola, most of us have, though it's said to be unlucky. But how can you bet on yourself? Yourself doesn't exist.'

'Doesn't exist?'

'Not apart from your number. Without a number Jael or Judith is just no one.'

'But surely you and I exist and should go on existing whether we had numbers or not?'

By this time a little crowd had collected and were staring speechlessly at the poster.

'Bet on yourself—that's a good one!'

'I'm not sure if I have a self—I used to have, but I think it has withered away, like my tonsils. In any case I wouldn't bet on it.'

'Oh, wouldn't you? I would.'

'What, on yourself? You wouldn't have a hope.'

'How do you know I shouldn't back a winner?'

'But what would you win? Life isn't a race.'

'Well, a place in the sun.'

'But there isn't any sun.'

'There is, only we don't see it because the war has

changed the atmospheric conditions. But we might see it some day, and then——'

'And then?'

'Well, I'd be sitting in it.'

'And what about the rest of us?'

'You could damned well bet on yourselves.'

By now more people had collected round the placard.

'What does it mean?'

'What does it mean?'

'This chap here says he wants to bet on himself.'

General laughter followed.

'Does he think it will make him better-looking?'

'Does he think it will restore his potency?'

At least half the men in the New State were impotent.

'Does he think he'll make himself an Inspector?'

'Or does he think he'll step into the Dictator's shoes?'

'Darling Dictator, darling Dictator, darling Dictator!' came the automatic chorus, and then more laughter.

'You're laughing out of turn,' the man said. 'You'll be having the Inspectors after you. It'll be a fine, you know, or ten days' sackcloth. I'll see you get reported.'

At this there was a pause, and several people turned their heads and looked apprehensively up and down the quiet street.

'Who said we weren't to laugh?' asked Jael, with all the truculence she could muster.

'Who said we weren't to laugh? I like that! Don't you know your regulations?'

'I hope so,' Jael said stiffly.

'Well, there's a new Edict. Until further notice, a quiet, reserved, downcast demeanour, suitable to delinquents of both sexes. Tears are recommended, but smiles are permissible, and laughter lasting not more than half a minute. On and off, you've been laughing for five minutes. I wish you could have heard yourselves, and seen yourselves.'

'It's a shame,' said someone.

'What's a shame?' asked Jael.

For a moment nobody seemed able to answer, but sporadic, ragged cries of 'It's a shame' continued to go up.

'What's a shame?' demanded Jael when at last she could make herself heard above the din.

'That we can't laugh when we want to!'

'That we're made to cry when we don't want to, and there's nothing to cry about!'

'It's a shame, it's a shame!'

The angry wailing rose and fell, to Jael the most exciting sound she had heard since they danced round the tower at Ely.

And she had started it and got it going! She looked about for Judith, but Judith had disappeared, and she must disappear, too, for in the distance was the golden gleam that heralded the approach of the Inspectors, and it wouldn't be healthy for her to be caught among the rioters. But something made her stand her ground, longer than she meant to, longer than was safe, and it wasn't till the crowd had begun to flee that she fled, too.

Had they recognised her, the Inspectors, had they seen the veil? Too much excited to go straight back to work, she made a tour of some of the posters she had put up last night. The tour rewarded her: around each poster an angry buzzing threatened violence.

'Good morning, Jael,' said Joab. 'You're very late this morning. Did something happen to you, or did you just over-sleep?'

Jael was still shivering from excitement, and afraid her brother would notice it; but she need not have been.

'No, nothing happened,' she said. 'Nothing to speak of.' That was literally true. Oh, that she had someone to confide in! She was tired of consuming her own smoke. Her brother was the last person she could talk to.

'I was afraid you might have got caught up in that regrettable little incident,' said Joab.

'What incident?' asked Jael. 'Tell me.'

'You mean to say you haven't heard? I can't think what you were doing.'

'To tell you the truth,' said Jael, 'I wasn't well this morning, and was in two minds about coming here.'

'Not well?' echoed Joab, amazed.

'No, not well. Nobody is well all the time. I wasn't well, this morning.'

'But whose fault is that?'

'Need it be anybody's?'

'I suppose not,' Joab said grudgingly, 'unless you wilfully reduced your efficiency. However, I'm glad you escaped the . . . the demonstration.'

'Tell me.'

Joab told her about the posters. 'They were stuck up all over the town. "Bet on yourself", whatever that may mean. For some reason the Inspectors didn't spot it until some fellow started making a scene.'

'And then what happened?'

'The Inspectors came and broke the meeting up and tore down the posters.'

'What will happen to the man?' asked Jael.

Her brother lowered his voice.

'He'll be R.E., I shouldn't wonder.'

Jael shivered. Returned Empty! That meant, it was popularly believed, being sent back to the Underworld, either dead or alive. The victim would be 'emptied' in some way; but how, and of what?

'But no one ever has been, have they?' she asked.

'A murderer was. But there's never been a serious rising before against the régime. The thing that you took part in at Ely—well, it was just a farce, though you were lucky to get off so lightly. The Dictator is merciful, we know——'

166

'Darling Dictator,' said Jael irreverently.

'But he'll have to take some notice of this. People will expect it of him. He'll . . . er . . . lose face if he doesn't. They'll expect a scapegoat. I wouldn't be in that chap's shoes.'

'How did you know about all this?' asked Jael.

'Man with some figures about Facial Rearmament told me about half an hour ago. It'll be all over the town by now. How are you feeling—better? Good, then take down this. The heading is "Facial Rearmament".'

Jael had evolved a technique for taking down dictation and at the same time listening to her own thoughts. At this moment her thoughts were very busy. Could it be possible that the incident that Joab referred to was not the one she had assisted at? He hadn't mentioned another. If it was the same one, how had she escaped? But had she escaped?

'Facial Rearmament,' she tapped out, 'is now practised by $17\frac{1}{2}\%$ of the female population of the New State, out of which total $10\frac{1}{2}\%$, rather disappointingly, are Betas. As is, or should be, well known to patients and delinquents of the New State, a Beta skin is already automatically provided with every aid to the wearer's looks, which cosmetics, in the past, were believed to provide. It is now established that make-up on a Beta skin is definitely harmful, and may result in indelible staining like grease on a mackintosh; while face-lifting, in which .05% of the female population have indulged, against the advice of their medical attendants, destroys the Beta facial tissue, and these unfortunates have sometimes been left literally without face. It cannot be too frequently emphasised that a Beta face must not be tampered with; it is there for good. The designs were chosen by a committee of connoisseurs in facial appearance, to be suitable for all occasions, including the most intimate, although, in this respect, care was taken not to make the design so physically alluring that the opposite sex would be impeded in the performance of its daily, non-amorous duties . . . to be psychologically, as well as aesthetically, satisfying . . . Any deviation from uniformity brings its own penalty, not only in Bad E, but in the derision which some of these experimentalists have unhappily incurred . . . The movement known as Facial Rearmament is sanctioned by the Dictator, who, as always, supports the Voluntary Principle, but it is discouraged . . .'

Had anyone seen her in the mêlée, wondered Jael, and denounced her to the Inspectors? Her veil made her conspicuous. Perhaps even now they were planning her arrest.

' . . . A somewhat disturbing feature of the so-called Facial Rearmament campaign is that men delinquents are now taking part in it. Before the question of Facial Justice had become a major issue, there were, of course, men who, for one reason or another, chose to paint their faces. They amounted to only .1% of the population, the Dictator is merciful, and they were ignored. The Dictator thought, and still thinks, that the male appearance is not a matter of sufficient interest to arouse Bad E, the virtue of a man lies in what he is, not what he looks like. Psychologists have estimated that only 18.5% of the female population are affected by a man's looks; whereas 79.5% of the male population are affected by a woman's looks. To what end, then, these misguided creatures seek to improve on the work of Nature it would be kinder not to ask . . .'

Rat-tat. Rat-tat—Rat-tat.

It was not Jael's typewriter, it was a loud knocking on the door that interrupted Joab's level, droning voice.

'Come in!' he called irritably, and when the visitor, seemingly deafened by his own knocking, failed to respond, he shouted still more loudly, 'Come in!'

The door opened at last, to reveal a man's frightened face, and then the rest of him, clutching to his body a long envelope. He did not speak, but his face, and especially his mouth, worked alarmingly.

'Well?' said Joab.

The man gasped out: 'They're everywhere!'

'Pull yourself together,' Joab said. 'What are everywhere?'

'The . . . the disturbances are. Wherever there's a poster. And they are shouting "Bet on yourself!" and "Down with the Dictator!"'

Joab turned pale, and the lines deepened on his face. Jael could not change colour or show what she felt, but her eyes glowed behind her veil and her heart beat exultantly.

'But what are the Inspectors doing?' she asked.

'They're taking them away as fast as they can.'

'The people or the posters?'

'Both. They're sweeping them up, but fresh ones keep coming. Can't you hear the noise?'

They listened, and a sound louder than the sighing of the March wind came through the windows.

'They're sweeping them up, they're sweeping them up!' the man repeated, shivering uncontrollably. 'I daren't go out again.'

'Well, stay here then,' said Joab. 'What's that you've brought for me?'

The man stared about him, dazed, and then suddenly saw the envelope in his hand. 'Why this—some figures, I think they are. They said you wanted them.'

'Yes, I expect I do. Sit down, and rest yourself.'

Trembling, the man obeyed, and Joab opened the envelope with hands that also trembled.

'Oh,' he said, trying to control his voice, 'it's nothing much. Nothing very secret. But you'd better not let on that you've heard.' The man nodded, as if he only half-understood, and the three of them involuntarily stiffened into listening attitudes.

169

'I don't hear it now,' said Joab, in an indifferent voice, as who should say, 'the rain has stopped.' 'I think you might take this down, Jael.' He cleared his throat, and took a turn up and down the room, glancing at the papers in his hand. 'The heading is "Facial Disarmament".

'Facial Disarmament. This is a very small movement compared with the other, affecting only .89% of the total population.' Again he cleared his throat and his eyes wandered: he was finding it difficult to concentrate. 'Perhaps we might put this in the form of a footnote, Jael. What do you think?'

Making a great effort, Jael wrenched her mind round to the subject in hand.

'But I suppose it involves a question of principle,' she said.

'Er . . . yes. Very well, then . . . Where had I got to?'

' ".89% of the total population." '

'Yes,' and with a wavering voice he again started to dictate. 'Trifling as the matter seems, a question of principle is at stake. The League for Facial Disarmament——'

Jael held her pen poised.

'I'm sorry. The aims of the League for Facial Disarmament appear to be obscure. Strangely enough, this self-styled League includes both men and women. There seems to be an idea that the Beta standard of facial appearance has been set too high, and those with Gamma countenances are suffering from a sense of inferiority and Bad Egg. They demand that the Beta standard should be lowered, and as a protest are taking every step, short of actual facial disfigurement, to make their appearances as unpleasing as possible, and, remarkable as it seems, they have found sympathisers in the Beta class—to uphold their claim. They say it is unfair—what was that?'

They all listened to the silence, which seemed as thick and impenetrable as a wall.

'There's no reason for uneasiness,' said Joab testily.

'Where was I, Jael? Oh, I remember now, you needn't remind me. They, the malcontent Betas, say it is unfair that the Gammas should be facially less well off than they are. They say they suffer from guilt in the presence of a Gamma, and do all they can to bring their faces down to Gamma level. They think that one face ought to be as good as another, and feel intense sympathy and compassion for the facially under-privileged. They want the standard of looks lowered. They say it involves an overwhelming psychological effort to live up to a Beta face.'

'I don't find it so,' said Jael, stung into championing her face. 'I don't look at myself if I can help it, but——'

'Your case is different,' Joab said. 'Your face was lowered, not lifted. Naturally you felt relaxed when, facially, you had been reduced to a lower level and no longer felt the emanations of Bad Egg from those with under-privileged faces. You could confront them on equal terms without the gnawing sense of superiority that was haunting you——'

'But it *wasn't* haunting me,' cried Jael, 'until . . . until . . .' She stopped, wondering at what moment it had begun to haunt her, and urge her steps towards the threshold of the Ministry of Facial Justice. 'Doesn't it ever make *you* uncomfortable,' she demanded, 'to think that just because you happen to have been born with this gift for statistics, which others haven't got, you should be allowed to keep your Failed Alpha status, when others——'

'Certainly not,' said Joab. 'It is quite different for men.'

'Just because the Dictator is a woman-hater——'

'Jael!'

'Well, everyone knows he is. Why should you be at liberty to feel superior, just because, in this one particular, you have more brains than other people? And do you find it a psychological strain to be better off mentally than they are?'

'I've told you it's different for men.'

'How would you like having your brains lowered?'

'Brains,' said Joab, wearily, 'are not a cause of Bad E, Jael, like money or beauty.'

'They might become so. It isn't fair that you should be cleverer than other people.'

'Don't be absurd. Where had I got up to?'

' "They say it is an overwhelming psychological strain having to live up to a Beta face." '

'Yes. Then take this down. They also say that after a time Beta faces smell. This is untrue, of course. They demand the lowering of all women's faces to a Gamma standard, as a result of which, they claim, women would cease to be face-conscious, and the nervous energy absorbed by face-saving would be released for more valuable ends.'

'What utter rot!' Jael interrupted.

'Of course it is. But one must be realistic. It is easier to lower a standard than to raise one.'

'But surely the Dictator——'

'The Dictator has to consider his human material. He has often said that he interprets, he doesn't initiate.'

'I see,' said Jael, and the thought slid into her mind, any discontent, any unrest, is better than none. This might be the tiny rumble, felt more than heard, that precedes the earthquake, just as——

Without warning a terrific hullabaloo started in the street outside their window. Cries, screams, grunts, a tumult of all the uninhibited sounds the human larynx can give voice to. The clamour displaced the air; it seemed to be going on inside the room, inside their own heads, as the three of them cowered against the wall that was furthest from the window. Their outstretched arms and hands, trying to support their sagging bodies, slid down the slippery surface, and even the men's faces lost all expression; the messenger collapsed in a heap. How long the din lasted they did not know, but gradually the volume of sound thinned and grew sparser, they could distinguish separate cries that were stifled into sobs. Little by little these, too, died away and silence fell, but still the trio did not move; it was as if every flicker of animation had been blown out, and not until the familiar strains of 'Every Valley', twice repeated, recalled them to themselves did they stand up and with bent heads await the Dictator's message.

CHAPTER TWENTY

'PATIENTS and Delinquents and My Dear People.'

A long pause followed, increasing every second in intensity and significance, for the Dictator's hearers to take in this novel salutation. Joab's head drooped; the messenger lifted his; Jael's veil seemed suddenly to become opaque, even her eyes disappeared behind it.

'My dear people,' the Voice at length repeated, in tones blurred by emotion, 'a very strange phenomenon has happened during these last hours which I feel may have puzzled and disturbed you. I will explain it.'

Another pause.

'As you well know, my concern for you is sleepless and it has been occurring to me, my dear ones, that of late you have not been altogether happy under my guardianship. There have been signs of what I can only call unrest. In the place below, from which I rescued you, such signs would have been visited with condign punishment; none of those guilty would have lived to tell the tale, they would have perished from a hundred forms of lingering torture. I need not remind you of this; it is all written in the Book, and what is more, only a mile or two below us, it is still going on. I need not have reminded you, but even with you, my precious people, memories are sometimes short, and in a time of prosperity it is easy to forget the hard times that went before. Some of you are old enough to remember how hard those times were: I do not intend to dwell on them. But the younger members of our beloved community only know of them by hearsay and it is chiefly to them I speak.

'Patients and Delinquents, you are all dear to my heart, and the thought that you might be suffering in spirit has filled me with the deepest grief. Repressive measures are abhorrent to me, recalling as they do the world from which we have escaped; my plans for your welfare have taken many forms, but never that one. As you know, our Constitution is based on equality, equality of the most deep-seated and all-embracing order. But it is a flexible not a rigid equality, inspired by a compromise between what I want for you and what you want for yourselves; it is not imposed, it is, in the good sense of the word, voluntary, the expression, through my Edicts, of your own Free Will. What that will is, it has always been my study to find out and gratify; what I have done for you, the modifications and transformations in your social life over these many (to me) happy years of our association, have been done by you yourselves through me. This is a fact, patients and delinquents, that you once realised, and a fact that you are now in danger of forgetting.

'Patients and Delinquents, whose welfare is in my charge, I decided to put you to the test. I wanted to discover whether your sense of free-will, without which no community, or member of a community, can lead a healthy and useful life—whether it still existed. That was to be my first discovery. And the second was, if, as I hoped and prayed, it still existed, that you were still free to exercise it. And my third discovery was to be, supposing you still had free-will and the desire to exercise it, whether you realised, my dear, dear fellow creatures, that it was to me you owed the power to express your individual longings. Did you realise that my provisions for you are the form your free-will takes?

'So my first two inquiries were soon answered, and in the way I hoped they would be! You had free-will and the desire to exercise it. And the third was answered, too, but not in the way I hoped. They were interpreted—these outbreaks, these manifestations of free-will—as a protest against the régime, against me, in fact. It was put about and, strangely enough, believed, that those posters had been put up by persons hostile to our administration, by persons who wished us ill, by persons who hoped to overthrow our Government. Free-will, yes; but free-will that consisted in opposition to ourselves.

'Patients and Delinquents, it was I who devised the slogan, "Bet on yourselves", I who designed the posters, I, or rather my agents, who put them in position. The whole idea was mine, and without me could not have taken place. I staged the revolt, which some have thought was a revolt against me. But it was really, as you must now all see, a demonstration for me, a vote of confidence in me. I wanted you to exercise free-will and you exercised it, not against me, but for me.

'But I am not infallible, my beloved people, any more than you are; and when I called on you to show your free-will, to act for yourselves, to bet on yourselves, I did not, I confess, anticipate the form your longing to express yourselves would take. I had visions of actions of ideal beauty—I myself hardly know what they would be, but actions far transcending in meaning and interest the communal enjoyments that I have devised for you. Those enjoyments, how tame and insipid they were—singing, dancing, love-making, games, sports, concerts, cinemas, work, your daily avocations—they were all—may I say it?—meant to be compromises between the harsh régime of the Lower State from which I rescued you and the anarchy I feared for you. They were repressive, that I freely admit; they were meant to repress those elements in you which refuse to live in harmony. Some, indeed, enthusiasts for the régime, have denied that they were repressive, have seen in them outlets, safety-valves, through which the elements that will not live together in harmony could harmlessly escape. It is not for me to say if they were right. But I sensed the growing unrest among you, an unrest which some would call divine; so I permitted the Country Expeditions, and then, when ardent spirits wished for more intense sensations, I allowed them to be dangerous. Oh, how my heart bled for you, my precious people, when after the expedition to Ely the hospitals were filled to overflowing. There are still amongst you cripples whom all the skill of our doctors could not heal; there are, alas, gaps in your ranks, the dead, who cannot be replaced.

'After Ely, I made another Edict. Of the six coaches three, not one, were to meet with an accident. This, I thought, will certainly deter them: no one will take the coaches. But you know what happened. Every seat was booked; many would-be passengers could not find a place; a cheering crowd, larger than the one that assembled before Ely, watched the coaches start on their disastrous journey. They waited hours and were still there when the six coaches returned intact, with all their passengers safe and sound. I now confess to you, my dear ones, that I had seen to that; it was a pious fraud, an innocent deception on my part, meant to save you from yourselves. And what was the result? Deep disappointment; you all felt cheated of your blood-bath; no risk, no ride, you said; and when the next expedition was due to start, without the promise of an accident, not a single patient and delinquent took a ticket; the coaches and the Square were empty but for the drivers and conductors, who did a Dawdle Dance to pass the time; and the service had to be discontinued for lack of patrons.

'Yet I knew I had done right; for, made as you are, your natures need that stimulus. Once it did not; once the thought of what you had suffered in the Lower State made you as clay in my hands. Anything, anything, to avoid a recurrence of those conditions when torture and mass-executions were the rule—as they still are, my precious ones, in the place that you have left. But your memories of it

177

have grown dim; some have forgotten, some, whom we have cherished with difficulty into life, have never known them. You have come to take the present for granted, and yes, you are tired of it, tired of the harmony it has been my study to bring about in you—you seek stronger incentives. Of this I have grown increasingly aware; and I said to myself, why treat my beloved subjects as if they were children? As if they did not know their own minds? As if they did not know what was good for them? And why, why above all, did I think that what they would want, if left to themselves, if left to their own devices, would be some form of activity that would fill the hospitals and the coffins? Why have I been so cynical? I asked myself, and my face, the face you will never see, burned with secret shame. Why had I directed you into that most destructive of all inventions, the motor-car, thinking it was that you wanted, the lure of danger, the excitement of bloodshed, the heady smell of death? Oh, what agonies of remorse I went through, when I thought how I had misunderstood and misdirected you! Of course, I told myself, my darling people wanted no such thing; left to themselves they will at once pass into another state of being, a state of bliss which even I cannot conceive, in which all my ambitions for you will be realised in a way my poor finite brain could never picture. The Golden Age—my dear ones, the door to which can be opened by each one of you with a special, private key. Not my key, not a master-key common to all, such as now you use for your houses, but the latch-key which in olden days every householder kept for locking up his goods. So each should have his paradise, her paradise, to be enjoyed by him or her alone, and inaccessible to the others. And yet not inimical to the others—oh no! Side by side, touching but not colliding, each cell enshrining a perfect individuality, that owed nothing to and took nothing from the rest. A hive of private paradises, fashioned not by working together, or playing together, or talking together, or thinking together, not created by any communal activity—perish the thought! But coming insensibly, miraculously into being by the simplest of all expedients: the exercise of free-will, all your free-wills, all operating on their own, without reference to others, guided by that inner light, that infallible sense of the right direction that, as is well known, we each of us possess.

'And I, dear Patients and most dear Delinquents, what part should I play in this paradise? These paradises, rather, since the term is individual, not collective? What room would there be in them for me? None; for as the poet says: "Two paradises 'twere in one—To live in Paradise alone." So I should give up, resign, abdicate; you would hear this voice no more, and I should in the quaint old phrase retire into private life, a private paradise like, and yet quite unlike —since each is individual and distinct—your own.

'And now I must let you into a secret, my dear fellow-angels. I have been called every name, I know, from tyrant downwards. It has been my duty to find out these things, and my Intelligence Service tells me that two hundred and seventy-one bad names for me are now in common usage. Formerly, I believe, there were far fewer, for (and now I will let you into another secret) my pride as a potentate was hurt to know you spoke so hardly of me. I even took measures of repression: as you will remember, there were edicts, there were fines, there were threats (never carried out) of Permanent Sackcloth for offenders. But then I asked myself, why curtail their liberty? What harm does it do me, whom they have never seen and never will see, if they speak of me with disrespect? So I gave orders that your freedom of speech should be encouraged, not discouraged, and believe me, I have had many a good laugh from some of the names you have invented for me.

'But, my beloved people, I wander from the point. What

I meant to say was this. You, or some of you, picture me as a remote official, hard-headed and hard-hearted, with only one thought behind all I do—how to cling to power. That, you say, those of you who are historians, is the way Dictators have always acted; they cling to power until another power is born strong enough to unseat them. If you only knew how untrue that is of me! If you only knew how much I should like to resign, abdicate, vanish (if what is unseen can vanish) into one of those private paradises which each of you, my precious subjects, is preparing for himself or for herself.

'I know better than to use this as a threat; for would not every one of you, my dear ones, call my bluff and take me at my word? I can imagine how heartily sick of me you must be, for I know how heartily sick I sometimes, but not always, am of you. It is for your sakes I stay on, exercising this power which you did not give me and therefore cannot take from me. None of you knows how I got it or by what means I keep it. Do you suppose it is fun for me to watch over your interests and your welfare, when I get nothing out of it but the knowledge that without me you would be far, far worse off than you are now?

'So at least I thought, Patients and Delinquents, if I may still call you by those sweet old names, until yesterday. But yesterday, I thought, perhaps I do them wrong to believe that my unsleeping vigilance is an advantage to them; perhaps they would be better and happier without me. And it also occurred to me, perhaps I should be happier and better without them, a private person, exercising my free-will for myself, and not for them. No more responsibility! No more wondering whether the morning will bring a two-hundred-and-seventy-second opprobrious epithet to mark your disapproval of me (I am told that more than two-thirds of these, 198 to be exact, have been invented by women, once called the gentler sex). Do not imagine that because I am a Dictator my skin is too thick to be penetrated by these barbs. No, each one of them rankles; you may think of me sitting here, wherever that is, with tears pouring down my face. So I thought, I cannot cure their restlessness, and perhaps I am wrong to think that their natural inclination is towards violence. Perhaps it was a mistake to send the coaches to Ely; and it was I, not you, who plunged you into a blood-bath. Let them have their heads, I told myself. Let them do what they like, without any prompting from me. I shall see actions that will astonish me, and bring to the New State a beauty of living you could have never dreamed of. I shall wither away; but they will go on, exploring the dimension of height which I have forbidden them, enriching their consciousness with experiences of beauty and completeness quite beyond my ken.

'So I put up the posters, begging, entreating, almost ordering you to bet on yourselves, to give the rein to your own instincts for your welfare. And what happened? Patients and Delinquents, a terrible thing happened— terrible that is, in my eyes. For blood has been shed in quantities quite unknown to our New State; the streets have run with it. What happened after Ely was like a cut finger by comparison. The hospitals are overcrowded; new hospitals are being improvised, but even so the wounded, the dying and the dead are still lying in the streets untended, for we have no organisation capable of coping with them. The whole town of Cambridge, dear Patients and Delinquents, has become a shambles. Yes, and other cities, too, for Cambridge alone could not contain all the casualties. Hundreds are known to have perished; thousands may have.

'Patients and Delinquents! The situation is now under control, and you may walk abroad without fear of bodily injury or of sights of horror that might haunt you for the rest of your lives. So go—those of you who remain—in peace.

'But what is to happen now, after the disastrous results of my experiment? Punish you I cannot; it was I who put the posters up, to test your reactions under the influence of free-will. I expected an earthly paradise, an assemblage of private paradises making one elysium which should include and transcend them all. It was to be the answer to my prayer, the justification of my faith in you. Instead, what have I found? A battlefield.

'Patients and Delinquents, it is all my fault, and I have done all I can to make amends. The dead are buried, the casualties are being cared for. It is not my first mistake, but it is my first big mistake.

'But was it a mistake? That is a thing, my dear fellow-citizens, that I still cannot quite believe. For are you not all good at heart, as good at least as I am? Did I not promise myself that when the time came for me to abdicate, that I could safely leave you to your own devices? Was I not sure that after so many years in leading-strings, so many years of seeing how life could be lived, tolerably if not excitingly, without the stimulus of blood-shed or any of the major crimes, you would be conditioned to this new gentle life, so that you could not hurt each other, even if you wanted to? That you would have a sense of what was due from one to another, that mutual forbearance, even mutual love, would have become a habit?

'I cannot think I was mistaken, and so, Patients and Delinquents, to show my trust in you I am going to repeat the experiment. This evening the placards, "Bet on yourself", which so inflamed you today, will appear again in the streets, and in far greater numbers than before. Then it will be for you to choose, and for me, too, to choose. If there is a repetition of last night's incident, then you must make what you can of it, for I shall not be there to help or hinder you. If, as I hope, there is no repetition, but instead a new vista of joy and happiness, if "Bet on yourself" means what it should mean, a new confidence in your power to help each other through the force of a good example, then I shall be there to share it with you; but if it means a recurrence of the dreadful scenes of last night, then, Patients and Delinquents, I shall wash my hands of you. I have never been present, but then I shall be absent, I shall disappear; and with me will disappear the organisation I have built up for you—the safeguards, the interests, the stimulants and sedatives that have made up my rule of peace. My rule of peace! How you once longed for it! Once it satisfied all your aspirations and stilled all your fears. Now it seems you desire something quite different, something in which I can have no part. There is a place ready for me, for us, I should say, where we shall have no one to look after but ourselves; there is also a place ready for you, which some of you will remember, for you once dwelt in it.

'Patients and Delinquents,' here the speaker's voice quavered—'it is for you to choose.'

The strains of 'Every Valley', those mounting phrases which belied the meaning of the words, sounded through the room, but they fell on unheeding ears. Joab was in tears; the messenger's face had gone lifeless; and Jael's, behind her veil, told nothing of what she felt. Joab was the first to recover.

'Please take down this,' he said.

The Dictator was not quite as good as his word; the posters did indeed reappear, but interspersed with them were some which said not 'Bet on Yourself' but 'Beta Yourself'. The public, who never tired of Beta jokes, thought this wonderfully funny. They were hysterical with relief at the Dictator's clemency, it assured them of his forgiveness and was the one thing needed to reinstate them in their own esteem.

The Dictator's triumph was complete. Never had he been

so popular. At the next meeting of the conspirators it was resolved, with only one dissentient voice, that the League for liquidating him should be disbanded. Jael made an impassioned plea for its continuance. 'How could you be taken in,' she stormed, 'by all that clap-trap? That sob-stuff, and those hypocritical endearments? And the repetitions and the contradictions! Whatever else he's doing he's losing his grip! And yet he can still fool you, still make you think he's acting for your good! He's even persuaded you that he put up the posters, whereas you all know I put them up. I put them up, I put them up, I tell you!'

But they didn't believe her and her solitary voice was shouted down. In their delirious enthusiasm for the Dictator they wound up the proceedings with a ballet in his honour that was a parody of the Assassins' Dance. Jael tried to run away but she was caught and dragged back and made to take a part. She was roughly handled by her late confederates, especially by the women; they pushed her about and hustled her and held her up, sometimes literally, to derision. And when she would not cry 'Long live the Dictator!' the whole pack fell on her and pommelled her.

When she recovered from her ritual death she was alone, alone on the dry mud of the hollow; and alone she slowly and painfully limped her way back.

CHAPTER TWENTY-ONE

'A CONCERT,' Dr. Wainewright said.

'That would be very nice,' said Jael. 'When?'

'On Saturday. Two pianists are playing, Brutus 91 and Cassius 92. It will be interesting to compare their styles.'

'I used to play the piano once,' Jael said, who now found it easier than she had to talk to Dr. Wainewright.

'Did you really? Why did you give it up?'

Dr. Wainewright spoke as if playing the piano was an unheard-of accomplishment.

'Because I was getting too good at it.'

'Why was that a reason for giving it up?'

'Because the others didn't like it.'

'Oh, I see. Bad Egg, I suppose.'

'Yes, they made me stick to easy pieces.'

'What a shame.'

'You ought not to say that,' said Jael.

'Why not?'

'Because none of us ought to be able to play anything more difficult than "The Merry Peasant".'

'Oh well. We have to make exceptions sometimes.'

'I thought that was just what we mustn't make,' said Jael.

'Oh, I don't know. Simply because you don't like the Dictator's rules, 97, you interpret them too rigidly. He never said we weren't to fall in love.'

'No, I suppose he had to stop somewhere.'

'And love implies a preference. Couldn't you feel one for me, Jael, even the smallest one?'

Seeing him darkly through her veil, Jael got a confused impression of his squarish face, dark hair, and pronounced features—the Roman nose was specially strong. She saw how another woman might have loved him, but the thought was bitter to her, for it brought back all that she had lost, her personal life, which, though it had been a dream, might also have been a reality but for Dr. Wainewright and his cruel fingers carving up her face, depriving her of the one love she could have responded to. Dr. Wainewright had made her in his own image, that was why he loved her. If he hadn't committed this outrage, someone else would have, she had to admit that, and it was her punishment, as the Visitor had told her—that nice old woman, whom she still thought of with gratitude. It wasn't his fault that she had to hate him. But did she hate him? Might not the understanding that sometimes goes with hate bring with it a warmer feeling?

'Couldn't you have the smallest preference for me?' he repeated, moved to hopefulness by her long silence.

'You know what I feel,' she said.

'But it's your mind saying that,' he said. 'Your hand doesn't hate me, at least it didn't last time.'

He bent forward and took it, unresistingly, in his.

'But,' she said after a moment, 'you were going to tell me something.'

'Tell you something? What do you want to know?'

'Something about him.'

'Who?'

'The Dictator.'

Dr. Wainewright hesitated. 'I told you he existed.'

'How do you know that?'

'Because of the Sign.'

'What is the Sign?' asked Jael. Without taking away her hand from his, she pushed her veil back. She didn't want to look at the world, or to be looked at by it, but sometimes she had to look, and be looked at.

Plainly now she saw the face of her destroyer, and he as plainly saw the face he had created, the face of his beloved.

186

He didn't answer her question.

'If I were to kiss you——' he began.

'But you have kissed me.'

'Yes, but you haven't kissed me.'

'Why should I?' Jael said. 'You haven't told me——'

'Is telling the price of a kiss?'

Jael looked at him again. Yes, other women could have loved him, probably had loved him, for the questing male urgency that, in asking for surrender, confessed its need of love. Jael shrank from it, as a prostitute might shrink from the too ardent glance of her first customer; but her senses had never fallen asleep again after their brief awakening in the sky. Perhaps she could bring herself to desire him just a little; then it would be easier. She had no doubt of his desire for her: but to what lengths of telling her what she wanted to know would it take him?

'You were going to tell me how you knew the Dictator existed,' she reminded him.

'Can't you guess?'

'How can I? Why should you know more than any other man, or woman for that matter? You aren't even an Inspector!'

'How do you know I'm not?' he teased her. 'Not all Inspectors look like old-time guardsmen. Some wear plain clothes and are quite inconspicuous.'

'I didn't know that.'

'Well, now I've told you something. Can I claim a kiss?'

'No, because you still haven't told me how you know the Dictator exists.'

'I told you about the Sign.'

'Yes, but not what it is. Is it something you can see? Could anyone recognise him by it if they knew what it was, and where to look?'

'This is not a guessing game,' said Dr. Wainewright, 'and I've told you too much already.'

Jael moved her chair away from him and changed the subject.

'At least you can tell me,' she said, 'why the Dictator is so down on women.'

'But is he down on them?'

'He's always trying to standardise us, and make us sex-machines instead of human beings.'

Dr. Wainewright gave her a sly smile.

'Perhaps he thinks that's what you really want to be.'

'It isn't true!' cried Jael. 'We want it less than men do. And anyhow he doesn't go the right way about it. If he knew anything about sex——'

'How do you know he doesn't?'

'Isn't it obvious? He makes us as unattractive as he can——'

'That's what *you* think,' the Doctor interrupted. 'I made your face according to a Beta pattern approved by him, with some slight variations of my own, and I find it very attractive, I can tell you, and so do a good many more.'

'But they can't see my face.'

'They could, before you pulled the blind down on it.'

'Who, for instance?'

Dr. Wainewright reeled off a list of names.

'Oh,' cried Jael, 'it makes me hate my face all the more, because they like it.'

'What nonsense!' Dr. Wainewright said. 'How can you hate your face if other people like it? It's a psychological impossibility. You see your face through other people's eyes—every woman does.'

'I hate my face,' said Jael. 'And I never look at it if I can help it.'

'Then you must hate yourself,' said Dr. Wainewright. 'You hate yourself and therefore you hate other people, including me, I'm afraid. That's what I'm trying to cure you of.'

Opening his black bag he took out a pad and began to scribble on it.

'What are you prescribing for me now?' she asked.

'A love-philtre.'

'Why do you think I need it?'

'I'm not going to leave any stone unturned.'

'I wish you would prescribe it for the Dictator!'

Dr. Wainewright smiled.

'No, he's too old for loving in that sense. Besides, he's full of love, that's why he keeps so well.'

'Keeps so well? You talk as if he was a food-tablet in a fridge. And love? How does he show it?'

'In heaps of ways. He goes about . . . well, helping people.'

'Disguised, of course.'

'You wouldn't recognise him,' said the doctor.

'Except by the Sign.'

'Not even then. You'd still think it was someone else.'

'Why?'

'You'd be looking for somebody to hate, not somebody to love.'

'Do you suppose I can't recognise people whom I hate?' demanded Jael. 'It's love that's blind. If he was a woman, of course, it wouldn't be so easy.'

'Why not?'

'Because she might have been betafied. She'd have to be, if she lived up to her principles. Quite often my best friends don't recognise me.'

'The Dictator would.'

'I don't count him as a friend, but does he know me?'

'I shouldn't be surprised. You've made yourself conspicuous, you know, on various occasions.'

'How can a Beta be conspicuous?'

'Oh, in more ways than one, or I shouldn't be here.'

'How do you know so much about the Dictator?' Jael asked.

'Ah!'

She turned away with an indifferent shrug. The gesture was not lost on Dr. Wainewright.

'You're rather dense, my dear. How do I know so much about you?'

'Because you're my doctor.'

'Well, then.'

When she still didn't see his drift, he said:

'If you give me a kiss, I'll tell you.'

'If you tell me, I'll give you a kiss,' said Jael.

For a moment it was a stalemate; then he saw he had won. He embraced her greedily and did not loose his hold until his molten mouth had poured itself round every curve of hers.

But how cold the kiss was to her Beta lips, and how distasteful to her unresponding heart.

Breathless, he said: 'If that's done you half the good it has done me, we shan't either of us need a doctor for a long time.'

Outraged, Jael answered:

'What a hygienic view of love! Doctors need doctors, I suppose, but I don't, nor, worse luck, does the Dictator.'

'That's where you're wrong,' he said. 'He does need a doctor.'

'How do you know?' she cried.

'Because I am his doctor.'

CHAPTER TWENTY-TWO

JAEL stared at Dr. Wainewright as if he had been another man, a complete stranger. Then incredulity came to her rescue and she gasped:

'But you can't be!'

'Why not? Dictators have to have doctors, just like other people.'

'Yes, I suppose so.' Jael's mind was whirling: a score of questions crowded to her lips.

'But where do you attend him?'

'I never said I had attended him.'

'But have you?'

'Yes, once.'

'Where was it?'

'Where he happened to be. He isn't always in the same place. But we are sensitised to his whereabouts.'

'What was the matter with him?'

'Nothing much. I just gave him a check-up.'

'But you're a plastic surgeon. What could you do for him?'

'We don't only arrange faces.'

'Are you a sign-painter, by any chance?'

Dr. Wainewright laughed uneasily.

'The Dictator is never ill,' he said.

'Then why does he need a doctor?'

'In case he should be ill.'

'Did you get your knife into him?'

'Oh, just a scratch.'

'It doesn't sound very likely to me. Are you telling me the truth?'

'Of course I am.'

'You told me a lie before—you told me somebody you knew had seen him.'

'Well, aren't I somebody I know?'

'You're a tricky customer, whatever else you are.'

'All doctors have to edit the truth,' said Dr. Wainewright. 'It's part of our profession. Should doctors tell? You must have heard of that.'

I'll worm it out of him somehow, Jael thought. His longing for me will unloose his tongue, but I must go warily.

'Has he other doctors besides you?' she asked.

'Yes, I believe so.'

'But you haven't been called in for a consultation?'

He shook his head.

'I wish I could be fond of you,' she said.

'You could be if you tried,' said Dr. Wainewright. 'I may not be an Alpha type to look at, but I'm sound and healthy. If we had children——'

'They might take after you,' said Jael.

'Or you.'

'Which me?' asked Jael.

'The one I love.'

Love! Love! The word gave out a sullen sound, like a false coin that spins itself to silence on the table.

'But how could I hand on my imposed characteristics?'

'It has been known. The image in the mind may reproduce itself on the face.'

'The Dictator forbid,' said Jael, but she spoke half-heartedly. Suddenly a panic fear came over her that he might get his way before she got hers; she might give in to him before he gave up his secret. It was a race between them. Which would win? The odds seemed balanced evenly. If she couldn't wheedle his secret out of him, could she wheedle something else—a better weapon than the regulation pocket-knife with its two-inch blade?

That would be an asset, even if she only used it against him.

At this and every subsequent encounter she must give ground a little, as he would. But giving ground really meant coming closer, until . . . until . . . At the idea of the last forfeit her mind shied away. No, she was the clever one; she would never pay it! But she might have to; for her mission's sake she might have to take the risk that he, out of the gratitude which men were said to feel on such occasions, might give her the vital piece of knowledge which his unsatisfied senses, however much they were being tantalised, would withhold.

She couldn't tell. She didn't know what he was really like. She only knew him as a man in love; she didn't know him as a man. As a man he might be shrewd, suspicious, realistic, set on his pound of flesh. She must keep him in love, and the best way of doing that was not by loving him, even if she had been able to; men fled from a loving woman. No, she must vary her demeanour, so that it never quite chimed in with his, or was quite discordant with it. He must find her different each time. Hitherto she had been too openly contemptuous of him, rude in fact, and it had seemed to work: he had always come back for more. Perhaps in his present mood of overpowering physical desire it was the best policy. But it would not always be. He would tire of it, and look for a woman less tart, if more like a tart, than she was.

How distasteful it all was. At times, and this was one, she was visited by a sense of unbearable, irreparable loss, remembering what it had felt like to be herself, before this trouble with her face began; like Eve in the garden, she had roamed from flower to flower, from fruit to fruit, until she tasted the forbidden one. But how could she have avoided it, without surrendering her personality? She had had to make the choice, and still would not have made it differently. The Fall! She hadn't fallen yet, but spiritually she had;

193

spiritually she couldn't have fallen lower, and all in an attempt to reach the heights.

Height, oh height.

But, of course, when this was over, when whatever had to happen would have happened, then she would go back to being what she had been. The episode—whatever it was, however it ended, would have left no mark on her at all . . . She wouldn't be anything horrid, certainly not a murderess —though a political assassination wasn't really a murder— she would just be the old Jael, good old Jael, who liked so many people and whom so many people liked, not taking ideas seriously, least of all political ideas, not even taking herself seriously, for what, after all, did it matter what she looked like? Then she would have no preoccupation with her conscience, no conviction that this was right and that was wrong and she must give up everything to prove it. No, she would be the old Jael, at whose appearance faces brightened (for even a Beta face could brighten a little), and who was once wooed by an angel—in the clouds, in the sky, no matter where—and it had changed her life, but not embittered it, only enriched it with a lovely memory.

She looked up from her reverie and there was Dr. Wainewright's rough-hewn face, to remind her of reality and her mission.

'I thought you had gone to sleep,' he said.

She started, still unable to focus him with her inner vision.

'I didn't like to disturb you,' he went on, 'in case you were thinking kind thoughts of me.'

'Of course I was,' she lied.

'Then may I hope?'

'Yes, indeed yes.'

'May I hope now—this minute?'

'Isn't once enough?'

'I can't have enough.'

'I'm not in the mood,' said Jael. 'I don't feel like it.' But there was something she wanted from him, wanted as passionately as he wanted her. She must be in the mood, she must feel like it.

'When did you last use your carving-knife?' she asked.

'My carving-knife?'

'The knife you cut our faces up with.'

'I don't remember . . . A few days ago.'

'I was thinking of my Beta-dom,' said Jael.

'Your Beta-doom, you said.'

'Yes, and I call my veil my Beta-hood. Silly, isn't it? But the Dictator likes us to be childish. If I had a memento—'

'What sort of memento?'

'The instrument—the knife—the scalpel or whatever you call the thing, that you did it with.'

'What do you want it for?'

'Just a keepsake. Was it the one you scratched the Dictator with?'

'It may have been.'

'It's become a sort of fetish to me. If I had it——'

'Well?'

'It would reconcile me to all sorts of things. Myself, yourself, even the Dictator's self.'

'It's very sharp, you know,' said Dr. Wainewright.

'Yes, but if I thought of your hand guiding it over the skin, my skin, the Dictator's skin——'

Dr. Wainewright took her in his arms but she pushed him away.

'No, give it to me first.'

Again the trial of strength between their wills; again the stalemate; but this time she won.

He rose, opened the bag, and brought out a long, thin, flat container, which he handed her.

'I don't like giving it you,' he said, 'but as long as you keep it sterilised, and don't hurt yourself or anyone else——'

She drew the knife out of its case and ran her thumb along the blade.

'For the Dictator's sake don't do that!'

Ignoring him, she said:

'So I came out of this?'

'Well, in a way.'

How easy it would be to stick it in him!

Putting the scalpel back in its sheath, she thought: 'Shall I disappoint him now? No, better not,' and true to her promise she held her arms out. Their embrace was long and close and mounting in intensity when Jael heard footsteps in the street and the door-handle turning.

'That's Joab,' she said. 'You must be going.'

'Oh, must I?' he grumbled like a child, and sighing deeply disengaged himself. Standing before her, bag in hand, he looked like a proper doctor.

'Well, thanks a lot, and don't forget about the concert. And you'll come home with me afterwards, won't you?'

'All right.'

'Is that a promise?'

'Yes, I think so . . . Joab, here is Dr. Wainewright who has come to give me some medicine.'

Joab shook hands with the doctor.

'Nasty medicine?' he asked hopefully.

'I don't think so, but tastes differ,' the doctor said.

'Oh no they don't,' said Jael. 'We all have the same tastes.'

He smiled indulgently.

'Well, mind you take it, 97, mind you take it.'

Joab walked with him to the door.

'How do you think she's getting on?' he asked. 'I can't see much wrong with her myself.'

'Her personality still needs adjusting,' Dr. Wainewright said. 'I'm afraid I shall have to continue the . . . er . . . treatment a little longer. She's still lacking in the sense of co-operation; until she gets that back, she'll always have these headaches.'

'Headaches? She's never mentioned them.'

'Not to you, perhaps. Sometimes women don't tell their nearest relations about these things.'

They parted and Joab went back into the house.

CHAPTER TWENTY-THREE

'The programmes were different, except for the interesting experiment that each pianist played the Moonlight Sonata. It was therefore possible to compare their respective styles and general status as performers. It would have been possible to do this in any case—perhaps impossible not to— but the juxtaposition gave point to the contrast.

'The Moonlight Sonata is a popular work but it is also classical—that is to say, above the heads of some members of the audience. At the moment I will make no comment upon this, except to say that the jazz section at the end (the rest of the programme was classical), which all could enjoy, came as a welcome relief. Classical music has, of course, long been tolerated by listeners who might be called under-privileged in the higher reaches of musical knowledge; even those who are unfortunate enough to have no ear for music have seldom openly resented it—much as they must have suffered from boredom and even from active irritation under the meaningless blare of sound. Not enough sympathy has been shown with a section of the public which has suffered more than most from the priggishness and fancied superiority of the Failed Alpha class, in whom the cult for "serious" music has always been strongest. How can music be "serious"? Seriousness consists, and consists only, in the effort to realise the theme song or signature tune which heralds the pronouncements of our darling Dictator (blessed be his name). Every valley must be exalted, every mountain and hill brought low; and how can this aim be achieved if the category "serious" is allowed to include any other activity of the human mind and body? Games perhaps; in games the anti-social instinct to excel is slightly counter-balanced by the fact that some are born with bodies stronger or more agile than others. Of those whom this superiority has raised to the pure Alpha class we do not speak; the Dictator in his infinite and inscrutable wisdom has decided that they should form a corps d'élite, a chosen and choice body with whom we should never dream of comparing ourselves. They are indeed the standard of our littleness, a littleness we embrace all the more eagerly because it absolves us from any effort, except the effort to be little, an effort that is becoming less with every day that passes. But we should not embrace it so willingly if it contained within itself gradations and degrees which enabled some to boast that they were not so little as others. We must be level in littleness and equal in insignificance, or what are we here for? And if I may presume to read the Dictator's mind, I should hazard the conjecture that he does not view with favour the bodily advantages that one man, and, still more, that one women, has over another. I say one woman, because it is no secret that the Dictator, with unerring insight confirmed by the latest psychological research, has decided that women are better subjects for complete equalisation than men. The virus of individuality is much less strong in them; by nature they differ from each other only in inessentials, in such minor matters as figure, voice, capacity for affection, etc. Their natural colouring, it has been well said, is protective colouring, and though some of the more ill-advised among them have often striven, and still strive, to assume a false individuality by divergencies of dress, they are at bottom *all alike*, and will be happier, as well as more useful, when they realise that this is so. Let us permit ourselves to hope that the Dictator, who has done so much for them by regularising their faces (for it's oh to be a Beta, when a Gamma's near), will proceed to regularise their bodies, which are a source of Bad E, just as their faces were; and even endow them with a common mind, pitched, let us hope, at no exalted level. And if it is discovered that the same beneficent process can be applied to men, without too much interference with their naturally more individualistic cast of body and mind (the Dictator does not wish any of us, least of all a man, to suffer), well, so much the better. Instead of sports at which this or that man *wins*, stirring up, it has to be admitted, a faint whiff of Bad E in his "rivals" or "competitors" (to use words which, some of us dare to hope, will soon vanish from the language), we shall have sports at which all the entrants win, or lose. And those two words, which have occasioned so much needless heart-burning in the past, will become indistinguishable and so lose their sting. For what does Good E signify, so long as any man, on whatever pretext of superiority, innate or acquired, can boast himself above the others? In the case of women, our minds already revolt from such a disturbing and reactionary thought.

'This is by the way, and a wistful and wishful vision of the future, inspired by a presumptuous effort to imagine what may be in the Dictator's mind. It may be totally mistaken. But we know that he is all for fairness, and more power to his elbow.

'But to return to classical, or "serious" music. In so far as the so-called appreciation of it results in distinguishing one man (or indeed one woman, though they hardly count) from another, it is retrograde. If this be heresy, I cannot help it. As a student of music, I have to admit that I did once understand to a small degree and even enjoy classical music: the climate of thought at the time made this possible and some thought even desirable. But now things have changed and it seems priggish and superior to enjoy what the majority, or even a minority, are by some congenital deficiency, or accidental lack of training, debarred from enjoying. We experience the same kind of discomfort, akin to shame, that a person in perfect health feels in the presence of someone physically or mentally less well off than himself. In this connection I need hardly remind you of a growing feeling, amounting almost to resentment, among the physically handicapped and under-privileged against those who go about too obviously enjoying their good health. Far be it from me to offer suggestions to a régime which has brought us all so much happiness; but since the Dictator, in his infinite mercy, has said that such suggestions are acceptable, may I most humbly propose that an effective way of eliminating Bad E (which is always breaking out in new places) would be to inject the healthy with some form of not necessarily serious illness, so that the level of physical and mental well-being in the New State should be roughly regularised—no one too ill, no one too well? Thus the healthy could no longer swank about it, nor those with unfair physical handicaps have to endure the mortification of seeing others fitter than themselves.

'Again I wander from my subject, but it was only to assure my readers that in writing about so-called classical music I am uncomfortably aware of a certain intellectual priggishness, and it is a positive relief to me to feel that many of my comments, if not all, would almost certainly be regarded by musicians of the old school (a supercilious set) as hopelessly wide of the mark. For how it warms the heart to know that one is erring with the majority, sharing their collective mistakes, and adding to the blessed mucilage of misinformation that holds us all together!

'By the old standards Brutus 91's rendering of the Moonlight Sonata would have been highly praised. His technical proficiency was admirable: he scarcely played a wrong note. He realized to the full the intention of the slow movement, which lulls the listener into a sense of false security, though a hint of coming storm is never quite silenced. He entered into the delicious gaiety of the allegretto, which Liszt called *une fleur entre deux abîmes* (please pardon this parade of un-general knowledge). He remembered the important direction to attack it at once; and when he came to the last movement, he surmounted its technical difficulties with so much ease that one was only conscious of the storm in the composer's mind and never of the trouble to the fingers of the executant. Those wild rushes up the piano over which we used to stumble were rendered effortlessly. The passion was like the passion of a thunderstorm; we did not ask ourselves by what technical means the heavens produced this soul-shaking uproar, where the electricity came from, and the thunder-claps; we were content to listen and admire. The audience, many of whom were experiencing for the first time emotions they could never have experienced for themselves, sat spell-bound, and when, after a breathless interval, the applause broke out, Brutus was recalled many times and at last induced to give an encore—a Moment Musical of Schubert's, which again brought down the house.

'These were the final items on Brutus's programme; I will not describe the others, though by old-time standards they were equally well played. After the interval, Cassius 92 took Brutus's place at the piano.

'From the first note he struck it was clear that he was not Brutus's equal as a pianist, and by not equal I mean he was inferior. He used the pedal far too much, especially in difficult or fast passages, thereby blurring the sound; his touch was heavy and rigid, and he played a great many wrong notes. He galumphed his way through Chopin's Ballade in A flat, making the delicate, dancing music sound like a stampede of elephants. Nor did he seem to know what the music was about or in what mood the composer had written it; he approached each piece as if it was a task that will-power alone would get him through. It seemed rather cruel to put him on the same platform with Brutus, and I wondered who was responsible for such an ill-judged juxtaposition. Surely the Dictator—blessed be his name—who (I say with all respect) is rumoured to have a hand in everything, could not have had a hand in this . . . this painful exhibition of one man's superiority to another. I mean, of course, superiority in the pianistic art; in all other respects, I am sure, Brutus was exactly Cassius's equal. As men, as patients and delinquents, not a pin to choose between them. The audience was puzzled, too; fair-minded as they must be and are, they began by giving Cassius exactly the same amount of applause, not a hand-clap more or less, than they had given Brutus. It was a splendid exhibition of fairness, the way they rewarded both men equally, as if their merits had been just the same. But after the third piece, in which, I must say, the unintentional discords had been very noticeable and the pianist, who was playing without his notes, lost his way and left out sixteen bars, the volume of applause fell off considerably and there were murmurs and shufflings. At this the pianist seemed to lose his nerve, for he left the platform abruptly and returned carrying rather sheepishly the music of his final piece, which was to be the Moonlight Sonata.

'At first I felt sorry for him and, I must confess, a little angry with him, he was making such a mess of it. He played the andante rather fast and with continuous use, which the composer expressly deprecates, of the soft pedal. He took the allegretto slower, and the presto, it seemed, slower still, and even so with a plentiful sprinkling of wrong notes. Instead of a whirlwind rush, laborious arpeggios climbed up the piano, like an unskilful workman going up a ladder, and the repeated chord of the climax was as often as not mis-hit. Of agitation there was plenty, but it was the nervous agitation of the bungler, not the headlong sweep of passion. The audience grew more restive, and even the Beta faces, as a rule so magnificently impassive, were ruffled by disapproval. And when the air made its first entrance, the pianist's left hand lost liaison with his right, with the result that at least an extra bar was added to the proper number. At this the audience made a low sound not unlike a groan, and I was inclined to join in, when suddenly a thought struck me that changed my mind and my whole outlook.

'If I had been called on to play the Moonlight Sonata, this was the way I should have played it—indeed I might even have played it worse: so who was I to demand that Cassius 92 should play it better than I could, or the audience either, few of whom, I suspected, in spite of their ungenerous attitude, could have bettered his performance? By playing it "badly" (advisedly I put the word in inverted commas) he was only playing it as *we* should have played it—those of us who could play. By playing it "badly" he was keeping us in countenance—a gracious act not so important for us Betas, but an inestimable boon to the male part of the audience, whose faces had begun to work alarmingly. "Betafy them! Betafy them!" I mutely cried (but that is for the Dictator to decide), "reveal to them that this performance, in spite of its faults, indeed *because* of its faults, is worth far more than the other, because it is in line with our common humanity: we all have faults, we all make mistakes. Brutus, by the very faultlessness of his rendering, has put us out of countenance, he has made us look up to him, which we should never do to anything or anyone, except, of course, the Inspectors and the Dictator! By taking up a superior position he has made us guilty of Bad E—yes, I could feel its poison stealing into me, destroying my sense of unity with my fellows. Cassius is one of us because he made mistakes, just as we should. What right has Brutus 91 to play more correctly than we can, to humiliate us? It isn't fair, it isn't! And almost simultaneously I had another revelation: that it was the object of whoever planned the programme (could it, could it have been the Dictator himself?) to teach us a lesson in humility, to keep us in our proper places, and prevent us trying to outshine our fellows by an exhibition of our so-called superior powers.

'After that it was the mistakes and the worst-played passages that pleased me the most, for I felt in them the strongest evidence of our common humanity—that is, our liability to err, and my resentment grew against Brutus and the flawless performance by which he had separated himself from us on his pinnacle of excellence. Crash! Bang! With each deviation from the music my heart rejoiced, for this, I knew, was the way I should have played it myself; and I felt that more and more I was entering into the mind of the Dictator, who has never wanted us to do anything well, for "well" is our highest common factor, which excludes the many who fall by the way, whereas "badly" is the lowest common denominator, and includes us all. Darling Dictator, blessed be his name, who does not require of us more than we can give, more than the least of us can give! Long may he live to make the New State safe for mediocrity!

'And the excitement of these thoughts was still seething in my head when the Sonata came to an end and the pianist rose shakily to make his bow. At that a storm of boos, hoots and hisses broke out, and Cassius turned away as though blinded. But I clapped madly, overcome by the sense of our common humanity revealed to me by his incompetence, I could not sit, I had to stand, and I shouted: "You are all wrong, you are hopelessly wrong! Cassius has done us all the greatest service. Cassius is you, he is us! He has fulfilled the will of the Dictator, who wants us to be all alike!" But I doubt if anyone heard me; or if they did, they only thought I was adding my bit to the abuse that they were heaping on the pianist.'

CHAPTER TWENTY-FOUR

JAEL laid down her pen, it was after three o'clock, but she hadn't noticed how the time was passing. The typewritten sheets had mounted up; later she would have to correct them, perhaps rewrite the whole thing, perhaps destroy it. But no. She saw how weak it was, how it fell short of what she had imagined. In theory, of course, that was right. It must not be a masterpiece. To be consistent with its own thesis it must be mediocre, or very bad indeed. Jael pushed these logical objections irritably out of her mind. It must be something that would get across—a low enough ideal anyhow—it must fulfil its purpose, which was, of course, to hoist the Dictator on his own petard, to push his ideas to a reductio ad absurdum. If you are going to be an *agent provocateur*, you must try to be a good one. How this question of standards kept cropping up! Good! Good! It ought not to be good; it ought to be no better than the stupidest members of the audience could write, supposing they were inspired by her grievance against the Dictator and wished him overthrown. It wouldn't do that, of course. But it might start a doubt in people's minds, and make them wonder just how silly he had hoodwinked them into being. She didn't think that anyone would doubt its genuineness. Much sillier articles than hers had found their way into print—and besides, and besides, such is the hypnotic power of creative effort, she had actually believed in some of it when she wrote it. Conditioning, no doubt: there were moments, still, in which she felt the tug of popular opinion, the compulsion to think other people's thoughts. Yes, it would get by; if only it could do more than that!

It was Dr. Wainewright who had given her the idea of

206

writing the article. 'If you are fond of music,' he said, when they went back to his rooms after the concert, 'why don't you write something about the performance we've just heard? It would do you good, take your mind off——occupational therapy, you know.' 'But how should I get it published?' Jael asked. 'I know an editor,' said Dr. Wainewright, 'a chap who was a patient of mine. I helped to pull him through a long illness. He'll publish it, anything you write,' he said, fondling her knee, 'if I ask him to.' 'Supposing I make mistakes in grammar?' 'I'm not sure that there are any rules now,' said Dr. Wainewright, drawing his chair closer to hers. 'Didn't you read that correspondence in the *Daily Leveller*—all about "who" and "whom", and the tyranny of the Objective Case? Lots of people thought that the cases should be standardised—it wasn't fair for a word to be governed by a verb, or even a preposition. Words can only be free if they're equal, and how can they be equal if they're governed by other words?'

'I'd never thought of that,' said Jael.

'They want to standardise the language,' Dr. Wainewright said, 'so that no one shall be better at writing than anybody else. Only quite simple words will be allowed, because it's so embarrassing for other people not to know them. But it won't be altogether easy, because the simplified language will have to be learnt. We can't have people writing just as they like. Or talking either.'

'Who started all this?' asked Jael. 'The Dictator?'

'Not to my knowledge. Somebody wrote to the paper.'

'I could try,' said Jael, doubtfully. 'There are some things I should like to say. But I don't want to make a fool of myself.'

'What does it matter if you do? The world is full of fools—you'd only be swelling the majority. Now if you set yourself up to be an expert, you might find yourself in trouble.'

'All right,' said Jael, 'I'll have a shot.'

'Are you grateful to me?' asked Dr. Wainewright.

'Well, not very. Perhaps just a little.'

'How can I make you more grateful?'

'You know the subject I'm interested in.'

'I hoped you were interested in me.'

'Well, so I am,' and she gave him a slight proof of her interest.

Jael knew little about love-making, nothing, perhaps, for she did not know, and now would never know, whether her strange experience in the sky had anything to do with love. She might have dreamed it. Like a dream it had coloured her life, leaving her with an almost unbearable nostalgia for it and the sense of oneness and wholeness that it gave her. Only then had she been herself, no, not herself but much more than herself, because for the first and only time she had wanted nothing; her being had been fulfilled in someone else's. Now she was much less than herself, for she was living only by her will, living on a grievance, living to get her own back. Get her own back! But how could she, since 'her own', the essential part of her, was irretrievably lost—lost in the sky, scattered among the elements, like the ashes of someone who has been cremated. Perhaps she had really died then, and this new self was a changeling who occupied her body in the same way that her new face occupied the site of her old face. But no, it couldn't have been then that she lost herself; even a spiritual experience recognises facts; and the fact was that until she saw herself in the mirror—shamed, parodied, outside, she had remained more or less the same inside. Michael's bewilderment when he saw her in the hospital, his embarrassment, his coldness, might have warned her; but it hadn't. It had shaken her, but she had tried to believe it was a passing mood, which Time would put right.

She would never get her own back, in the sense that

mattered most. But something she would get back, if she caused the Dictator's downfall, or better still, if she destroyed him with her own hand: the sense of counting for something, of being fulfilled as a person, even if she died in the attempt. And there were still moments when her moral indignation against the Dictator seemed to her noble, as if she was doing humanity a service, not just avenging herself.

She tried to think so now, while Dr. Wainewright's eager hands travelled over her, above, below, around, sometimes caressing the skin of her body, which was so much more responsive than her face—so much more responsive that every now and then, between her bouts of almost anguished resistance to him, as if he were the one creature in the world with whom she had nothing in common, she felt twinges of physical desire that bitterly distressed and shamed her. At such times she found herself breathing almost as heavily as he was and half wishing that every breath might be her last.

'Does the Dictator have these pleasures?' she managed to bring out. 'If so, they are too good for him. But I suppose all men need physical love, just as women do,' she giggled.

'As a matter of fact he doesn't,' Dr. Wainewright giggled, too, and fondled her still more intimately.

'You mean he is too old? I thought men never were.'

'It's not exactly that. No, don't take your hand away.'

'You mean he doesn't like women? He prefers his own sex, as some people have always said—and it may very well be true—the way he treats us.'

'I didn't mean that either.'

'Darling, you are so mysterious.'

'I should be less mysterious, if you were kinder to me.'

'But aren't I being kind?'

'You could be kinder.'

'How?'

'By taking off this sackcloth that you will insist on wearing. It discourages me.'

'But it's Sackcloth Day today.'

'It was, but midnight is just striking, and you know what that means.'

'What does it mean?'

'It means that all who love each other should show it by their acts.'

'Is it a law?'

'No, just a *memento amare*. The Dictator doesn't make laws, as you know, or very few—he just issues edicts.'

It's now or never, Jael thought, and started to take off her clothes. They had been messed about so much that she couldn't at once find the fastenings.

'No, let me help you.'

But his eager fingers fumbled and shook so much that her dress was being torn, not taken, off her. And not only her dress, all of her was being torn; her skin was coming off with her dress; she was being flayed.

'Ah, here it is!'

'What is?'

'Your skin—your own dear skin—it's mine at last.'

He began to babble incoherent endearments, pressing his head against her neck. Then he remembered and with many a long-drawn chuckle—ha-ha, ha-ha, ha-ha—he began to take his own clothes off.

'Oh please!' cried Jael. She didn't know for what she was imploring; was it to be let off, to be released? Or was it for guidance, for inspiration?

How different he looked without his clothes. Pathetic, in a way, with nothing but his flesh to recommend him. All at once he seemed to feel himself inadequate. He shivered slightly and murmured:

'Darling, let's talk.'

'But do people talk when they are making love?'

He scented a trap in this, and answered; 'I'm told they do. It wouldn't be quite . . . quite friendly, would it, if they didn't? There's such a lot to say. I mean, we've such a lot to say, to explain why—well, no, not to explain, because it explains itself, doesn't it?—but to say something—that goes *with* the feeling. It should spring to the lips, shouldn't it? If it doesn't, something must be missing. It isn't an occasion like any other, is it? I mean, it's every part of us that is involved—our voices, too. Nothing must be left out or forgotten.' He looked at her appealingly and a little timidly, seeming like some strange shaggy animal in his nakedness, and vulnerable and defenceless for all his brave intentions. And he was shivering, whether from desire or cold or nervousness, he himself could not have told.

'Say something, please,' he said, 'just . . . just to start the ball rolling.'

'What shall I say?'

'Say that you love me, even if you don't mean it.'

She tried to say it and couldn't, there were so many other things she wanted to say. Mouthings in the tone of love escaped her, but without loving words, for she couldn't bring her tongue to frame them. Panic seized her, for during her wordless monologue he had pulled back the bedclothes, and half pushed, half lifted her into the bed. She felt against her the hardness of his body which his clothes had softened and concealed. She sat up straight in bed and cried:

'Oh no, oh no, I can't!'

'All right, all right,' he soothed her, confidence returning to him with the warmth that was stealing through his limbs from her and from the bedclothes. 'Easy does it. If you're not in a hurry, darling, nor am I. I like it better this way— just a little at a time so that we can find out about each other. You're my very dear friend, don't be frightened. I'll put the light out, if you like.'

'No, no,' she muttered, looking downwards at his tousled head, half-wishing she could love it.

'All right, then. This is my arm, you see, that just goes round you. It's nothing to be afraid of, is it, I'm really rather proud of it.' And he flexed the muscles so that they dug into her side. 'And this is you—but I'm not greedy, darling, I don't want to know all your secrets straight away —I'll give you plenty of time, if you'll give me time. Ask me to look for something and I'll find it. Have you a little mole, perhaps, that you've kept hidden from me?'

She didn't answer.

'I ought to know,' he coaxed her, 'because I've seen you before, for duty, not for pleasure—though it was a pleasure, too, and then you didn't mind, so don't mind now, dear, darling 97. If you have a birthmark, I should love it. Some people have birthmarks in the most unexpected places. It's like their signature, written on them, a sign to know them by. I knew someone once——' he stopped.

'Yes?' said Jael.

'Oh nothing, darling.'

'But I want to know, because perhaps I have it, too, and then I could show it to you.'

'Oh no, you haven't. No one else has, and it isn't interesting, only just a birthmark.'

'How do you know? It might be interesting to me—most interesting. I felt so happy, I was just dropping off to sleep and now you've spoilt it all.'

'I've told you, it was only a birthmark.'

'Yes, but what?'

'Why do you want to know?'

'Because I want to love you.'

She looked down at him, with all the tenderness her Beta face could muster. Once more he hesitated, and then said:

'If you want to know, it was shaped like a heart.'

'How touching, how romantic! And where was it?'

'Just below . . . just below . . . the heart itself.'

'But how wonderful, how symbolical, to have two hearts —one inside, and one out! And whose was it?'

'Oh, somebody's—a patient's.'

'A man patient's or a woman patient's? You don't seem sure.'

'Being with you confused me—it was a man patient's, of course.'

'Why "of course"? A woman might have a heart-shaped birthmark just as well as a man.'

Looking down, she saw how agitated he was; the sensuality had left his face: it was all wariness and apprehension. His nakedness seemed a separate fact, apart from him, and an unpleasant one, and his whole body, that had looked so proud and sure of itself a moment since, seemed drained of life, as if it had been punctured.

'Don't be silly,' he snapped. 'I know my patients like the palm of my own hand.'

'Was it the Dictator's?' she asked casually.

At that he jumped straight out of bed, and stared at her with terror—yes, with terror—in his eyes.

Almost her first thought was: I shall never see him again.

CHAPTER TWENTY-FIVE

DAZED with shock and triumph, Jael walked slowly home and softly let herself in. Joab was asleep; she could hear the gentle, regular snores which seemed so typical of his personality. Far too excited to go to bed, she paced the sitting-room feeling as victorious as if she had already beaten the Dictator to his knees. Yet as her pacing gradually calmed down her excitement, so it also chilled her spirit; for what, after all, did her success amount to? She knew now what the Sign was: paradoxically it was a heart, the very organ the Dictator lacked. But just as he didn't wear his heart upon his sleeve, neither did he wear the sign in any place where you could see it; he would not, like the Emperor in the story, parade his nudity through the deserts and streets of the New State. Nudity! The thought of it made her flesh creep; it was only tolerable to the eyes of love. Her thoughts belittled it and with it the birthmark, which seemed a trivial physical sign to distinguish the Dictator. Much as she hated him, her thoughts had invested him with grandeur; they had never been able to comprehend him, any more than if he had been God. And now a birthmark, just as if he was the most commonplace of mortals! The long-lost child, with a strawberry-mark on his right arm! What a let-down, what an anti-climax.

And yet to her tired mind and changing mood the mystery persisted, indeed was reborn in a different form: the mere idea that a man, distinguished by nothing more remarkable than a birthmark, could make his will, his wicked will, prevail over the wills of thousands, bending them to his, and never with more public acclaim than now, when he had turned their little rising into a vote of confi-

214

dence in himself! Not without violence, not without bloodshed, as he had pretended; no one knew, no one would ever know, what the Inspectors with their pulverising arts had done to the insurgents. Yet she had escaped; she, a marked woman, who had done everything to make herself conspicuous, had never been molested. Why? Not for the first time she asked herself, why had she been spared?

The question struck her almost like a blow, and in the midst of her pacing she stopped dead. Her eyes mechanically sought the window-sill where, hardly alive but certainly not dead, stood the cineraria, whose dark blue velvet petals, long since shrivelled, had once enshrined a hope so strong that it seemed like a fulfilment. Tending it, trying to find out what was good for it, she had nourished something in herself that perhaps was still alive, however overlaid by the destructive impulses which governed her now. Was it that which had preserved her, the unknown spring in her own life, which wanted to create, not to destroy? But how could it have preserved her? How could a hope exist without an object? And she had ample proof that the object had ceased to exist—she had seen its extinction in his face, she had seen it in her looking-glass, no other proof was needed. Had some virtue from the giver lived on in his gift, protecting her? In a world of substitutes, this plant alone was real. Battered and untidy as it was, fit only for the dust-bin to which her brother had often bidden her consign it, it had something which was rare in the New State—an organic personality, a life of its own that was nourished on the mystery of its growth. No doubt it was a hot-house flower; to some extent its human cultivators had tampered with it. In days long past they had experimented with flowers, altering the type, producing larger but less fragrant blooms. But now that there were so few flowers left upon the earth—a handful, perhaps, in every country—men's one idea was to keep them alive, to promote their natural growth, to make them happy in their own way. Nothing was imposed on them, no regimentation, no standardisation, their slightest whim was gratified. How spoilt they were, the darlings! And none more spoilt than hers. On it she had lavished all the love and care that she would have lavished on the giver, had not he— Could it be that the flower, more faithful than he was, had shown its gratitude, and through by-paths of the spiritual world, which even the scientist Inspectors had not yet explored, lent her a helping hand, so that instead of being pulverised and scattered to the elements, she was still in being, still able to think and feel for herself, and plan revenge?

In the hospital ward those other cinerarias, the plastic kind, still stood by every bed-head; and the patients liked them just as much as if they had been real. Even at its best, hers had never reached their artificial perfection; her fellow-patients had condoled with her on hers. Theirs came from a factory; and if one was knocked over, or damaged in some way, the matron got in touch with the factory, and the factory replaced it. But hers came who knew how, or who knew whence, and was an emblem of love, the love she had known for such a short time, the love she had been robbed of when she was robbed of her face.

She did not blame him, she had never blamed him, for who could go on loving something which no longer was the thing he had loved, more and worse than that, which had been changed to resemble every other object of its kind— the Beta face? Beta is best—but best for what? Not for a god-like Inspector, whose fancy was at liberty to roam where it chose, until it lit on her. She did not blame him, but she did blame the Dictator.

Had the Dictator, she wondered, muddled by sleepiness and all the experiences she had been through, a Beta face? And was this ridiculous heart implanted on the skin, the only means by which the Head of the State could be identified? Did even that august personage have to bear some

216

sign of mortal weakness, some trivial token of individuality so that those who knew (of whom she was one) could say, beholding it: 'This is the Dictator!' ? Of course not, for the Dictator was a man, and had the privilege of looking like a man, not a mere replica of other men.

Was it possible that the idea of standardisation could ever really bore people? Could it ever be rammed down their throats too hard? Could she, Jael, add one more to the infinite number of variations which the Dictator had invented to make it appetising, which would somehow show it up? Could she inoculate them against it by giving them an over-dose of it?

But as she sat down before her typewriter a thought came to her that made her jump to her feet. Why write when what she wrote would never be printed?—for Dr. Wainewright was now her mortal enemy, as she was his: he would never approach the editor on her behalf, and without his intervention, the article would never be accepted. By drawing his secret out of him, she had drawn her own sting. Sickened with frustration and defeat, her head drooped till it nearly touched the table. And then, as suddenly, it jerked upwards. For, of course, he would persuade the editor to print it. He would have to! All she need do was to enclose with the typescript a covering note—'Dear Dr. Waine-wright'—the 'Dear' could be left out—'In view of what you told me last night—this morning—a piece of information which will be all the more interesting to the outside world as coming from you—I have no doubt at all that you will see your way to get this printed. Otherwise—but I need not say what "otherwise" means to a man of your discernment, exemplified unprofessionally, as well as professionally'—something like that.

Blackmail, perhaps; but it would bring him to heel.

Jael sat down again: the typewriter looked much more co-operative this time.

CHAPTER TWENTY-SIX

JAEL's article duly appeared but the manifestations did not start at once: it was several days before the rumours and whispers and jokes, and the furtive conversations at street corners, suddenly broken off, began to affect the surface of life in Cambridge. At first they took the form of an outbreak of mistake-making which was especially active among typists and female secretaries, with one of whom every businessman and civil servant, however unimportant, was provided. These went out of their way to make mistakes in grammar and spelling, to put words in the wrong order, and make nonsense of the simplest statement. When reproved they either giggled or pertly remarked that they understood that it was not good form, or the Dictator's wish, that their work should be accurate. 'As long as anyone makes mistakes, we ought all to make mistakes,' they argued. 'It wouldn't be fair to the others if we didn't. They can't help it if they're not as quick as we are, but we can help it if we're not as slow as they are.'

'That's all right, my girl,' the employer would say; 'but if you go on doing it, you'll be fired.' To which they replied: 'All right, Armstrong 93, but you'll find that we all do the same.' And this was true: the citizens of the New State were so highly suggestible, and so well aware of what was passing in each other's minds, that they not only used the same arguments to justify their mistakes, but made the same mistakes.

'I can't think what's come over you, Jael,' said Joab. 'You used to be a first-rate, no, I won't say a first-rate, but quite a good Beta-rate typist. And now you seem all over the place. What's this you've written? "The birthrate

among chiropodists has declined from 111% to 92%."
It should be, of course, "from 11% to 9.2%". If what you
wrote was correct, we should have to be building the
chiropodists a new housing estate. As it is, we shall have to
allocate 1.8% of their present dwelling-space to the french
polishers, who for some reason, which is no concern of my
Department, are more procreative.'

'I can't help it,' Jael replied, who had taken some trouble
to think up this particular blunder, 'it just slipped out. But
I don't regret it, nor must you, because it's just an example
of the New Outlook, according to which any mistake is
valuable, because it emphasises our common humanity, by
showing we are all liable to err.' She spoke patiently as to a
child. 'You wouldn't like me to shame my fellows by not
making mistakes, would you? Nor would the Dictator.'

'I can't answer for the Dictator,' replied Joab, tartly,
without that drop in the voice with which he usually uttered
the great name; 'but unless your work improves I may have
to speak to Dr. Wainewright about you. Besides, how do
you know the Dictator does encourage, or even sanction,
mistakes as such? He hasn't said so. It all comes from that
article in the *Leveller*, which many people think ill-advised.'

'We are waiting for his pronouncement,' Jael said
demurely. 'All we know is that a respect for mistake-
making, and a belief in the essential desirability of mistakes,
is inherent in his political theory.'

Joab smiled. 'I shall believe it when I hear it from his own
lips,' he said. 'In the meanwhile will you kindly make the
necessary corrections? I don't want the new Housing
Scheme ruined, especially not by mistakes made at this
office. By the way, how are your headaches?'

'My headaches?'

'Dr. Wainewright told me you were suffering from
headaches.'

'He was my only headache,' Jael said.

'Oh, really? I thought you were rather partial to him.'

When the time came for Joab to sign his letters, he found this piece of dialogue embedded in one of them.

'Gracious Dictator, Jael, are you mad?'

'You mustn't expect perfection.'

'Why ever not?'

'Because it would be very anti-social.'

In a few days' time, however, he was obliged to accept her errors with a shrug, so much headway had the New Outlook made. Conditioned into being suggestible, the population had no tradition of behaviour to oppose to it; they went down like ninepins, as before an epidemic. Besides, it was such fun, both to act upon and to talk about. The general drop in standards made everybody happy. People vied with each other as to who could produce the most ingenious blunders, and make others make them, for it was even more fun to watch than to do. The spirit of the practical joke took hold of them, and every day became an April Fools' Day. People were always sending their friends running on false errands, often to non-existent destinations; loaded with letters, parcels, baskets or sacks they trudged along, to be greeted at their journey's end with shrieks of laughter, and sent back to where they had come from. All this provoked intense hilarity, never had there been so much laughing in the New State, and the only time when the mirth seemed to abate was during the official 'Five Minutes' Laughter' programme—then they all wore long faces and could not squeeze a smile out of themselves. Daily life was becoming seriously disorganised, even the essential services were being interrupted, when Jael launched her second bomb-shell.

'It has reached our ears,' she wrote, in the course of a long article, 'that certain people are devoid of birthmarks. Whether it can be considered an advantage to have a birthmark, or an advantage not to have one, I hesitate to say, but clear it is that whichever way you look at it, *it isn't fair*. People who haven't what they feel to be the privilege of a birthmark will want to have one, and those who regard them as a blemish will want to get rid of them. It is essential to the success of the New Outlook—and in saying this I feel sure I am only echoing the wishes of the Dictator—that the position *vis-à-vis* birthmarks should be regularised. Either we should all have one, or none of us should have one. No doubt in his good time the Dictator will give us a ruling. It is obvious that the accident of birth has nothing to do with the ethical problem involved, except to aggravate it, for who can help what he is born with, whether it be regarded as a blessing or a curse? The great thing is that we should be all alike. I myself, being without a birthmark, regard my condition as an intolerable hardship, and when I think of someone having, for instance, a heart-shaped birthmark just below his heart, as I am told some person has, Bad Egg floods my system and my blood-pressure is dangerously increased. Why should not I have such a birthmark? Why should not any of us? The owner of this birthmark is, to my mind, the luckiest man alive. Indeed, I have sometimes wondered whether anyone so lucky *ought* to be alive! Surely he is a menace to the State, being such a cess-pool of Bad Egg. Who is he, that is what we all want to know! Let him come forward and declare himself! But I don't think he will, for he is someone, so I have been told, who shuns publicity and works in secret. He would not like his identity to be revealed, for if it was, who knows what might not happen! But if he won't declare himself, can we not drag his secret out of him?

'I have an idea, and I am sure that it will win the approval of the Dictator. It is this. Let any P. and D. be free to challenge any P. and D. he meets to bare his breast and prove that he, at least, is not the owner of the birthmark.

And let the one so challenged have the right to challenge the challenger! If neither party has anything to hide, if neither is guilty of harbouring the birthmark, then with a brief exchange of courtesies the examination will quickly be concluded to the satisfaction of both sides. But should the challenge be resented, it will be for the challenger to extort, by force if need be, the essential proof, and if he cannot do this unaided, to call on the bystanders to help him.

'We do not believe that such an occasion will arise. We believe that every patient and delinquent, not only in Cambridge but in all the land, will be only too glad to demonstrate his innocence, by offering his bare breast for scrutiny—knowing that, when he does so, one drop at least of the poison that infects the State will be dissolved.

'And should the culprit be discovered, should the tell-tale heart at last be revealed to the pure daylight, what then? What punishment is great enough for the wretch who from his birth has enjoyed a privilege denied to all his fellows? It is not for us to say what the penalty should be, but in the name of the Dictator, let it be swift and short!'

A day or two passed and nothing happened. The craze for mistake-making went on unchecked. On the whole it was good-tempered, for few escaped the attentions of the practical jokers, and those who had suffered made others suffer in their turn, so there was no feeling of unfairness. And then the pastime seemed to lose its hold; the fun went out of it and instead of laughter pealing through the streets, an ominous silence fell. Men eyed each other with suspicion and hostility. The man so scrutinised would give himself a quick look, wondering if something was amiss with his appearance, or, if he guessed what was in the other's mind, give him a look as straight and hostile as his own. And this went on for several days, the tension growing, until at last someone—nobody ever knew who—stopped a man and challenged him.

A knot of onlookers collected, and formed a ring round the two challengers. The chill March wind made it essential to wear plenty of clothes. The first man took his coat off, then his pull-over, then his shirt. The onlookers came closer, excited by the striptease, and when at last he fumbled with his vest and lifted it above his head, they made a strange expectant sound, half-way between a growl and a groan. But the hairy chest was innocent of a birth-mark. When the challenger was called on to disrobe, the same sound followed, and the same result: his naked chest, white as a baby's, showed no blemish. But when the two men, who happened to be friends, shook hands and parted, another sound rose up from the spectators, relief mingled with disappointment; then smiles broke out on their faces; they slapped each other on the back and went their way.

Now that the ice had been broken, and the age-old convention, that a man's body should be treated with respect as something personal and sacred, to be struck, perhaps, in anger, but not exposed in public unless its owner wanted it to be, the challenges became more frequent. For the spectators, if there were any, they took on the quality of an entertainment. Often it was a slapstick comedy, which evoked shouts of laughter, sometimes good-natured, some-times cruel; but in not a few cases, when either of the men was hot-tempered and resentful, or when both were, it degenerated into a gladiatorial show, and aroused extreme excitement and partisanship among the lookers-on. Fights became frequent; shirts were torn from backs; bloody noses were common; sometimes there were more serious injuries, and the contestants were carted off to hospital. And the behaviour of the spectators deteriorated likewise. From keeping the ring and egging on the combatants, they joined the fray and it became a free-for-all.

So popular were the challengings that attendance at the recognised places of entertainment began to fall off, especially at the churches. Sometimes, particularly at night, these heart-searchings, as they were often called, took the form of pitched battles between rival factions, each of which had its own ringleader and attacked the others at sight.

The newspapers had always been allowed extreme latitude of expression, even when criticising the régime; now they excelled themselves. The cartoonists above all were in clover; they had never very strictly observed the bounds of decency but now they threw discretion to the winds. Challengers and challenged were portrayed in every degree of dishevelment, and often in dubious or even obscene conjunctions, their bodies plastered with enormous and fantastic birthmarks, with captions and letterpress to correspond. 'Where is your heart, old man? You're not looking in the right place, chum.' The variations on this sort of joke were endless. For a time it seemed as though the humorous aspect of the thing might get the better of the serious; for the citizens of the New State loved a laugh—for which, for so many years, they had had very little opportunity and still less inclination. But they had also been for many years denied the outlet of violence, and the appeal of this was stronger. To their extreme suggestibility the presence or absence of a heart-shaped birthmark became an overwhelming symbol of inequality; and the owner of it, wherever he might be, the best-hated man in the New State. Almost every day rumours got abroad that he had been discovered; but they all proved to be unfounded. Many birthmarks, even some heart-shaped birthmarks, were forcibly brought to light (for their owners did not show them voluntarily), but they were never in the right place. 'Is your heart in the right place?' the cartoonists playfully inquired; but in fact they never were.

To begin with, the female population adopted an aloof attitude to all this: it was just ordinary men playing at being he-men; nothing else could be expected of them. If only they had had their faces betafied, it was suggested, there would be none of all this nonsense. So when they saw a scuffle, they passed on with heads held high. But they could not long resist the infection of it; where men led, they had to follow. They could not forever be indifferent to what was happening to their husbands and boy-friends. Some of them became fanatical partisans of this or that challenger (for there was no limit to the number of times one man might challenge another) and made a cult of him amounting to hero-worship. Sometimes they even threw themselves into the rough-and-tumble, getting their faces scratched and hit, and their clothes torn off. On such occasions they were like Maenads, half beside themselves. The soberer sort did not venture out at night, except in little groups; and even then they often had to take to their heels.

At last the inevitable happened, and a man was killed. There he lay, stark naked, with his eyelids feebly fluttering; then the fluttering ceased. After a moment of shocked silence, one of the participants stole forward, and almost reverently closed his eyes. The day following was a day of mourning, and not a single outbreak took place. But the day after there were one or two sporadic outbreaks of a rather half-hearted character, and soon, to nearly everyone's relief, the movement was in full swing again. Nor, when the second man was killed, did an interval of mourning follow. Indeed, the very next day there was another death. This time it was Jael's friend Judith, who had taken no active part in the affray, but who received on her temple a brick-bat meant for someone else.

CHAPTER TWENTY-SEVEN

AND what were the Inspectors doing all this time? Nothing, it seemed; they were seen going about as usual, but astonishingly they did not interfere. At first the gangs of rowdies melted away at their approach, but when they found that they were not being pulverised, or arrested, or even followed, they took heart and soon started again in another place.

There were, of course, law-abiding citizens of the New State who regretted these demonstrations, which were making their lives both difficult and dangerous. The more timid spirits did not like to go down a street even by daylight where birthmark baiting was in progress, and wasted time and shoe-leather by making long detours to reach their work. Of such was Joab, who had a natural aversion to danger. Usually he chivvied Jael, reproaching her with her habits of lateness, and often started out in the mornings before she did. But now, however late she was, he waited for her, and during the walk stayed close by her side, sometimes even taking her arm, which he had never done before.

Jael herself could hardly believe in her success, but as each day brought new proof of it, new proof that the surface of the régime, at any rate, was cracking, she could not doubt and her exultation mounted. She lived in her idea of the Dictator's downfall: no other life was real to her. She had rid herself of Dr. Wainewright: the blackmailing letters with which she accompanied her articles, and which, naturally, were never answered, except by his acceptance of them, were the only form of communication she had with anyone—for with her brother her relations, never easy, no longer meant anything to her. For Judith she did feel a twinge of remorse. She remembered the old days when friendship was the main interest of her life and Judith her chief friend. Was it not Judith who had advised her against having her face changed, and so altered the whole course of her existence?—for had she done it voluntarily, as she meant to, she would never have had the grievance which came from having had it forced on her by a trick. And then she would never have met Michael, or if she had, he would never have noticed her, let alone taken a fancy to her: she would have been just another Beta, and she knew how he felt about Betas. He would have made her pay the nominal fine for not knowing the right epithet for Alpha—what was it today? she idly wondered—and never seen her again. It was generous of Judith—a sign of true affection—that despite the fact that she herself was plain and welcomed betafication both in principle and practice, she hadn't wanted it for Jael; she wanted Jael to keep her flawed, fragile prettiness.

Afterwards Jael had drifted away from her, as she had from all her former friends; she had lost her craving for friendship, she did not even remember what it was like to be attached to another human being by those ties. She lived a dedicated life, with but one aim, and that aim excluded friendship; even the Beta women with their common faces, and almost common consciousness, knew more of it than she did. Yet a tear for Judith welled up and flowed down her unfeeling cheek; she felt almost like a murderess, and wondered if she would ever be one.

Meanwhile, daily life in the New State was coming to a standstill. The process was not regular; on some days the outbreaks were more serious than on others; days would pass without a fatality, and then on some one day several people would be killed. Sometimes the excitement of bloodshed resulted in sexual orgies; the women who hung about

227

the outskirts would not only throw themselves into the fray but rely on their immunity from birthmark risks to receive a warm and tender welcome from the combatants. Nor were they disappointed, though sometimes the welcome was rougher than they expected.

The newspapers, which had begun by making capital out of these disorders, were puzzled, the happenings were too fantastic and surprising for the cartoonists to satirise them; their lampoons lagged far behind the reality. So they looked for other subjects which might have the appeal of novelty; but there was no other subject, violence and destruction held the field and would admit no rival. Even the expedient of making individual cartoons of the most popular heroes and heroines of the affrays began to pall; the public were more interested in their feats than in their faces.

There came a moment when the craze seemed to have reached its peak. Inconvenience is a powerful enemy that even violence has to reckon with, and the disturbances, thrilling as they were, were also highly inconvenient to many. In certain quarters there was a shaking of heads and a shrugging of shoulders; would these demonstrations, the most picturesque and exciting the New State had ever known, end in boredom? Or in a laugh that turned against itself?

In this almost imperceptible lull people began to ask themselves: 'What has happened to the Dictator? Why doesn't he make some comment on all this? It isn't going to be easy for him, of course; how will he explain this breakdown in his theories? His policy, he has always told us, was to make violence impossible: hence the daily dose of bromide, the dancing, the sackcloth, everything. He has been made to look a fool, of course; all his theories have been proved wrong; we have given up taking bromide, or wearing sackcloth, we only dance when we think we will; we have done everything he told us not to, and yet

228

here we still are, flourishing and enjoying ourselves: but it would be fun to know what he has to say about it. I suppose he is too frightened to say anything. But he ought to say something, or what is a Dictator for? Where is that voice we used to hear, in and out of season? Why this silence? How long has it been going on for? A week, a fortnight, a month? It's all very well, but a Dictator has his duties, just like other people. He ought to give us a lead. All these years he has been making us dependent on him, and then when we want his advice—no, not his advice, we've had too much of that, but his opinion—he doesn't say a word! If he would just tell us what he thought about this birth-mark baiting, or beating, so that we could do the opposite— or even do what he told us—it wouldn't be the first time! It isn't fair that he leaves us to ourselves! We've been very good subjects; not many people would have put up with what we've put up with! He ought not to neglect his business so! If he was one of us, he'd have been fined for it, or made to wear P.S.! It isn't fair! He's always down on privilege, yet no one is so privileged as he is!' and much more in this strain.

Jael seized upon this moment of uncertainty to write a third article. She pointed out that the bungalows on the new Housing Estate were larger than the old ones: this discrepancy, she explained, was most unfair; the lucky dwellers in the new bungalows were already giving themselves airs, whereas their under-housed neighbours were stinking of Bad Egg. The only remedy was to pull down all the older houses, and replace them with houses of the new type. While the work of demolition was in progress, the evicted householders could be accommodated in the bungalows of the New Estate; and if the squatters or their hosts felt that they had a grievance, well it was just too bad. Share and share alike applied to houses as to other things.

As before, nothing much happened for a day or two.

Then a group of men assembled outside the last house in a row, looking at it with a purposeful and measuring eye. They did no more; but the next day they came again with crowbars, pick-axes, and sledgehammers, and after piling these in a workmanlike manner against the low wall that divided the little square garden from the pavement, one of them strode up to the door and rang the bell. 'Maybrick 92,' he said to the woman who opened it, 'we've come to knock your house down.'

'Knock my house down?'

'We're doing it for your sake, of course. We're the slum-clearance squad. Didn't you realise you were living in a slum?'

'Slum my foot!' said the woman angrily; as with all Betas her age was difficult to guess. 'This house is as good as the next one, or as any of the houses in the row, and I'll thank you to keep your dirty feet off my doorstep.'

'You're right,' the man said, 'it is as good as the other houses in the row, but they're not good enough, and you ought to be ashamed of living in it. Anyhow, they've all got to come down.'

'Who says so?'

'We do, and so would the Dictator, betafied be his name, if he hadn't been struck dumb.'

'But what's wrong with this house?' asked the woman, astonished and bewildered.

'It's all right in its way,' the man said, 'but it doesn't compare with the houses in the New Estate. You ought to be ashamed to live here.'

'But I'm not, I'm proud to live here.'

'You may think you are, but underneath you're reeking of Bad Egg. We got a whiff just now.'

'Bad Egg,' shouted the woman, 'my husband will give you Bad Egg when he catches you!'

'There are a good many of us,' said the man, indicating

his companions, who moved forward and stared at the woman with expressionless faces. 'You'd better be reasonable. We've got you fixed up with Landru 91 and Bluebeard 92 in the first Section of the New Estate. You're lucky; there are only eight others besides you.'

Just then an Inspector, in all his panoply of plume and brass and silver, came striding by, and glanced incuriously at the couple on the doorstep and the knot of workmen standing on the pavement in attitudes of repressed activity.

'Here! Here! Inspector! Please help me!' the woman cried. 'They're trying to pull my house down.'

The Inspector raised his eyebrows, and his epaulettes, as who should say, 'this is none of my business.' Then he withdrew his gaze, and passed by on the other side.

'You see, Maybrick 92?' the man said. 'You won't get any change out of the Inspectors. Beta resign yourself; the State knows what's best for you.'

The woman looked past her tormentor, wondering if some passer-by would help her. Not far away another group, and a more familiar one, was forming. The challenged man had evidently refused to strip; he was digging his elbows into his sides, and thrusting his head forward. A snarl that chilled the woman's blood went up from the onlookers. 'On to him! Set about him! Worry him!'—so the cries rang out; and after a moment's hesitation the demolition squad joined in the fray. But when the victim, an under-sized fellow, who had had his clothes torn off him and was shivering in the March wind, revealed the fact (together with other facts) that he was innocent of a heart imprinted on his person, and when the challenger had done the same, the demolition men strode back to their pick-axes, wearing a businesslike air. At a sign from their leader up went their ladders, and soon the men were scaling them. Striding the flat roof they looked like giants, or devils, they were so black against the ever-grey sky. Certainly they looked like devils to the woman whose home the house was. When the first splintered slates came sliding to the ground, raising a cloud of dust (the dust that seemed to come from nowhere), she covered her face with her hands; but the workmen raised a cheer.

In the afternoon a pitched battle broke out, between the demolition squad and their supporters, and the dwellers in that row of bungalows and theirs; it raged till nightfall, many bodies lay spread-eagled where they fell. The demolition party were outnumbered, but they had the better weapons and the issue was still in doubt when all at once, amid the shouts and groans filling the air as liquid fills a glass, they heard the three-fold summons.

'Every valley . . . every valley'—then silence so profound it seemed no sound could ever break it.

'Patients and Delinquents,' said the Voice, 'I have been watching with much interest and some concern the latest developments that have been happening here. I did not comment on them, because I wanted to see how you would fare when I should be no longer with you. Patients and Delinquents, I am not immortal, nor (except for your sakes) do I wish to be. And now I am going to let you into a secret. This voice which you have heard from time to time, and which I shall still, for a few minutes more, call my voice, is not my voice at all. My voice is very different. If I said that none of you have ever heard it, that would not be true, but none of you, of this I feel sure, has ever connected it with me. I never meant that you should hear my voice, for I did not think that you would listen to it. The voice I am now speaking with is an Alpha voice, the best voice in the State: the voice with which I shall be speaking to you presently is a Beta voice, and you may have to listen hard to hear it. But I hope that you will listen for I have a special message for you, and one that must come from my own mouth, not through a mouthpiece. I am afraid you will be disappointed with my voice, for it is not the kind of voice you will expect to hear. It is not a commanding voice, or a mesmeric voice, it is the kind of voice for daily conversation —perhaps not even for that. I shall not try to raise it, I shall speak in ordinary tones to ordinary people, if I may call you such. For we have been living in a play, of which I have been the producer and stage-manager—yes, and perhaps the author. You have been—I will not say my puppets, but my troupe of actors: you have learnt your parts from me and played them under my direction. Perhaps you may have thought that it was not a play, that it was real life, but you were mistaken: real life is what you have been living just lately, searching for birthmarks and destroying houses. Who am I to say my play was preferable? I should not dream of saying it, but this I do say, the curtain has come down and the play is over.

'Patients and Delinquents, I must not keep you longer. You have urgent business on your hands: there are still houses to pull down, there is still a birthmark to discover. For many years (how well I realise it) I have stood between you and your desires: a solitary figure, made up of prohibitions and commandments; a Voice, not even a Voice, perhaps, just an abstraction. I existed in your thought of me, what a strange existence! A resentful thought, a contemptuous thought, a frightened thought, a frustrating thought, perhaps—dare I claim it?—an indulgent thought. So many thoughts which I, in thinking about myself, have had to take into account! We all live in the thoughts of other people; but not as I have, I have had no private life, except in the daily bulletins of pros and cons (the cons were in the majority) that my ministers brought to me. Yet I do exist, oh yes, I still exist; tired and old as I am, worn out in your service (but who will believe me when I say this?), I still have an identity of my own, independent of you and what you think of me. In my play I tried to rob you of your identities: for who is not happier without one? But you wanted them back, you wanted them back, and now you have them.

'The play is over, at least I think it is: there just remains this curtain call, and my last message to you. In the old days, when a play was popular, there used to be shouts of "Author!" "Author!" But that was on the first night, not the last, and in answer to the audience's applause. You have applauded me from time to time: even quite lately you applauded me, when I showed you the result of betting on yourselves. But during these past weeks the play has been growing stale: you all feel you ought to have a hand in it, and who shall blame you? You all would like to be the authors, so this author must stand down, but not before he has spoken to you in his proper voice and given you his last message.'

Suddenly the air was empty of sound, as if the gathering darkness had somehow quenched it. Then the Voice was heard again, the same voice: 'Patients and Delinquents, pray silence for the Dictator!' and the strains of 'Every Valley' once more soared into the air.

Afterwards a few people swore they heard a sound, but they must have been mistaken, for no one else did. No one else heard anything, least of all a voice, and after they had listened for what seemed a timeless period, they dispersed.

CHAPTER TWENTY-EIGHT

JOAB was dead; he was killed in the skirmishes that broke out on the night of the Dictator's abdication—as some called it. Jael felt his loss less than she had felt Judith's. This was not surprising, for her brother had never been close to her; from childhood he had been her keenest and most persistent critic. Yet in his way he had been fond of her and she of him. Unwittingly she had leaned on him, and she missed him as a prop, if not as a man.

But events had moved so quickly towards chaos that the ties of family and friendship had ceased to have much meaning. Who is on our side, who? That was what mattered. Jael's revolutionary activities, once known to a few, were soon known to many; more than one faction courted her— she could choose between them. She chose what was for the moment the most radical—the Demolition Squad: with her own hands she helped to break down some more houses. But this group soon lost its following, for it was clear that in the present conditions no new houses would be built, and the occupiers of the New Housing Estate were as unwilling to take in lodgers as the evicted were to seek their hospitality. In the last of several bloody encounters the Demolition workers were badly beaten, and soon became absorbed in other groups. Most of these groups were frivolous, or idealistic or destructive; everybody wanted something undone, hardly anybody wanted anything done. The essential services had almost ceased to work, no regular hours were kept; there had never been much distinction between employer and employed, now there was none. The collective consciousness which the Dictator had fostered lingered on; people still knew what their fellows were feeling, and would rally to anyone who seemed like a leader; but initiative they had none, they could only do what they were told. The most popular pastime was still birthmark baiting; the excitement of it never seemed to pall; and some of the victims had been stripped in public half a dozen times. Many more birthmarks had come to light, but never the right one.

Where were the Inspectors? No one knew; they had vanished, and rumour had it that they had founded a colony of their own, in some distant country, taking with them, some said, the Dictator. But the more general belief was that the Dictator had never existed; he was a hoax, and his last communication to his subjects was the greatest hoax of all.

So things went on, in growing anarchy and chaos, until at last the free-for-all existence encountered a sharp check. Food supplies were running out.

It had not occurred to the rioters that this might happen: the store of tabloid meals had seemed inexhaustible. But it was managed by the Inspectors; no one else knew where to get it, least of all the underlings who were accustomed to distribute it. They still did a job of work at the Food Office, when they felt so inclined, and recklessly handed out the rapidly diminishing store; but the day came when people were not getting enough to eat. Who was to blame? Who was to blame? The civil servants at the Food Office, of course; they were idlers and drones who had neglected their duties. An angry mob collected, and sacked the Food Office, incidentally killing the few employees who happened to be working there. Then the situation became acute: starvation threatened.

There was only one thing to do. It was known that during the Dictator's régime relations with the Underworld had never quite been broken off; as between countries at war, the means of communication still existed, though what they were, and how they operated, no one knew. The hole in the ground through which the Pretty Gentleman's child spokesman had led his followers into the light of day, before his mysterious disappearance, was still there: round and above it, masking it from view, was a low crematorium-like building, whose transverse lines were dominated by a fat, squat chimney, over which, at times, a plume of black smoke hung. The building was defended by an iron palisade, topped with spikes, an unnecessary precaution, for the place, which was only just outside the town, was always shunned by the citizens, who believed that it brought bad luck even to touch the railings. During the disorders many, if not most, of the buildings in Cambridge had suffered in one way or another from the Demolitionists or from gangs bent on pure destruction: but the Hole Hall, as it was called, had never been touched. No one had ever been inside it, except presumably the Inspectors, or the Dictator himself, though they had never been seen to enter it.

The famine created, almost overnight, a Government of a kind, a Committee of Public Safety whose decrees were harsh and peremptory; any infringement of them was punishable by death. Its first act was to impose a curfew, everyone had to be indoors by eight o'clock, so that there were no witnesses when, towards midnight, a handful of men furtively approached the Hole Hall and, with the help of pick-axes and crowbars and one oxyacetylene lamp, broke their way in. Nor did any member of the public know by what means they made contact with the ruler of the Underworld; but contact they did make, and the results of it were posted up in the market-place, next morning.

The Ruler of the Underworld had made his conditions, and as was only to be expected, they were severe. Before he would enter into any negotiations with the people of the so-called New State, he demanded that six of them, three men and three women, should be sent to him as hostages. How they would be treated when they arrived was not stated; but it was stated that they would not be permitted to return. The proclamation concluded by announcing that unless six volunteers for this service presented themselves at the Office of Public Safety before nightfall, the six would be conscripted.

Panic seized the people, at first a silent panic, for they were appalled by the examples which had just been made, some of whom were still hanging from hastily erected gibbets. Accustomed to being treated *en bloc*, the idea that half a dozen should be singled out for a special purpose was almost inconceivable to them. They were conditioned to identifying themselves with the mass, with each other, in fact; and the idea that six of them were to have a quite separate destiny, which they couldn't share with their fellows and which they would have to endure alone, appalled them. The notion of existing in oneself, apart from other people, receiving no support from their thoughts and feelings, was too terrible to be borne. And still more terrible was the fate itself. Under the Dictator, the severest punishment for any offence (apart from the rumoured pulverisations) was that of being sent back to the Under-world. R.E., Returned Empty, whatever it might mean, was still the worst thing that could happen. Unscrupulous kiddy-kuddlers sometimes used it as a threat to frighten refractory charges with. 'You'll be R.E.!'—and then the tears flowed faster, or, from terror, stopped.

The recognition, by each member of the community, of a self-hood that must suffer, and suffer alone, involved a reversal of all their mental processes that acted on them like madness. Being entirely without self-discipline, relying only on the stimulus of what others thought and felt, they had no idea how to meet a situation which was to affect each one of them alone. Mass-suicide, subject as they were to mass-suggestion, they might have understood and acted on; but solitary suicide! Or solitary martyrdom, long drawn out, among indifferent or hostile people, with whose thoughts they could hold no communication, while with the passing of each agonising minute they were driven deeper and deeper into themselves! The thought was so frightful that many went mad as soon as it had penetrated into their consciousness, while others died from shock.

The cry went round: 'A scapegoat! A scapegoat! Where is the Dictator, who has brought all this on us? Where is he? Let him be R.E., instead of us!' A few days before they had collectively forgotten him; now the thought of him once more flooded their minds and with but one association: that he had condemned them all to this terrible punishment—for each man and woman felt that it was he or she on whom the lot would fall. Starvation was bad enough, but that at least they could all face together; this was something far, far worse, a doom that threatening everyone would only light on six.

An outbreak of birthmark baiting started, but it was a feeble affair, for most of the hunters were so weakened by hunger that they could hardly stand; quite often the challengers and the challenged fell down in a heap on top of each other before they had had time to strip. The black-suited myrmidons of the Committee, who had appropriated what food there was left, had no difficulty in crushing the outbreak or in suitably punishing the ringleaders. When night fell, all was quiet in the streets.

CHAPTER TWENTY-NINE

JAEL was sitting alone in the house she had shared with Joab. For twenty-four hours she had eaten nothing and had only once been out. Going out, she had heard the news (her radio no longer worked) and seen the proclamation about the hostages. She had done something else, too, which made her feel light-headed.

It was raining. Rain was a rare phenomenon in the New State. The Inspectors knew how to get drinking water from the clouds; they could get it from the sea, too. But the ordinary patients and delinquents did not know. So in a sense the rain was opportune; for it meant that even if the population died of starvation it would not for the moment die of thirst.

Rain meant a rainy season. In the New State it never rained but it poured, and poured for days, turning the crumbling earthy surface into a swamp. Some parts of the country were flatter than others; the district north of Cambridge was the flattest of all, being part of the old Fens, and would soon be water-logged. How would the people, if there still were any, manage then?

Jael mused on this, and on many other problems connected with the future, though for her they were academic problems, the solution of which, if there was one, she would never see. For she had volunteered to be a hostage, to be Returned Empty to the Underworld. At seven o'clock in the morning, when the curfew was lifted, she would proceed to the Committee's Office and surrender herself. From what she knew and what she had heard, she did not think that anyone would steal a march on her. Only she retained the faculty of private judgment and the power of choice. The others could not act against their collective wish for self-preservation. Of the six hostages, she would be the only volunteer.

As this was to be the last night on earth, whatever happened to her below it, she had decided to spend it sitting up. She would be a long time dead and didn't want to waste her few remaining hours of consciousness. She would spend them communing with herself. The room next door was her bedroom; she had not imagined, when she made her bed that morning, that she would never sleep in it again.

How had she come to her decision? In a flash. In a flash she had seen it was the only thing to do, and the logical outcome of everything that she had done so far. She wanted to assert the uniqueness of her personality, which in its external aspect, at any rate, the Dictator had taken from her. Yes, and in other ways, too; for a time she had been ensnared by the collective consciousness and had reacted accordingly; she had seen herself through other people's eyes instead of through her own. Why did that matter? To Jael it seemed to matter tremendously, but she couldn't have told why.

Did it weigh with her, she wondered, that other people— the whole population of the New State, perhaps—might come to hear that she had voluntarily accepted the role of hostage, and regard her as a heroine? She didn't think so. Nor did she think they would be told; for hitherto the Committee had acted in secret, and suppressed the names of those who, for whatever reason it might be, had disappeared. You could not be a heroine if no one knew you were.

Was she doing it for anybody's benefit but her own? She tried to answer this question dispassionately. In a way, yes. Once she had loved her fellow human beings; she did not love them now, she had seen them do too many unpleasant things. When she reflected that now only five instead of six would have to be conscripted, she felt a certain warmth about her heart. Somebody would get off on her account; but the woman, whoever she was, would never know what she had escaped, and the general panic would be as great as ever. Even if they were told, and they would not be told, that someone had volunteered to be a hostage and by so much had reduced the odds against them, they would still identify themselves with the remaining five.

And Dr. Wainewright? How did she feel about him? He had been her stooge, just as, in a sexual way, she had been his, or would have been, if he could have made her. She had got the better of the bargain: she had used him, but he had not used her. She felt a certain compunction about him for he had loved her, whereas for him she had had no warmer feeling than a few unwilling twinges of sex. That gave him, in the moral balance, an advantage over her—an unfair advantage: for what was the use of being loved, if you could not return it? One-sided love was simply an embarrassment, an intolerable burden on the conscience and the feelings. Anyhow, she could do nothing about it now, for Dr. Wainewright was dead—he was one of the earliest victims of the riots. He had died, and half his secret with him.

Jael thought of the Dictator, her arch-enemy. But she could not think of him clearly, or personally, as it were; her thoughts of him were still mixed up with other people's thoughts; he presented no consistent recognisable picture, not even to her hate. If she couldn't think about him, she could still hate him, and she must; for had not he been her undoing, had he not undone them all? He had corrupted and betrayed the people and was worthy of death. There, almost within arm's reach, lay the scalpel, unsterilised, rusty from disuse, that she was keeping for him. At the sight of it, her resentment against him flamed up once more. And yet she resented her resentment, for it disturbed the calm that had come over her spirit with her decision to dedicate herself—to herself. It was a jarring note in the growing harmony of her feelings.

On the window-sill, beside the scalpel, stood the cineraria, the plant that Michael, while he still loved her, had given her as an earnest of his love. It had survived the outbreaks of violence that had carried off so many human beings. It was still alive, though only half alive, and it would outlive her. It was the only thing she cared for in the world, she cared for it far more than for herself; for herself, except as an emblem of identity, she cared not at all. If only she could give it to someone—someone who would cherish it! But there was no one, no one to whom she wanted to make a gift.

How the rain beat down! It pattered and sometimes drove against the window, it filled the street outside with a soft humming sound. Suddenly she remembered having been told, by a friend older than herself, who had heard it from her mother, that in the old days when plants abounded, and some people had as many as half a dozen in their houses, they used to put them out of doors when it rained, for the rain did them good in a way that artificial watering could not; it washed their leaves, put them in touch with Nature and refreshed their entire beings.

Flower-pot in hand, she went to the front door and opened it a crack. All was dark; the street-lamps no longer functioned; there was no sound but the hiss and patter of the rain. No one would see her if she stepped outside and stood the plant on the earth beside the doorstep.

How the mud squelched! Tomorrow it would be ankle-deep, or worse. Tomorrow was of no interest to her, but she must remember to take the plant back when it had its drink—when she went out at seven o'clock to give herself up. She must not forget. Would they perhaps let her take it with her? In the past, people condemned to death had sometimes been allowed a final boon. She did not think

243

they would; the New Committee had as little respect for personal wishes as the Dictator had had. Yet something she must do, to try to preserve it after she was gone. How hard it was to rid the mind of all desires, to attain the peace she strove for! She would write a card, 'Live cineraria, very precious—please preserve,' and perhaps whoever lived in the house after her, supposing anyone did, would read it and respect her wishes.

She wrote the note. No good putting it with the plant now; it would be washed away or smudged too much to read. She must remember this little duty in the morning, when she put the plant back in the house. Two things to remember, and she didn't want to remember anything! Consciousness wasn't such a blessing after all. Just close her eyes and lose it.

CHAPTER THIRTY

A KNOCKING on the door awakened her, or had she dreamed it? Not on her door, for that was open, but on the street door. There it was again, a soft insistent tapping. When she listened the sound ceased, as sounds so often do. She went to the door and opened it a little, but could see nobody. Opening it wider she saw the outline of a figure, crouching on the doorstep with its back to her.

'Come in, come in!' she said, mechanically; but no sooner were the words out than her whole being tingled with alarm, for the orders were to let no one in during the curfew.

As her visitor crossed the threshold something about her seemed familiar and then Jael knew why: it was the old lady who used to go round the hospitals and had once stopped and talked to her. A nice old thing, the ward sister had called her, and Jael remembered her as a nice old thing. But what a terrible state she was in now! The fur cape that gave her narrow shoulders the breadth of a man's was soaked and matted; her full silk lilac dress, which Jael remembered well, was nearly as black with wet as the black lace over it, and clung to her frail figure pitifully; her indoor shoes were squelching, and oozed bubbles of water at the instep with every step she took: every feeble step, for she could hardly totter, and Jael had to support her into the sitting-room. Shivering uncontrollably she dropped into what had been Joab's chair. There was nothing to be said; the poor old woman's appearance was its own best comment; but there was something to be done, and at once.

'You must change your clothes,' said Jael. 'I have some dry ones here.' She remembered that she would not need

245

the clothes again, and added: 'You can keep them if you like.'

The old lady did not seem to understand, so Jael fetched a dress from the bedroom, and held it out before her.

'I'm afraid it's not as nice as your dress,' she said, as one woman to another. 'Your dress was so lovely. It will be lovely again,' she went on, 'when it's dry.'

The old woman didn't answer, but made a feeble gesture, as though to push the clothes away from her.

'You must take them,' Jael insisted. 'Please take them. It might be serious for you if you didn't.' She spoke slowly and distinctly, as though to a child, and a little doubtfully, too; for in the New State no one, in her experience, had ever got wet through, and she didn't know what the consequences might be.

'You are very kind,' the old lady muttered weakly, in a voice that was like, and yet unlike, the voice that Jael remembered, 'but you mustn't put yourself about for me.'

'I'm not putting myself about,' said Jael. 'I only wish I had something better to offer you.'

The old lady, like most old ladies, wore her own face, she had not been betafied; but she had little or no command over her features, and Jael could not read her thoughts.

'Have you no sackcloth?' she at last brought out.

'Sackcloth?' said Jael. 'Sackcloth?' she repeated. What a strange request! 'Do you mean F.S. or M.S.?' (F.S. meant Full, M.S. Modified Sackcloth: they were always known by their initials.)

'F.S., please.'

Jael had a suit of F.S., though she had not worn it since the time, many years ago, when everybody wore it.

She fetched it, smelling of moth-balls, from a cupboard, and held it diffidently for her guest's inspection.

'Do you really want this?'

The old lady fingered it with a trembling hand.

'Yes, please,' she said.

'Then may I help you on with it? And I have some other clothes here.' She indicated shoes, stockings and under-clothes, a complete outfit that she had brought from her wardrobe.

A look of fear came into her visitor's eyes.

'You are very kind,' she said again, in her low, weak, but curiously distinct voice. 'But I think I would rather do it by myself.'

'Are you sure you won't let me help you?'

'No thank you, I can manage perfectly well.'

She spoke with authority, as well as dignity, and Jael, who found herself obeying, at once betook herself to the next room.

'I'll give her five minutes,' she thought. What was five minutes in this timeless night? Something—for it brought her by so much nearer to her end; the end she had begun to long for; yet somehow she couldn't think about it, she could only think about the old lady and her present plight. To do something for somebody! It seemed years since she had done that. Make her warm, bring her back to health, restore her! For what? For a life that she would enjoy after Jael was gone—but that did not seem to matter much.

Five minutes passed. No sound came from the next room. Give her a little longer, Jael thought. She is too old to be the object of anybody's vengeance. Even the Unholy Office will let her off. She can't have many years to live, but let her live them! In her time, she did nothing but good, going round the hospitals, trying to find out if the patients were comfortable and happy. How the Sister and the nurses laughed at her! And yet they half respected her; when she came into the ward, in her funny old clothes, there was a kind of hush. She said something to me about having been punished: 'Poor child, you've been punished enough.' I wonder how she knew. She doesn't recognise me, why

247

should she? I don't suppose I shall see anyone who recognises me before I am R.E. What would it be like to be R.E.? To be empty, but empty of what? Of life? She didn't think she minded. Of self? Perhaps they would drag the self out of her by some kind of spiritual suction. In her mind's eye she saw the open nozzle of a tube writhing towards her; it would fasten on some part of her where the self was nearest to the surface, a powerful vacuum would form inside it, and then her sentient self would be sucked in and pass like excrement along the tube ... Ugh! But yet, how many problems it would solve! A body going about, unconscious but not inanimate, just surviving, like the cineraria. A sort of sleepwalker.

At the thought, the thought of a selfless state, she had a moment of ecstasy. To be free of herself at last, the self she had so passionately defended from attack! What use had it been to her? It had been the cause of all her troubles. Oh, to be free of it! And free of the collective self, which sometimes visited her—which visited her now, and chilled her ecstasy—investing her conception of R.E. with all its former horror, the horror in which everybody held it. R.E.! R.E.! The poor old creature in the chair, she might be called R.E., for she was drained of almost everything that makes a human being.

She must have been pretty in her time, very pretty. I wonder if it meant anything to her, as it did to me. It must have; it means something to every woman. She doesn't wear a wedding-ring, or any ring: perhaps she was crossed in love, as I was. Perhaps the Dictator had a grudge against her. I can't see much future for her, but I'd like her to live on. I think I'll ask her to take care of my cineraria for me: old ladies like having pets. I needn't tell her why: it would only upset her, and she's been through quite enough already. I'll put her wet clothes in the airing-cupboard and show her where to find them. I shall just say I'm going out. I can't give her anything to eat, though, because there isn't any-thing. I suppose they have some tablets left at the Unholy Office, but no doubt they are keeping those for themselves.

I wonder if the Underworld will really help us in this matter of food. I suppose they will; but what will the price be? Will they want a certain number of us (them, I mean) to work for them, as ants do? Work until they drop down dead, as used to happen in the Labour Camps? Or will they let us go on living up here, and pay a sort of tribute? It won't matter to me what they do, but it will to her; I should like to think that she will end her days in peace.

If the Dictator could see what's happened as a result of all his pretty theories, I wonder what he'd say? Would he kill himself, which is what I am doing? If he didn't, he would find plenty of people who would gladly do it for him, I for one—not only for my own sake, but for the sake of the poor old thing in the next room, who never did anybody any harm, and now look at her!

I haven't looked at her properly. It was rather touching the way she didn't want me to watch her undress—she's too old to mind, one would have thought—especially with another woman, a fellow-sufferer from the Dictator's spite. I could have made it easier for her, but no doubt she has some quirk of modesty dating from days before we took most of our clothes off to dance.

But what a fool I am! I have some food—some tablets which I saved up for an emergency. I quite forgot them yesterday, so much was happening. Now where did I put them? In some safe place, I know.

Jael rummaged in a drawer and at the back, under some handkerchiefs where she had hidden them, she found three tablets, yellow, pink and blue. Breakfast, lunch and dinner they represented—a whole day's rations. At the sight of them she realised how hungry she was, and would have liked to eat the lot, if she was to be R.E.! The yellow one

249

would keep her going till then, but at the thought of 'then' her throat contracted and would hardly let the pilule pass.

No, not in my fingers, Jael thought, that is too squalid, and she looks as if she likes things nicely served, so she went into the kitchen and got out her best dish. It was the size of an old-time butter-dish and divided into three compartments, yellow, pink and blue to match the pills. A pity one of them was empty, but that couldn't be helped. But for the food inside her she might not have been able to attend to the old lady; it was odd how much she wanted to do something for her.

The clock caught Jael's eye.

Gracious Dictator!—oh, that awful phrase—a quarter of an hour has gone by—it's nearly three o'clock—it's nearly three o'clock, only four more hours to zero hour. I must go in and see her—I hope she won't keep me chatting all the time, though. I don't want to be bored my last four hours.

Holding the dish in one hand, Jael knocked at the door, and getting no answer, knocked again. When still no answer came she went into the room.

The old lady was asleep in Joab's chair. She had put on the stockings and struggled into the skirt, but then her strength had failed her and from the waist upwards she was naked. Her back was bent and her head had fallen forward so that it nearly touched her knees. Of her face only her forehead caught the light, the rest was in shadow. Perhaps from some impulse of modesty she was holding her left arm across her breast, the wrist clasped in her right hand. Beside her on the floor her wet clothes were still oozing water. They were not thrown down, she had made a pitiful attempt to fold them.

I mustn't wake her, Jael thought, but is she really asleep, or is she dead? She didn't want to touch her so she came nearer and looked closer: was her heart beating? Her thin arm lay across it, but underneath was something that Jael could only half see. Was it a bruise, perhaps? Or a wound? Some injury she had received from a fall or a blow? Poor darling, even that had not been spared her. Jael bent closer. It was pinkish brown, the colour of dried blood, and tapered almost to a point, as blood might, running down. But no, it wasn't blood, because it was below the skin or in it, not above. And then she saw: it was a birthmark, a heart-shaped birthmark underneath the heart—the Dictator's heart.

She shivered convulsively. Yes, there it was, the Sign that he had spoken of, the Sign that had cost so many lives. And now, thought Jael, it must cost one more.

For a moment she had doubted, but now she didn't doubt. It was too unbelievable not to be believed; all the capacity for belief that Jael had left was re-born into that one conviction. The creeping thing, the snake! Every feeling of love and pity she had had for the fugitive was suddenly reversed, transformed into the hatred that had swayed her heart so long. Thankfulness was an emotion to which she had long been strange; she could not have remembered a time when she felt thankful. But now she felt thankful, overwhelmingly thankful, that she had been spared for this last office. Taking her own life, she was also taking another —that other—that had made her life—everybody's life— unbearable.

She stole across to the window-sill where lay the scalpel that had carved her face up, solitary now, bereft of its habitual companion. As she stood by the window, a sound reached her from the street, which was not the sound of rain, though that sound still persisted. It was another, fuller sound, a kind of roaring, that suggested a dark-red colour, shot with black. But she did not ask herself what it was, she hardly noticed it, for the same noise and the same colour were in her mind, as her hand closed on the scalpel. Now that it was in her hand, she suddenly became conscious of her movements and of the need for secrecy and silence. She tiptoed back and stood behind the chair. The Dictator's head was lolling sideways, exposing a length of withered neck. It would be easier to do it if she could not see her face. Now! Now! But still she could not do it; she needed a moment—two, three moments—to realise exactly what the act meant, its full significance, to her and to history; it was the Dictator she must kill, not an old woman who had taken refuge with her from the storm. She could, she must kill the Dictator, the old woman she could not kill. How keep them apart in her mind—be murderous to the one, compassionate to the other? Need she decide at once? It would be the perfect crime, done under cover of curfew, when nobody could reach her, done too, as few murders had been, under sentence of death, for her own life was already forfeit.

How quiet the room was, and how familiar, except for this red sound, red motes, like drops of blood, beating upon her ear. Keep her mind steady, that was the thing; remember that action was a thing-to-itself that happened after the cessation of thought. From where she stood, there was nothing pretty about the old lady; grey hair, thin and wispy where not matted; shoulders too scraggy to be shown; and this inviting length of corded neck——

The drumming, throbbing noise grew louder, died down, returned with increasing force: it was almost like a tune. Was it really going on in her head? Was it caused by the pressure of her thoughts, or of her blood, and would it stop as soon as she had done what she had to do? Thought would take her no further forward, it would only take her further back. She must act at once. But how could she act when somebody was knocking at the door?

A wave of fury came over her. How dare Fate interrupt her like this? Knocking or no knocking, she would complete her task. Yet to be caught red-handed!

She stopped and listened, and all at once, with the opening of the street door, the sound became much louder, it paralysed her thoughts. She had just time to lay the scalpel down when the room door opened, and Michael stood upon the threshold, in all his gleaming array. 'Why isn't he wet, too?' she thought, but before she had time to speak, the figure on the chair between them stirred and moaned, and the grey untidy head struggled to raise itself.

Michael fell upon his knees in front of it, and Jael, at last able to move, knelt by his side.

'Most gracious——' he began.

Recognition seemed to dawn in the Dictator's eyes. She tried to lift her hand, the right one—her other arm still clutched her breast, as though to keep its secret—but it fell to her side.

'God bless you all, my children,' she murmured in a whisper, 'God bless you.'

Her eyes closed.

'She was trying to say that,' said Michael, 'when she broke down before the microphone. She's been saying it ever since. We had her with us till tonight, and then she slipped away.'

'What is that noise?' asked Jael.

'It's the people in the streets—they're shouting for her, they want her back. It's the fire, too. The whole town is on fire.'

Now that both doors were open Jael could hear the repeated rhythmic cry: 'We want the Dictator! We want the Dictator!'

Jael rose to her feet and on an impulse touched the Dictator's forehead.

'But will they get her?' she said.

Michael, still on his knees, gave a long sigh.

'We must do something for her, Michael,' Jael said, 'or we shall lose her. Quick, some water.' She poured it into a glass and held it to the Dictator's lips, who seemed to drink some. 'And I'll put the jacket on—she couldn't do it.'

Somehow she managed to get the Dictator into the jacket, and drew the sides together across her breast. Then she looked up and for the first time smiled.

'P.S.!' she said. 'Permanent Sackcloth!'

Full of pity, they gazed at the brown figure helplessly.

'They want you back,' said Michael. 'They're crying for you. Can you go to them?'

The old woman shook her head.

'I can't,' she said. 'I'm dying, didn't you know? But you can go to them—only don't let them see you.'

'We can go?' said Jael and Michael, in the same breath.

'Yes, you can go, for all they want's a Voice—a Voice to tell them what I didn't tell them. You have learned by my mistakes.'

'What shall we tell them?'

The dying woman made a great effort.

'Say what I tried to say . . . And then . . . And then . . . You must think out a new play for them—a better one than mine. Together you can do it . . . I had to do it alone . . .' She smiled, an open, child-like smile. Then a line appeared between her brows and her hand fidgeted. 'God bless you both,' she said mechanically. 'Michael knows . . . he knows where everything . . . he was the Announcer . . . He knows how to . . . Take me away from here, because I shouldn't like to stay here . . . and the birthmark . . .'

'I'll see to it,' said Michael.

'But it's the play, the play that matters. Some sort of play, with a happier ending . . . Jael, do you forgive me?'

'If you will forgive me.'

Outside there was a burst of cheering, and renewed cries for the Dictator.

'They're cheering you, not me,' she said, and her head fell forward.

254

Michael couldn't, it was Jael who closed her eyes.

When they realised that they were alone, Jael said:

'Did you come here to find me?'

'No,' said Michael, 'I was looking for her.'

'Then why did you come here?'

'Because I'd always wanted to come here.'

'Why didn't you come?'

'Because I hadn't any excuse. An excuse was what I needed. An excuse.'

'Why did you need an excuse?'

'We all need an excuse.'

'What was yours for?'

'Mistaking the appearance for the reality.'

Why was it that Michael's kisses were real to her, when no one else's had been, not even his, that one time at the hospital? Was it because he loved her now, and hadn't then? After the fullness of his lips the whole room seemed empty; even the silent witness in the chair had disappeared. The cheering, the delirious shouts, the dull red glow beyond the window were like a protection, enfolding them in a ring of flame. A ring of flame! And presently the ring drew nearer, so that what had seemed a metaphor announced itself as a reality, crackling and hissing and darting tongues of fire that licked the window. Releasing each other, they stood looking out; the whole street was ablaze. And not only the street. A furtive rustling started in the room behind them, gnawing and scratching sounds. Turning, they saw puffs of smoke spurting out of floor and ceiling, and at the heart of each a flame. The fiery intruders ran along the floor. Some small, soft, black thing lay in their path: it flared up, glowed and went out, leaving a thin trickle of ash: the last of Jael's veil.

A fire solves all problems but itself. Looking with smarting eyes towards the figure in the chair, which they could hardly see, they did not have to tell each other that this problem had been solved. The fire would keep her secret, guard the anonymity she had so much desired, and, for them, soften the harsh necessity of leaving her. No one would ever see her now. Was it not fitting she should feed a flame, who in her lifetime had been fed on one?

Coughing and choking, they somehow reached the passageway, where it was clearer. Through the opening, in the glare, a tormented shadow seemed to lash the doorstep. Feebly it struck at Jael as she went by, as though in a last spasm of reminder, and she saw the cineraria, scorched by fire and drenched with rain.

'Oh, can we take it with us?'

'Yes.'

'But how?'

'You take it and I'll take you.'

Mounting, she held it in her arms, as he held her; mounting, she saw, through a drifting curtain of prismatic rain-drops, lines of fire running along the roofs, a blue-print of the township drawn in red: the world that Jael knew was being destroyed. Mounting, she felt power flowing into her, she knew not whence. The place they came to was unknown to her, as were the faces that surrounded her. She was clothed in authority, a ritual began of which she seemed to be the centre; Michael bent his knee. Wordless they watched her but she recognised her mission in their eyes and knew what she must say.

'Every valley . . . Every valley . . .'

It was a triple summons.

'Ladies and Gentlemen,' the Voice said. 'God bless you all.'

But Jael did not speak with her own voice, she spoke with Michael's.

January 1953–September 1959.

256

OXFORD

MORE TWENTIETH-CENTURY CLASSICS

Details of a selection of Twentieth-Century Classics follow. A complete list of Oxford Paperbacks, including The World's Classics, OPUS, Past Masters, Oxford Authors, Oxford Shakespeare, and Oxford Paperback Reference, as well as Twentieth-Century Classics, is available from the General Publicity Department, Oxford University Press (JH), Walton Street, Oxford, OX2 6DP.

In the USA, complete lists are available from the Paperbacks Marketing Manager, Oxford University Press, 200 Madison Avenue, New York, NY 10016.

Oxford Paperbacks are available from all good bookshops. In case of difficulty, please order direct from Oxford University Press Bookshop, Freepost, 116 High Street, Oxford, OX1 4BR, enclosing full payment. Please add 10 per cent of published price for postage and packing.

THE ESSENTIAL G. K. CHESTERTON

G. K. Chesterton

Introduced by P. J. Kavanagh

The extent to which G. K. Chesterton is still quoted by modern writers testifies to his outstanding importance in twentieth-century literature. In this selection from his work, P. J. Kavanagh fully explores the many sides to Chesterton's personality and writing. Chesterton the novelist is represented by a complete work, *The Man Who was Thursday,* and his poetic gift is displayed in a fine selection of verse. But the lion's share of the volume goes to Chesterton as essayist and journalist. Here we can enjoy his lively writings on the issues and debates of his day.

'Mr Kavanagh's selection is extremely rewarding.' John Gross, *Observer*

AN ERROR OF JUDGEMENT

Pamela Hansford Johnson

Introduced by A. S. Byatt

Dr William Setter exchanges his plush Harley Street consultancy for a job, unofficial and unpaid, as rehabilitator of social misfits. One such misfit is a juvenile delinquent whom he suspects of having kicked an old woman to death. Slowly becoming convinced that the boy is a callous murderer, Setter finds himself obliged to make a moral judgement, not only on the boy but on himself.

THE SMALL BACK ROOM

Nigel Balchin

Introduced by Benny Green

Sammy Rice is one of the 'back-room boys' of the Second World War. The small back room of the title may also be Sammy's own living quarters, where he tries to control a drinking habit, and lives with a woman he loves but won't marry for fear of imprisoning her in a life he sees being slowly eroded by the unreality of war.

As an account of the war experience, the book is realistic and unsettling, and as a study of a personality under stress, it reveals perennial truths. As Benny Green says, 'to the battle which Sammy Rice wages against himself no precise date can be attached. The struggle goes on.'

'His theme is of intense and irresistible interest.' *New Statesman*

C

Maurice Baring

Introduced by Emma Letley

' "In this parcel," he said, "you will find a bundle of unsorted papers. You are not to open it till I die. They contain not the story but the materials for the story of C . . . I want you to write it as a novel, not as a biography, but write it you must." '

It is from C's personal effects, passed on by his dying friend, that C the novel is finally written; no ordinary novel, as Maurice Baring says, but one in which the truth of events and personalities is rigorously observed.

Throughout his short, unhappy life C is accustomed to hiding his true feelings. Belittled by his parents, misunderstood at Eton and Oxford, and out of place at the high society functions he is obliged to attend, C acquires a reputation for secrecy. It is only after his death that the details of his private life are discovered.

IN ANOTHER COUNTRY

John Bayley

Introduced by A. N. Wilson

John Bayley's only novel explores the effect of 'the first cold winter of peace' on a group of British servicemen stationed in a small town on the Rhine. Some, like the ruthless Duncan Holt, use army life to further their own ends; while others, like the naïve Oliver Childers, must fight against their own personal defeat in the wake of national victory.

'now that you can't get "books from Boots" any more, and country lanes and democracy seem to be going the same way as "proper drains", there is every reason to savour an intelligence as extraordinary as John Bayley's, and a novel as good as this' A. N. Wilson

RICEYMAN STEPS

Arnold Bennett

Introduced by Frank Kermode

Bennett's reputation as a novelist waned after the publication of his great pre-war novels, *Anna of the Five Towns, The Old Wives' Tale,* and *Clayhanger,* but it was emphatically restored by the appearance in 1923 of *Riceyman Steps,* the story of a miserly bookseller who not only starves himself to death, but infects his wife with a passion for economy that brings her also to an untimely end.

THE DEATH OF VIRGIL

Hermann Broch

Translated by Jean Starr Untermeyer

Introduced by Bernard Levin

Broch's magnificent novel describes the poet Virgil's last hours as he questions the nature of art, and mourns the death of a civilization.

'One of the most representative and advanced works of our time . . . an astonishing performance.' Thomas Mann

'Broch is the greatest novelist European literature has produced since Joyce.' George Steiner

'One of our century's great novels.' *Sunday Times*

HIS MONKEY WIFE

John Collier

Introduced by Paul Theroux

The work of this British poet and novelist who lived for many years in Hollywood has always attracted a devoted following. This, his first novel, concerns a chimpanzee called Emily who falls in love with her owner—an English schoolmaster—and embarks on a process of self-education which includes the reading of Darwin's *Origin of Species*.

'John Collier welds the strongest force with the strangest subtlety . . . It is a tremendous and terrifying satire, only made possible by the suavity of its wit.' Osbert Sitwell

'Read as either a parody of thirties' fiction or just crazy comedy, it deserves its place as a 20th-century classic.' David Holloway, *Sunday Telegraph*

ACADEMIC YEAR

D. J. Enright

Introduced by Anthony Thwaite

Three expatriate Englishmen teaching in Egypt towards the end of King Farouk's splendid and shabby reign live through the academic year of this novel. Apostles of an alien culture, they stand somewhere between the refined English aesthetics of Shelley and T. S. Eliot and the chaotic squalor of the Alexandrian slums, trying to balance the unattainable against the irredeemable, the demands of scholarship against the dictates of reality, while making a modest living for themselves. Their consequent adventures and misadventures are either hilarious or tragic, and sometimes both. And, we suspect, as near the truth as makes no difference.

'This first novel is funny, extremely funny; it is an Alexandrian *Lucky Jim* with much more humanity and much less smart lacquer.' *Daily Telegraph*

THE VIOLINS OF SAINT-JACQUES

Patrick Leigh Fermor

Epilogue by Simon Winchester

The Violins of Saint-Jacques, originally published in 1953, is set in the Caribbean on an island of tropical luxury, European decadence, and romantic passion, and its story captures both the delicacy of high society entanglements and the unforeseen drama of forces beyond human control. Throughout, the writing is as beautiful and haunting as the sound of the violins which rises from the water and conceals the story's mystery.

'Beautiful is the adjective which comes uppermost ... outstanding descriptive powers.' John Betjeman

NEVER COME BACK

John Mair

Introduced by Julian Symons

Desmond Thane, hero of *Never Come Back,* is a cynical, heart-less, vain, cowardly smart-alec with a flair for seductive charm, an inexhaustible capacity for deceit, and a knack of bending pokers in half. He is also a very desperate man, who finds himself pursued by the agents of a shadowy political organiza-tion bent on turning wartime uncertainty to their own advan-tage. Unwittingly, he becomes the prime obstacle to the success of their operations.

John Mair was one of the most promising literary figures of the 1930s, and a man whose charisma is still remembered. When first published in 1941, *Never Come Back* was immediately recognized as worthy of his promise. George Orwell saw in it the beginnings of a new kind of thriller: a powerful, politically astute burlesque. This is the first reissue for over forty years.

'Don't on any account miss *Never Come Back*—lively, exciting, and intelligent.' Maurice Richardson, *Observer*

'vigour and imagination, and humour as well as nastiness: a drink with a kick in it' *Sunday Times*

THE ROOT AND THE FLOWER

L. H. Myers

Introduced by Penelope Fitzgerald

Myers's great trilogy, is set in exotic sixteenth-century India and records a succession of dynastic struggles during the ruin-ous reign of Akbar the Great Mogul. It is an absorbing story of war, betrayal, intrigue, and political power, but Myers's ultimate interests lie with the spiritual strengths and weaknesses of his major characters. The book explores a multitude of discrepancies—for example between the vastness of the Indian plains and the intricacy of an ants' nest—and yet attempts subtly to balance them. Throughout the trilogy Myers persists in his aim to reconcile the near and the far. *The Root and the Flower* demonstrates both his determination and his elegance in doing so, and, it has been said, 'brought back the aspect of eternity to the English novel'.

THE DEFENCE

Vladimir Nabokov

With a Foreword by the author

This novel, by one of the twentieth century's most accomplished novelists, has attracted widespread critical acclaim but not the popular attention it deserves. All Nabokov's characteristic power and grace are much in evidence in this sad but sympathetic story of a Russian Grandmaster of chess who comes to perceive life as a great game of chess being played against him.

'Nabokov treats the theme of obsessive genius in a light comic vein with superb results.' *Birmingham Post*

'Endlessly fertile, overflowing with an energy and intelligence that converts whatever it touches to literary gold.' *Observer*

'marvellously executed, with wit and precision and a shining newness of vocabulary' *New Statesman*

'The style is dense and allusive, the intelligence vast. *Lolita* was a best seller because of its theme—a perverseness which lubricious readers gloated over while missing the beauty and intricacy of the writing. *The Defence*, less regarded, is more metaphysical and more typical of Nabokov's large talent.' Anthony Burgess

BIRD ALONE

Séan O'Faoláin

Introduced by Benedict Kiely

In late nineteenth-century Ireland Corney Crone grows up in a family marked by poverty, pride, and spoiled aspirations. The recurring theme in his own life is the Faustian one of solitude, present in the private dreams of his boyhood and the insistent independence of his manhood. In old age the note of loneliness is more dominant: he is the 'bird alone', reliving the experiences of his youth, above all the secret love for his childhood sweetheart, which began in innocence and happiness, and ended in tragedy and shame.

Everywhere the book shows a poetic mastery of its material and a deep understanding of human nature. Corney Crone's private joys and sufferings belong to a common humanity, and as we read, his experiences become ours.

TURBOTT WOLFE

William Plomer

Introduced by Laurens van der Post

When this novel first appeared in 1925 the wide critical appreciation it attracted in England was matched by the political
controversy it caused in South Africa. It remains acutely rele-
vant, and if, as Turbott Wolfe declares, 'Character is the determination to get one's own way', then history bears the marks
of this book and testifies to the depth of its perception.

Plomer records the struggle of a few against the forces of
prejudice and fear. The book is full of images of exploitation
and atrocity. Yet it is also the love story of a man who finds
beauty where others have seen only ugliness. The narrative,
which never shrinks from witnessing the unforgivable, is also
characterized by sensitivity and self-control, and in the end
manages perhaps the most we are capable of: continuing brav-
ery, the voice of individual affirmation.

MR BELUNCLE

V. S. Pritchett

Introduced by Walter Allen

'At twelve o'clock Mr Beluncle's brown eyes looked up, moving
together like a pair of love-birds—and who were they in love
with but himself?'

The imposing figure of Mr Beluncle more than fills his world.
Neither his home life in the London suburbs nor his failing
furniture business can contain his fantasies. He speculates in
imaginary businesses and prepares to move into smart new
houses he cannot possibly afford. He spends profits he has not
earned. His motto is 'Give Love'. Yet as Mr Beluncle's suits
become more fashionable and expensive, his wife's dresses
grow shabbier, his sons are morbid or foolish, and his mistress
and business partner, Mrs Truslove, desperately tries to shake
off her infatuation with him. Throughout Mr Beluncle steps
grandly towards financial ruin. This is his novel, and by the
grace and consummate art of V. S. Pritchett, a novel not only
of laughter, but also of tears, and often both at once.

BEFORE THE BOMBARDMENT

Osbert Sitwell

Introduced by Victoria Glendinning

Written in 1926, *Before the Bombardment* was Osbert Sitwell's first novel, and also his favourite. It studies change, both social and psychological, when a world of obsolete values come under the bombardment of a new and harsher era. Set in an out-of-season seaside hotel, it portrays the loneliness of the few remaining guests with a masterly satiric humour.

'It is a book which you will never forget; a book which nobody else could have written; a book which will frighten you, yet hold you with the richness of its beauty and its wit.' Beverley Nichols, *Sketch*

'Few novels that I have read during the past year have given me so much pleasure . . . a nearly flawless piece of satirical writing.' Ralph Straus, *Bystander*

NOCTURNE

Frank Swinnerton

Introduced by Benny Green

Frank Swinnerton (1884–1982), critic and prolific novelist, was a familiar figure in the literary life of the first half of this century.

In *Nocturne*, a masterly portrayal of relationships and the way they work, Frank Swinnerton takes a romantic theme and casts it in a realistic mode. As a result his lyrical evocation of the night's changing moods is matched by its powerful insights into his characters' anxieties and jealousies as two sisters struggle to make sense of their feelings for their father, the men they love, and each other. One of the novel's admirers was H. G. Wells, who wrote of it: 'this fine work . . . ends a brilliant apprenticeship and ranks Swinnerton as Master. This is a book that will not die. It is perfect, authentic, and alive.'